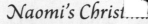
"[Perry] never disappoints."

—*The Mary Reader*

Hannah's Joy

"An enjoyable Mennonite romance starring two fascinating individuals . . . Fans will enjoy this warm tale of love and belonging."
—*Genre Go Round Reviews*

"Amish book lovers . . . you are *ferhoodled* if you don't go out and pick up a copy of *Hannah's Joy* RIGHT NOW."
—*The Mary Reader*

"The characters in this book are great . . . As usual, I loved my visit to Pleasant Valley."
—*Night Owl Reviews*

Katie's Way

"Superb . . . Magnificent Marta Perry provides another engaging Pleasant Valley tale."
—*Genre Go Round Reviews*

"*Katie's Way* stands alone, but readers will love . . . all of the novels in the order they were published . . . Great characters and a bit of mystery . . . A delightful novel!"
—*Romance Reviews Today*

"A great story of friendship, second chances, and faith . . . Wonderful."
—*Reviews from the Heart*

"While this is a love story, it's also a very complex story . . . I highly recommend this book and this series to anyone who loves Amish romances."
—*Night Owl Reviews*

continued . . .

Sarah's Gift

"Perry's fourth Pleasant Valley book places her well-rounded characters in a sweet, entertaining romance." —*RT Book Reviews*

"Perry's narrative keeps a nice pace as things develop credibly . . . between Aaron and Sarah; the legal challenge makes for more than merely romantic tension. Minor characters are also clearly sketched and differentiated." —*Publishers Weekly*

"The latest Pleasant Valley inspirational Amish romance is a superb contemporary that focuses on the role of a midwife in modern America . . . Another powerful Pleasant Valley tale."
—*Genre Go Round Reviews*

Anna's Return

"Those who enjoyed the first two series titles will eagerly await this third entry, which does not disappoint. It will also appeal to fans of Amy Clipston and Shelley Shepard Gray." —*Library Journal*

"Perry crafts characters with compassion yet with insecurities that make them relatable." —*RT Book Reviews*

"A story of forgiveness, redemption, and mistaken ideas . . . Full of wonderful characters . . . A wonderful book!"
—*Romance Reviews Today*

"In today's fast-paced society, it's a joy to sit back and enjoy a book that can combine romance, faith, and a bit of a thriller . . . I look forward to reading more of Ms. Perry's books."
—*Night Owl Reviews*

Rachel's Garden

"Sure to appeal to fans of Beverly Lewis." —*Library Journal*

"A large part of the pleasure of this book is in watching Rachel be Amish, as she sells snapdragons and pansies to both Amish and 'English' at an outdoor market, taking in snatches of Pennsylvania Dutch." —*The Philadelphia Inquirer*

Leah's Choice

"What a joy it is to read Marta Perry's novels! *Leah's Choice* has everything a reader could want—strong, well-defined characters; beautiful, realistic settings; and a thought-provoking plot. Readers of Amish fiction will surely be waiting anxiously for her next book."

—Shelley Shepard Gray,
New York Times bestselling author of *Hopeful*

"A knowing, careful look into Amish culture and faith. A truly enjoyable reading experience."

—Angela Hunt,
New York Times bestselling author of *The Offering*

"Marta Perry has done an exceptional job describing the tradition of the Amish community . . . A wonderful start to what is sure to be a very memorable series." —*Romance Junkies*

"I loved *Leah's Choice* by Marta Perry! More than just a sweet Amish love story, it is a complex mix of volatile relationships and hard choices. I couldn't put it down. I highly recommend it!"

—Colleen Coble, author of *Butterfly Palace*

Pleasant Valley novels by Marta Perry

LEAH'S CHOICE
RACHEL'S GARDEN
ANNA'S RETURN
SARAH'S GIFT
KATIE'S WAY
HANNAH'S JOY
NAOMI'S CHRISTMAS

The Lost Sisters of Pleasant Valley

LYDIA'S HOPE
SUSANNA'S DREAM

SUSANNA'S DREAM

The Lost Sisters of Pleasant Valley
BOOK TWO

MARTA PERRY

BERKLEY BOOKS, NEW YORK

THE BERKLEY PUBLISHING GROUP
Published by the Penguin Group
Penguin Group (USA) LLC
375 Hudson Street, New York, New York 10014

USA • Canada • UK • Ireland • Australia • New Zealand • India • South Africa • China

penguin.com

A Penguin Random House Company

This book is an original publication of The Berkley Publishing Group.

Library of Congress Cataloging-in-Publication Data

Perry, Marta.
Susanna's dream / Marta Perry. — Berkley trade paperback edition.
pages cm. — (The Lost Sisters of Pleasant Valley ; Book two)
ISBN 978-0-425-25375-5 (pbk.)
1. Amish women—Fiction. 2. Sisters—Fiction. 3. Amish—Fiction.
4. Amish Country (Pa.)—Fiction. 5. Christian fiction. 6. Love stories. I. Title.
PS3616.E7933S87 2014
813'.6—dc23
2013037391

PUBLISHING HISTORY
Berkley trade paperback edition / February 2014

PRINTED IN THE UNITED STATES OF AMERICA

10 9 8 7 6 5 4 3 2 1

Cover art by Shane Rebenschied.
Cover design by Annette Fiore DeFex.

This story is dedicated to my dear sisters-in-law,
Molly, Barb, Arddy, and Christine.
And, as always, to Brian.

LIST OF CHARACTERS

Lydia Weaver Beachy, wife of Adam Beachy; their sons: Daniel, eight, David, six

Diane Wentworth Weaver, Lydia, Chloe, and Susanna's deceased mother

Eli Weaver, Lydia, Chloe, and Susanna's father, also deceased

Susanna Bitler, Lydia and Chloe's birth sister, adopted by Jonah and Elizabeth Bitler, both deceased

Chloe Wentworth, Susanna and Lydia's birth sister, raised by their Englisch grandmother, Margaret Wentworth

Seth Miller, Englisch, son of Lydia's Amish neighbor Emma Miller

Emma Miller, Seth and Jessie's mother

Jessie Miller, Seth's younger sister

Dora Gaus, Susanna's partner in Plain Gifts, Nathaniel Gaus's mother

Nathaniel "Nate" Gaus, Dora's son, owner of Gaus's Bulk Foods

GLOSSARY OF PENNSYLVANIA DUTCH WORDS AND PHRASES

ach. oh; used as an exclamation

agasinish. stubborn; self-willed

ain't so. A phrase commonly used at the end of a sentence to invite agreement.

alter. old man

anymore. Used as a substitute for "nowadays."

Ausbund. Amish hymnal. Used in the worship services, it contains traditional hymns, words only, to be sung without accompaniment. Many of the hymns date from the sixteenth century.

befuddled. mixed up

blabbermaul. talkative one

blaid. bashful

boppli. baby

bruder. brother

bu. boy

buwe. boys

daadi. daddy

Da Herr sei mit du. The Lord be with you.

denke. thanks (or *danki*)

Englischer. one who is not Plain

ferhoodled. upset; distracted

ferleicht. perhaps

frau. wife

fress. eat

gross. big

grossdaadi. grandfather

grossdaadi haus. An addition to the farmhouse, built for the grandparents to live in once they've "retired" from actively running the farm.

grossmutter. grandmother

gut. good

hatt. hard; difficult

haus. house

hinnersich. backward

ich. I

ja. yes

kapp. Prayer covering, worn in obedience to the Biblical injunction that women should pray with their heads covered. Kapps are made of Swiss organdy and are white. (In some Amish communities, unmarried girls thirteen and older wear black kapps during worship service.)

kinder. kids (or *kinner*)

komm. come

komm schnell. come quick

Leit. the people; the Amish

lippy. sassy

maidal. old maid; spinster

mamm. mother

middaagesse. lunch

mind. remember

onkel. uncle

Ordnung. The agreed-upon rules by which the Amish community lives. When new practices become an issue, they are discussed at length among the leadership. The decision for or against innovation is generally made on the basis of maintaining the home and family as separate from the world. For instance, a telephone might be necessary in a shop in order to conduct business but would be banned from the home because it would intrude on family time.

Pennsylvania Dutch. The language is actually German in origin and is primarily a spoken language. Most Amish write in English, which results in many variations in spelling when the dialect is put into writing! The language probably originated in the south of Germany but is common also among the Swiss Mennonite and French Huguenot immigrants to Pennsylvania. The language was brought to America prior to the Revolution and is still in use today. High German is used for Scripture and church documents, while English is the language of commerce.

rumspringa. Running-around time. The late teen years when Amish youth taste some aspects of the outside world before deciding to be baptized into the church.

schnickelfritz. mischievous child

ser gut. very good

tastes like more. delicious

Was ist letz? What's the matter?

Wie bist du heit. how are you; said in greeting

wilkom. welcome

Wo bist du? Where are you?

CHAPTER ONE

*T*he shop was too quiet. Susanna Bitler straightened one of the paintings she had on consignment from an Englisch artist and moved on to the display of quilted place mats. Her partner in Plain Gifts, Dora Gaus, might return from her doctor's appointment in time to close, but Susanna certain-sure didn't need help.

A rainy weekday in September always meant few customers in the shop. Still, it didn't normally feel lonely, crowded as it was with baskets and candles, place mats and wall hangings, hooked rugs and table runners, all of them handmade by local craftspeople. The bright colors and myriad of textures would cheer anyone, wouldn't they?

Unfortunately, being alone gave her too much time to think. Susanna smoothed the skirt of her black dress, a reminder of her mother's death less than a month ago. She must stop feeling sorry for herself. Her mother would have been the first one to tell her so. Mamm's death had been God's will, and she wouldn't have wanted her mother to linger in pain. Still . . .

The sound of footsteps on the shop's small porch ended the stream of thoughts that might well have her in tears if she wasn't careful. Susanna turned toward the door, arranging a welcoming smile on her face.

The bell tinkled as the door opened, and the smile froze despite her efforts. It wasn't a customer. Her visitor was Nathaniel Gaus, Dora's son. A nice enough man, from all Susanna knew of him, except that he always seemed to regard his mother's young partner with a vague disapproval that Susanna found unsettling.

"Nathaniel." She moved toward him, more than usually aware under his observant eyes of her limp that was the remnant of a childhood accident. "Wilkom. I'm sorry, but your mother isn't here this afternoon."

Odd, that he wouldn't have known. He must have forgotten, occupied as he was with his own business. Dora had lived with her son since the death of his wife twelve years earlier.

Nathaniel slapped his black hat against his leg to shake off the raindrops that clung to it. With his fair hair and beard, blue eyes, ruddy skin, and broad shoulders, Nathaniel probably looked like the popular Englisch image of an Amish man, but he wasn't a typical farmer. He owned Gaus's Bulk Foods, a thriving store here in Oyersburg.

"Ja, I know." Nate came closer, so that she had to tilt her head to see his face. "I don't think I've talked to you since your mamm's funeral, Susanna. I hope you are doing well."

"Denke. It's been . . . a difficult time." She blinked, taken aback by the tears that seemed to come too readily when someone spoke of Mamm. "May I take a message for your mother?"

A slight frown wrinkled his forehead. "No, that's not necessary. Actually, I came to speak to you."

Susanna stiffened, thoughts jostling in her mind. "Was ist letz?" She couldn't imagine Nate seeking her out unless something was wrong.

"Nothing's wrong." But his tone seemed to argue with the words.

He glanced around the shop, his gaze skimming the pottery, the hooked rugs, and all the other things that she'd just been thinking made Plain Gifts so cozy and welcoming. Nate's look was assessing instead of admiring, she thought.

"The shop isn't busy," he observed.

Susanna tried to quell the defensive feeling that sprang up at what she felt was the criticism in his tone. "Now that school is in session, many of our shoppers come on Saturdays. And I'm certain-sure business will pick up again as we get closer to Christmas."

As a businessman, he should understand that, but Nate probably didn't have such cycles in his bulk foods business. Folks always had to eat, but they weren't always looking for gifts and crafts.

"I suppose." The frown settled between his straight brows. "That's why Mamm is always so tired around the holidays."

Susanna wasn't sure whether that was a complaint or not. What was he driving at?

"Ja, I suppose we both work extra hard then. We could always get a girl in to help out if needed."

His frown seemed to deepen. "Mamm has family to keep

her busy, especially at the holidays. It's different for you." He stopped, the color deepening in his ruddy cheeks, as he seemed to hear what he'd just said. "I didn't mean—"

"It's true that I don't have any kin here in Oyersburg now that my mother has passed. And that certainly gives me more time for the shop." She kept her normal, quiet tone, but Nate's attitude was beginning to bother her. Why didn't he just come out and say whatever he wanted to say? "What is it you wanted to talk with me about?"

He blinked, as if startled that she would be so blunt. "Ja, well, the point is that my mamm isn't getting any younger."

She could imagine Dora's reaction at hearing her son imply she was getting old. "None of us are doing that."

A flash of exasperation crossed his face, but he reined it in quickly. Nate was a man who didn't let his feelings show. He always had a pleasant smile for his customers, but his eyes seemed constantly on guard.

"True enough. I didn't come here to argue with you, Susanna. I want to ask for your help."

"*My* help?" That was surprising. Nate didn't seem to need anyone's assistance, as far as she could tell. He'd built up his successful business on his own, and according to his mother, he controlled every aspect of it, no matter how small.

His face relaxed into a smile, his usually cautious blue eyes warming in an expression Susanna had never seen before . . . one that gave her a funny, prickling feeling along her skin. "Ja. I apologize. I shouldn't beat around the bush, ain't so?"

Most women would have trouble resisting the genuine smile that appeared so rarely on his face, and she didn't seem to be an exception. "What do you need?"

He hesitated for a moment. "I would like your help with my mother."

"With Dora?" Her breath caught. "Is something wrong with her?"

"No, no." He touched her sleeve lightly in reassurance, and his warmth penetrated the fabric, startling her. "She is getting older, that's all, and I fear she's working too hard. She ought to be able to take it easy now that her kinder are grown."

Susanna tried to imagine the ever-busy Dora sitting in a rocking chair with her knitting instead of being up and doing. She couldn't. How best to convey that to Nate?

"Maybe your mamm doesn't want to take it easy."

"Sometimes people aren't the best judge of what's good for them," he countered.

"True enough." A frown wrinkled her forehead. "If you think Dora should take more time off, I am happy to work longer hours in the shop." Probably everyone in Oyersburg's Amish community knew she had little else in her life just now.

"Ach, we both know how she is." His smile invited her to agree with him. "She'd be in here every day anyway just to make sure things were running fine."

Susanna realized she was staring at him, studying the strong lines of his face for any clues to what he was really saying. "You know I would do anything for Dora, but I'm not sure what you want from me."

His gaze sharpened as if he'd finally reached the heart of the matter. "It's simple, Susanna. I want you to persuade my mother to give up the shop."

The words fell with such stunning swiftness that they

shocked her into immobility. Nate went on talking, but his voice was only a background to the panic that swept in as she realized the impact of his proposal.

". . . you might buy my mother out if you wanted to run the shop on your own, of course. Or I thought maybe since your mother is gone, you'd want to move back to Ohio, where you grew up. You'd have friends and kinfolk there. I'm sure the shop was a good solution when you had your mamm to take care of, but now you're free to—"

"No." The word came out with explosive force.

For a moment Nate didn't speak. "*No* what?" His brows gathered like thunderclouds forming.

"No, I will not try to talk Dora into doing something I don't think she wants to do." A few other words crowded her lips, words about bossy men and people who thought they had all the answers, but she held them back. It was not in her nature to start a quarrel.

"I think I know what is best for my mother." Nate's voice had hardened.

She hesitated, but she had to say what she felt. "And I think your *mother* knows what's best for her."

Nate's shoulders stiffened. "Then I guess we don't have anything more to say to each other." He settled his hat squarely on his head and stalked out, disapproval conveyed in every line of his body.

The door closed hard enough to make the bell nearly jangle off its hook. Susanna stood immobile until Nate had passed the shop window and disappeared. Then she clasped her hand over her lips.

She would not cry. She would not give in to despair.

But if Nate had his way . . .

The money she had left after her mother's final illness was nowhere near enough to buy out Dora's half of the business. What was she going to do? She couldn't lose the shop. She didn't have anything else.

Nathaniel was still brooding over his conversation with Susanna at closing time that afternoon. The woman had gotten under his skin with her pointed questions and outright refusal to do as he asked. He hadn't expected it—that was the trouble.

Susanna had always seemed such a quiet little mouse, with her halting walk and her habit of effacing herself until a person forgot she was even there. Well, apparently this mouse had teeth.

Closing out the cash register, he swept an experienced glance around his store. Everything seemed to be in order, with the floors swept, the cans neatly stacked, shopping baskets and carts returned to their places. He made a mental note to increase his order for the granola that Tibby Byler made for the shop. It had been selling wonderful well with the first few cooler days of September.

Susie and Anna Mae Mast, the two teenage girls he employed to help in the shop, were lowering the shades on the front windows. Anna Mae, the older sister, seemed to notice him watching them. She came toward him with a bit of a sway in her walk.

"All finished," she announced. "Susie has to hurry off home, but I can stay and help you with restocking, if you want."

The swift upward glance to see how he took the offer set Nate on guard. He must be close to fifteen years older than the girl, and Anna Mae had too much of an eye for the main chance. He'd become an expert at avoiding unwanted lures in the twelve years since Mary Ann had died.

"No, denke," he said crisply. "You go on home to your mamm. She can probably use your help, ja?"

Pouting a little, she withdrew. The two girls collected bonnets and sweaters and clattered their way to the door. Busying himself with an order sheet, he still couldn't help overhearing Susie's satisfied tone.

"See? I told you so. Everyone knows he's still in love with his wife, even after all these years." The door snapped closed on Anna Mae's answer.

He'd crumpled the order sheet he held. Annoyed with himself, he ripped it up and tossed it in the trash. He ought to be used to comments like that by now. He ought to feel as calm and unconcerned on the inside as he showed on the outside.

Too bad the bitter taste still flared at the unexpected mention of his supposed pining for his lost wife. If folks knew the truth—

Well, they didn't, and they never would. Whatever people thought or said was better than what had really happened. Truth was a fine thing, but not when it hurt innocent people.

Locking the doors of both shop and memory, he crossed the parking lot to his house behind the store. One thing he might thank Mary Ann for, he supposed, glancing back at the store. Thanks to her, he'd spent his twenties concentrating on building up a thriving business, turning the family farm over to his next younger brother, Jonah. He'd been able to provide well for his mother and all the younger ones, and that satisfied him.

He went in the back door, as usual, and found his mother

in the kitchen, browning some chicken in a pan on the stove. Her hair was entirely gray now, and her back bent from years of hard work. He crossed the kitchen and gave her a quick hug.

"Didn't I tell you not to bother with supper tonight?" His mock scolding had a serious undertone. "You'll be tired from your trip to the doctor's."

"Ach, what is there about a trip to the doctor to tire me out?" She swatted at him with a pot holder, her lined face crinkling into a smile. "I was back in plenty of time to stop by the shop before Susanna closed."

He couldn't help stiffening. If Susanna had told her about his visit, the fat would be in the fire for sure. "Everything all right with Susanna?"

His mother's eyebrows lifted. "As right as it can be. She's still grieving for her mamm, poor child."

Nate made sympathetic noises, relieved. Susanna hadn't said anything, then. Today seemed to be a day for her to surprise him.

Sitting on the edge of the heavy oak kitchen table, he studied his mother, concerned by the sudden awareness of how she was aging that he'd felt when he walked in. The wrinkles around her eyes and mouth were pronounced, but a person seldom noticed them because of her warm smile. Despite the briskness of her movements as she forked chicken onto a platter and stirred the homemade noodles that were his favorite, she was showing her age.

"What did the doctor say about your headaches?" He couldn't help the rough edge of concern in his voice.

"It's nothing, just like I've been telling you." But she didn't look at him as she said it.

"And the dizzy spells. You told the doctor about them, didn't you?" There had only been two spells, over quickly, that she'd told him about. He couldn't help worrying that there had been more that she'd kept to herself.

She hesitated, hand poised with the wooden spoon above the kettle. "All right. You don't need to be so nosy. I told him, and he said my blood pressure is a little high, that's all. He gave me some pills that should help, and I'm supposed to go back in two months." She glared at him. "Now you know everything, so stop worrying, ja?"

He stood and put his arm around her shoulders. "You should be taking it easier," he said, imperfectly hiding his concern. "You've worked hard all your life. Now it's time to let your kinder take care of you."

They both knew why she'd had to work so hard, though neither of them would mention it. His father had been that most unusual creature, a lazy Amish man, constantly worrying about his own health and doctoring himself with one quack medicine after another while his wife worked to feed their kinder. And it hadn't been his imagined ill health that had taken him in the end but a reckless driver and his own habit of walking on the road after dark.

"I'd rather wear out than rust out," his mother said testily. "Now stop bothering me with such talk."

He was wise enough to know arguing wouldn't get him anywhere, but he had to try. "You could at least think about giving up the shop."

He seemed to hear Susanna's voice, as sharp as a tack in his mind. *Maybe she knows better than you do what's best for her?*

"Why would I do that?" His mother looked at him in what

seemed to be genuine amazement. "I like the shop, and besides, Susanna couldn't manage it alone. I can't let her down."

"I'm sure Susanna could—"

His mother interrupted sharply. "Enough. I'm not in my dotage yet. And I forbid you to say a thing about this foolishness to Susanna. She has enough on her mind right now."

He nodded meekly enough, but his mind buzzed with the implication of what she'd said. It seemed to him that her devotion to running the shop had more to do with Susanna than with her own wishes.

It wasn't right. His mother had worked herself to the bone for Daad, for him, for his brother and sisters. He wasn't going to let her do the same for a woman who wasn't even kin.

Susanna might be a nice enough woman, but she couldn't stand in the way of his taking care of his own mamm. He wouldn't allow it.

The gift shop was busier the next day, with its bell tinkling happily as folks came in and out. Maybe the weather had something to do with it—a few days of rain had given way to a sparkling September day, warm and with only the slanting angle of the sunshine to remind a person that fall was on the way.

Susanna found herself watching Dora from time to time, looking for any evidence of . . . well, whatever it was that had Dora's son convinced she should retire. She was ashamed that her first instinct had been for her own future. She should have been concerned for her friend.

And Dora was a friend, despite the difference in their ages.

They had worked together for five years, with never a cross word between them. Dora, despite being older and the senior partner in their business, always treated Susanna as an equal, valuing her opinion and ideas.

Try as she might, she could see no sign of worry on Dora's face. Still, there had been that doctor's appointment yesterday.

They were working together at the moment, stacking the quilted place mats a customer had pulled out. The woman had, it seemed, looked at everything in the shop before deciding she didn't want to buy anything today after all. "Looky-Lous," Dora called people like that.

Susanna smoothed a nine-patch runner flat with her palm, sending a cautious sideways glance at Dora. "I didn't ask you yesterday when you got back, but how was your doctor's visit? Everything all right?" She made an effort to keep her voice casual, but she feared worry might show in it.

Eyes bright, Dora darted a quick look toward her. "You, too? You're as bad as Nate, fussing so over a little doctor's visit. I'm fine."

"So Nate's worried about you?" She carefully kept her gaze on the quilted pieces, not wanting to give away Nathaniel's visit.

"Ach, he's a gut boy." Dora's tone was indulgent. "He worries too much, is all. Just because I had a few headaches—"

"You didn't tell me that." Alarm threaded Susanna's voice.

"Pooh, everyone gets a headache once in a while. The doctor did say my blood pressure was a little high, and it was time I went on medicine for it. That's nothing for Nate to make a fuss about."

"I'm glad that's all it is." Relief swept through Susanna. That surely wasn't anything too bad. Lots of people Dora's age had to take medication for high blood pressure.

Maybe Nate had just reacted too soon with his talk of Dora retiring. "You wouldn't like it if your son wasn't concerned about you, ain't so?"

"I suppose that's true, but I don't want him to worry." It was Dora's turn to stare down at the place mats. "He's always been the responsible one, even before his daad died. I don't know how I'd have raised the younger ones without his help. He just seemed born to take care of others. Too bad he doesn't have a houseful of kinder."

Susanna wasn't sure what to say to that comment. Other folks mentioned sometimes how devoted Nate was to the memory of his beautiful young wife, dead before they'd been married even a year. But Dora had never talked about why Nate was the way he was.

"He's a gut son," she finally said.

He was also rather bossy and intent on having his own way, but Dora probably didn't see that aspect of him.

"Ja, he is," Dora agreed, smiling. "I'm not ready for the rocking chair just yet, but I suppose it wouldn't hurt to take things a little easier if that would make him happy."

Susanna nodded, but worry wound a tighter knot in her chest. If Dora wanted to make her son happy, how far might she go? Far enough to want to give up the shop?

"There, that's done." Dora gave the stack of place mats a pat. "I think I'll put the kettle on. Do you think our visitor would like a cup of your herbal tea?" She raised her eyes briefly to the ceiling.

Susanna smiled. Their visitor was not, as one might suppose

from the gesture, in Heaven, but only in the upstairs storage rooms of the shop.

"I'll ask her," she said quickly, and headed for the steps to the second floor.

Chloe Wentworth had started dropping by the shop several months earlier, but it had only been since she'd moved in down the street that she'd become such a frequent visitor. The young Englisch woman had such an interest in Plain Crafts that she was writing some sort of paper on them as part of her degree program. Dora and Susanna had been able to put her in touch with two of their craftspeople who were willing to talk to her, and Dora already had ideas of others.

In the meantime, Chloe was photographing and writing about the different items in the shop, using the upstairs storerooms as a work area.

"Chloe?" Susanna emerged into the upstairs, glancing around the two large rooms. "Where are you?"

"Here." Chloe's head popped up behind a stack of boxes. "Sorry. I was looking through this box of table runners. I'm surprised you don't have them on display."

Chloe was slim and quick, with a mop of auburn hair and a pair of lively green eyes. She wore, as usual, faded jeans and a T-shirt, and her black-rimmed glasses were pushed up on her head. Sometimes Susanna thought she used them more to hold her hair back than to see through.

"No room," Susanna said, making her way between boxes toward Chloe. "We could use twice the display space we have. Dora says if you're ready for a break, come down for a cup of tea."

"Sounds good." But Chloe was studying the postage-stamp quilting on a table runner with such intensity that Susanna wasn't sure she'd heard. "Just hold the end of this, will you, so I can get a picture."

Susanna took the end obligingly. "Take pictures of anything I own except my face," she said, only half joking.

Chloe, nodding, focused on the detail of the quilting. "I might not be an expert on the Amish, but I do know not to take your picture," she said.

"You know more than most Englischers," Susanna said. A totally unexpected friendship had formed between the two women in the past month. When Susanna thought about it, she couldn't really explain it, but there just seemed to be a link between them.

Maybe it was partly because Chloe was new in town, although she'd said she had family near here. Even though Susanna had lived in Oyersburg for seven years, she hadn't formed the close friendships with other women her age that she might have hoped for.

Natural enough, though. Amish women her age were married with families, and a maidal like Susanna was an anomaly. Since she hadn't moved here until she was in her twenties, she didn't have the shared history of school and rumspringa to create lasting friendships.

Daad had thought the move a smart idea when Mamm's cancer had been diagnosed. The doctors had given Daad a list of places where she might best be treated, and among them had been the big medical center in Danville, only thirty miles away from Oyersburg with its thriving Amish community. He'd been familiar with the area, and Susanna hadn't cared where they went as long as Mamm got the best of care.

Chloe slid the camera back in its case. "There, that's done." She smiled. "I got some great shots of Ada Klinger making her hooked rugs—only her hands, of course. And some even better stories. She loves to talk."

Susanna chuckled. "Dora said we should have warned you what a blabbermaul she is, except then maybe you wouldn't have gone."

"She was well worth it," Chloe said. She paused, studying Susanna's face. "What's up? Is something wrong?"

Startled that she was so transparent, Susanna tried to deny it, but the words died in her throat.

"Not . . . not exactly," she stammered. "I didn't know it showed."

"We're friends," Chloe said, reaching out to touch Susanna's hand lightly. "And it's a good thing you don't make a practice of lying, because you're not good at it."

Susanna chuckled, though she felt close to tears at the unexpected understanding. "I don't lie, anyway."

"You could tell me it's none of my business."

"I wouldn't do that, either." Susanna sighed. "It's probably nothing. I'm just exaggerating the whole thing in my own mind, most likely."

"Well, I'd give an opinion if I knew what we're talking about," Chloe said.

The urge to confide in someone was too strong. "It's Dora's son, you see. He thinks she ought to retire and let him take care of her. But if she does, the shop . . ." Susanna let that trail off, not sure she wanted to say that much.

"You're partners in the shop, right?" Chloe said. "Does he expect you to buy her out?"

Chloe grasped things quickly, that was certain-sure.

"I doubt he's thinking about the effect on me. Well, I wouldn't expect him to," she added hastily. "But Dora is getting on, and naturally I knew someday she'd want to give up working so much. I just didn't expect to face it now." She shook her head. "Anyway, I don't know that Dora wants to do any such thing. And if she does . . . well, I'll have to figure out what I can do."

Chloe's eyes were clouded with concern. "You wouldn't have to give up the shop, would you?"

"I won't." Her voice was sharper than she intended. "The shop is all I have now. Whatever happens, I won't let it go."

CHAPTER TWO

*C*hloe's thoughts were still on her conversation with Susanna as she walked out onto the deck of the tiny house she was renting just down the street from Susanna's shop. The deck was her favorite part of her new home. Surrounded by trees, which gave privacy, it overlooked the rippling waters of the creek.

This end of the town of Oyersburg was almost a peninsula, with the Susquehanna River flowing along one side and the creek dancing its way along the other. A glance upstream showed her the red covered bridge she'd noticed in several of the paintings in Susanna's shop.

But even the tranquil view couldn't quite settle her mind. She longed to pick up the phone and call her sister Lydia Beachy, but one disadvantage of having a sister who was Amish was that Lydia had no telephone. Chloe could drive over to Pleasant Valley, but . . .

A knock at the door interrupted her line of thought. She

slipped back inside, crossing the small kitchen and minuscule living room in a few steps to swing open the door.

"Seth." The lilt in her voice startled her. Seth Miller would think she'd been missing him if she wasn't careful. "I thought you weren't getting back until tomorrow."

Seth smiled as he loosened the collar of the blue dress shirt that reflected the blue of his eyes. "I wound up my business and managed to get an early flight. Thought I'd stop and see how everything's going before heading over to Pleasant Valley to check on my mother."

Seth's smile could charm the birds from the trees, her sister Lydia claimed. That was when he'd been Amish, like Lydia. But Seth had had dreams that extended beyond Pleasant Valley, and he'd left for the outside world when he was just a teenager. Now he was a successful designer with a software company, but that smile, combined with the cleft in his chin and the laughter in his eyes, was still pretty irresistible.

"Come in." She waved a hand toward the deck. "I was outside. Something to drink? Iced tea? Soda?"

"Tea sounds good." He stepped out onto the deck, pulling the two chairs to either side of the small round table. The breeze ruffled his wheat-colored hair, and he brushed it into place with an automatic gesture.

She opened the refrigerator door, relieved to discover that she did indeed have a pitcher of iced tea. Somehow she hadn't quite mastered the seemingly effortless hospitality of her Amish relatives, who produced food and drink for even an unexpected guest at the drop of a hat.

Seth had been her introduction to those relatives. He'd shown up in her office at the museum where she worked in Philadelphia a little over four months ago, shocking her with the announcement that the parents who'd died when she was a baby had other children—two sisters whose very existence had been kept from her by the grandparents who'd raised her.

She hadn't believed him, of course. True to her patrician grandmother's tenets, she'd suspected he was after something, probably money. But Seth had a dogged persistence behind that charming smile, and eventually she'd given in to his determination that she at least meet one of her sisters.

Her reunion with Lydia had been a bit rocky at first, but with a bit of give and take on both their parts, it had blossomed into a relationship she treasured. But Susanna—well, they hadn't yet told Susanna the truth. Lydia had been convinced that it would be too upsetting to tell Susanna when her adoptive mother was ill.

But now . . . Chloe had to fight back the words every time she was with Susanna. At least she could talk to Seth about her, she supposed. Chloe didn't want to lean on him, but it was a little late to start being reticent about her Amish relatives.

Chloe carried the glasses out on the deck. Seth leaned back in the chair, gazing at the rippling brook, the lines in his lean face relaxing. Did he realize how tense he looked each time he returned from a business trip that took him back to the world he'd thought he wanted? She wasn't sure.

He turned toward her when she sat down, his face easing into that smile again. "So, how is your project going?"

"You mean the paper on Amish folk art part of the project or the getting-to-know-Susanna part?"

"Either or both," he said.

She lifted up her glass, ice cubes clinking, and then set it down again. "I think we've waited long enough. We should tell Susanna that she's our sister now."

Keen blue eyes studied her face. "What does Lydia think?"

"I haven't talked to her about it in the past few days, but—"

"Susanna is Lydia's sister, too." His tone was one of patient reminder, and it annoyed her. "You can't make the decision without her."

"Lydia never thinks the time is right." She tapped her fingers on her glass. "First we had to wait because Susanna's adoptive mother was so ill. Now she thinks we should wait because Susanna is still grieving her."

He raised an eyebrow. "I take it *wait* is a dirty word in your vocabulary?"

"I'm not Amish," she reminded him tartly. "In my world, things move along, and if they don't, you push them."

"As I recall, you weren't exactly pleased when I broke this news to you." His lips twitched, which probably meant he was remembering her threat to have him thrown out of her office.

"I thought you were trying to con me." Because that sort of caution had been drummed into her by the grandmother who'd raised her.

People are always after the Wentworth money or influence. You can never assume people like you for who you are. Everyone wants something. Gran's mantra had been pervasive, and sometimes Chloe had almost believed it.

"I don't suppose Susanna would think that about you," Seth said. "But she might not believe you."

He let it rest there, but his silence was more powerful than any argument would be. If she told Susanna the truth—that she'd been adopted after the accident that killed both her parents, that she'd never been told about her sisters—and Susanna refused to believe it, their tentative friendship would be at an end.

Seth let her think, and he seemed to be following the progression of her thoughts fairly well.

"You'd lose what you have now," he said finally. "What's the rush? I thought you and Lydia agreed that it was best to get to know Susanna gradually before hitting her with the truth."

"I know that's what we talked about doing." She turned her glass on the table, absently watching the rings of condensation it made, intersecting and overlapping, like the circles of people in her life. "But she was upset about something today, and she probably told me more than she meant to."

Seth leaned toward her, face intent. "What?"

"Apparently, from what she said, her partner's son is trying to get Dora to retire. If she did, Susanna doesn't know what would happen to the business."

"She's a partner, isn't she?" He frowned. "But being Amish, they probably don't have a formal partnership agreement that would spell out her rights in that situation."

"She didn't say. But I have the impression she can't afford to buy Dora out, and the shop means so much to her." She could still see the pain in Susanna's face at the prospect of losing her store. "Maybe, if she knew she had family, she'd let us help her."

"Financially, you mean?" Seth considered it. "Could you actually do that, if she agreed?"

Chloe shrugged. "Depends on how much it is, I guess. I do have some money that my grandfather left me directly. Everything else is controlled by my grandmother." She hesitated, lips tightening. "She's Lydia and Susanna's grandmother, too, but she seems willing to forget that fact."

Her relationship with her grandmother, never exactly warm, had been fraying at the edges since Chloe had discovered that not only had her grandmother hidden the existence of her siblings, she'd had no interest in them. She'd only wanted Chloe, the baby, the one least likely to have been influenced by her daughter's new life among the Amish.

"Even if you could, Susanna might not be willing to accept financial help." Seth's tone was practical. "So there's no point in leaping ahead."

"Wait, in other words." Chloe met his gaze as she said the words, and they suddenly seemed to take on a different meaning. Wait. The way they seemed to be waiting each time the attraction flared between them, which it was doing more and more frequently in recent weeks.

What if they stopped waiting, and let whatever might happen between them happen? Her heart seemed to be thundering in her ears, and she couldn't tear her gaze away from Seth's.

He shook his head, as if chasing away something that clouded his thoughts. He drew back, but he was breathing as quickly as if he'd been running.

He cleared his throat. "At least talk to Lydia before you do anything. Once you tell Susanna, there's no going back."

"I suppose that's right." And maybe that's what was going on between them, as well. Neither of them wanted to take a step from which there would be no going back.

"I'd better get moving." He stood up, the action abrupt.

Chloe followed him through the house to the front door, opening it. "Say hello to your mother and sister for me."

He caught the door, stopping its movement. She looked up at him, a question on her lips . . . a question that was drowned by a quick, hard kiss. It tasted of longing, desire, and maybe regret. Almost before she could react, he was gone.

"Ach, yet another Looky-Lou," Dora exclaimed when the door closed behind a customer who'd examined everything in the shop and left without buying. "Sometimes I wonder why they think we're in business."

"Perhaps she'll come back and buy another day." Susanna straightened the row of handmade wooden toys that were a new addition to their stock. Dora, it seemed to her, had been out of sorts all morning. "I can handle things here, if you want a break."

Dora's annoyed expression smoothed out to her usual smile. "Don't mind me. I'm chust fratched this morning over Nate's fussing and this new medicine the doctor has me on. I think I felt better before I started taking it."

Knowing Dora was fully capable of throwing the medication away without telling anyone, Susanna sought for a comforting word. "Sometimes it takes your body time to get used to new medication, ain't so? I know it was that way with my mamm. The doctor would say to give it a few days, and most of the time, that solved the problem."

"You're right, and I'll stop my complaining, ja?"

Susanna nodded, smiling, but there was worry under the smile. She'd spent the previous evening going through her finances and come away more discouraged than she'd been before she started. Daad had been a careful man with his money, but the cost of Susanna's partnership in the gift shop, followed so soon by his death and the expenses of Mamm's illness, had gone through the comfortable bank balance at an alarming rate.

The bottom line was that if Dora did decide to give up the

shop, there was no possible way that Susanna could afford to buy her out.

"These wooden toys will sell fine come time for Christmas shopping." Dora lifted down a small train engine to examine. "Who did you say brought these in?"

"Lydia Beachy, from over in Pleasant Valley. Her husband, Adam, is the one who makes the clocks." She'd met Lydia in the spring, when she'd first come into the shop, and had seen her often now that they were handling her husband's work.

"He's a gut craftsman, that's certain-sure." Dora set the toy back on the shelf. "Someone was in just the other day asking when we'd have a new clock in. I can't call to mind who, but I wrote it in the green book."

The green book was nothing fancier than a schoolchild's notebook, where they listed items folks were looking for. A surprising number of repeat sales came that way. Oftentimes they were able to find exactly what a customer wanted just by asking among the craftspeople.

"I'll drop Lydia a note and ask her when we can expect another clock from Adam," she said. "They have an apple orchard, though, and this is probably a busy time of year for them."

Dora nodded. "True enough. The orchard must be a big part of their livelihood."

"Lydia says they're sehr thankful for the outlet for Adam's clocks. It means he doesn't have to work away from home now. So it helps us and them." That was a satisfying thing, to bring together a craftsman and the buyer who would love his work.

"You've done a fine job of finding new crafts, like the clocks," Dora said. "You have a gift for the business—I knew it from the first day you came to work."

"I love it," she said simply. Her gesture took in the displays . . . from hooked rugs to candles to quilted mats to pottery to paintings . . . Everywhere there was color, and every object seemed to express the personality of its maker. "Just walking in the shop makes me happy. I never dreamed something like this could be partly mine."

"More than partly, I think," Dora said. "Your heart is in the shop. I've been wonderful lucky to have you as a partner."

It was an unusual expression of feeling from the practical Dora, and while it warmed Susanna's heart, it also caused her a touch of wariness.

"Your daad was wise to see how much the partnership would mean to you," Dora went on. "Not every father would see the importance of a business opportunity for his daughter."

Susanna shrugged ruefully. "I think by then he realized I wasn't going to marry. It was a way of being sure I was taken care of."

"Ach, that's foolish talk," Dora scolded, her eyes snapping. "You talk as if you're a hundred and two. You're not even in your thirties, and any man would be lucky to have you as a wife."

Susanna just shook her head. Dora meant well, but Susanna had accepted the truth a long time ago. Her limp hadn't kept her from having all the usual friendships when she was growing up, but when boys and girls started pairing off during rumspringa, she'd been the one left behind, the boys talking to her, even seeking her advice about the girls they fancied, without ever seeing her as a possible mate.

"Just because you're not arguing doesn't mean I can't see what's in your mind," Dora chided. "It's true that a seventeen- or eighteen-year-old boy might not understand your worth, but a grown man ought to be a bit smarter. Mark my words, love will come along for you when you least expect it."

"Maybe you're right," she said, hoping to pacify Dora. But she certainly wouldn't count on it.

More to the point, was all this talk about Susanna's marriage prospects a prelude to breaking the news that Dora was thinking to give up the shop? She wanted to ask, but she was afraid to hear the answer.

"Well, I think . . ." Dora's voice trailed off oddly.

Susanna, spinning toward her, saw pallor sweep across Dora's normally ruddy face, bleaching it of color.

"Was ist letz?" She rushed to take Dora's arm. "Komm, sit." She shoved a step stool out from under the nearest counter.

"Chust a little dizzy-like," Dora muttered, sinking onto the stool.

Then, before Susanna could do a thing about it, she sank right on down to the floor.

"Dora!" Terror seized her throat, so that she felt she couldn't take a breath. She dropped to her knees, grasping Dora's wrist to feel for a pulse. "Dora, say something."

Dora's eyelids fluttered, as if she was trying to respond and couldn't.

What should she do? Stay with her? Run for help? If she left—

The bell jangled. Feet rushed across the shop toward them, and then Chloe was kneeling next to her.

"What happened?" She was already pulling a cell phone from her bag. "I'll call 911."

"No." Dora's voice was a thready whisper, but her eyes were open. "No ambulance."

Susanna exchanged looks with Chloe. Do it anyway? Chloe seemed to wait for her to make the decision.

"Call her son," she said. "There's a phone at his store." She gave the number quickly, and then turned to Dora, patting her hand. Nathaniel would know what to do.

"It's going to be all right," she said, trying to sound more positive than she felt. "Chloe's calling Nathaniel. He'll be here in a few minutes, I know."

Dora shook her head slowly, frowning as if trying to concentrate. "Nate will fuss," she murmured.

"Only because he loves you," she said. "Just lie still. I'll get a pillow for your head."

Almost before she got the words out, Chloe was handing her one of the quilted pillows from the display.

"He's on his way," Chloe said softly. "He said he'd bring a car and driver. I tried to tell him I'd be glad to drive, but he didn't listen."

Susanna suspected that listening wasn't one of Nate's strong points, but of course he almost always had a driver available, because he had several Englischers who did deliveries for him. "Denke, Chloe. I mean, thank you. That's kind of you."

Chloe's smile flickered, and she patted Susanna's shoulder. "I do know what it means. What about a blanket? Dora, are you chilly?"

"A little," Dora muttered. "What am I doing on the floor?"

"You fainted. You'll be better soon." Susanna's heart ached at the confusion in Dora's face, and she murmured a silent prayer.

"Here." Chloe knelt with a woven throw in her hands, draping it over Dora's body. "This will keep you more comfortable."

"I should get up. What if a customer comes in?" Dora's voice was stronger, and she attempted to raise herself.

"No, no." Susanna eased her back down. "You might get dizzy. Just rest for a few more minutes." Hopefully Nate would be there by then.

"I feel so foolish," Dora muttered, sounding more like herself every moment.

Before Susanna could answer, the door flew open with such force that the bell nearly jangled off its hook. Nathaniel surged into the shop, seeming to fill the room with his physical presence.

"Mamm, are you all right?" He glared at Susanna. "Why is she lying on the floor? She'll get chilled."

She couldn't take offense at his tone, not when she knew it came from his fear for his mother.

"We were afraid she'd be dizzy again if she tried to get upright," she said, keeping her voice low. "Best not to move her suddenly."

He frowned, but nodded. "I should get the emergency squad—"

"No." Dora's tone was decided. "I'm not going to let them cart me out of here on a stretcher. I'm fine." Some of the color was back in her face, and she seemed to be improving every moment.

"The hospital, then. I have a car and driver outside. We'll take you straight there."

"So I can sit in an emergency room for an hour? No, thank you. Just take me home. A nap is all I need." She managed to get up onto her elbows, not seeming to feel any ill effects, and frowned at her son.

"Don't be ferhoodled." He frowned back, the two of them looking remarkably alike in expression. "The hospital—"

"Why don't you take her to her own doctor?" Susanna suggested. "If this is a reaction to her new medicine, he'll know best what to do. We can call ahead so he expects her."

Nate stood, apparently for the sole purpose of frowning down at her. "I know best for my mother."

"Getting her more upset won't help her," Susanna pointed out.

"I will go to the doctor," Dora announced, sitting up with Chloe's help.

Nate held out for another second, and then he shrugged. "Ja, have it your way."

Before Dora could resist, Nate bent and scooped her up in his arms. Holding her easily as he straightened, he glanced at Susanna, and she had no difficulty in reading his expression. *You see, I was right.* That was what he was thinking. *It's time she retired.*

Nate strode toward the door. Susanna hurried to hold it open for them and then followed to help him get Dora settled in the backseat. Susanna recognized Jack Shaffer, one of the retired Englischers who did deliveries, behind the wheel. Nate climbed in next to his mother, and Susanna watched until they were out of sight, managing to keep a smile on her face.

Then, once they were gone, she could feel herself crumbling.

Chloe nudged her back inside. She reached out to flip the sign on the door to CLOSED, and then put her arm around Susanna and steered her firmly toward the back room.

"I shouldn't close in the middle of the day," she protested.

"Any real customers will wait. They'd probably just be the curious if they saw Dora's son carrying her out of here anyway. You don't want to answer a lot of questions."

"I suppose you're right, but . . ."

"No buts. You'll sit down. You can use my cell phone to call Dora's doctor. Meanwhile, I'll make you a cup of tea. You need a little recuperation time, too."

Susanna managed a shaky laugh. "I do feel a bit bowled over. It was so scary to see Dora pass out. One minute she was talking perfectly normally, and the next she was on the floor."

Chloe pushed her into the rocking chair and began to assemble the tea on the small stove in the back room. She'd shared a cup often enough with Susanna and Dora to know where things were. Susanna placed the call, explained matters to the doctor's receptionist, and then was glad to lean back and let her thoughts go where they would.

Unfortunately, where they chose to go was in the direction of what would happen now. Nate was no doubt convinced that this incident proved his point. He'd be even more determined to get his mother to give up the shop.

Susanna leaned her head on her hand. Naturally she couldn't want Dora to hang on to the shop just for her sake. If it was best for Dora to give it up, then Susanna would have no choice. She brooded over it, trying to see a solution.

Chloe pressed a steaming mug into her hand, and she took it automatically. The first sip seemed to ease the tightness in her throat.

"You're thinking this makes it more likely that Dora will have to give up the shop, aren't you?" Chloe perched on the edge of Dora's usual chair, looking a bit out of place in denim jeans and a bright blue sweater.

"I suppose so." Susanna rubbed her forehead. "I wish I knew what to do."

"I take it you can't afford to buy her out right now," Chloe said, with an air of fearing she was going too far.

"No, not now. Maybe in a few years, but I'm beginning to fear I don't have a few years."

"You might take out a loan. Or I'd be glad to help, if I can."

Susanna's cheeks grew warm at the thought of accepting what amounted to charity from an Englischer. "I . . . I couldn't impose on you. You hardly know me."

Chloe sucked in a deep breath, like a swimmer about to plunge underwater. "I know you better than you think, Susanna. We . . . Lydia Beachy and I . . . We thought we shouldn't tell you when your mother was so ill. But the truth of it is that we're not strangers. We're your sisters."

CHAPTER THREE

Chloe held her breath, praying she hadn't made a mistake in telling Susanna the truth. All she wanted was to help her sister, and surely this was the right way to go about it.

Uneasiness stirred. Susanna wasn't reacting at all. She sat and stared, the cup seeming forgotten in her hand. The deep blue of her eyes had grown even darker.

"Susanna, did you hear me? Lydia and I are your sisters." Still no response. "I . . . I guess I shouldn't have blurted it out. We were adopted—you, and Lydia, and me—after our parents died in a van accident."

Susanna shook her head slowly. "This can't be true. I would know. Mamm and Daad would have told me."

"I'm not sure why they didn't." She'd have to tread carefully around that part of it. "Lydia is the oldest. She was five when it happened. She had a head injury, and she doesn't remember anything from before the accident. She was adopted by our father's brother and his wife. She knew about our parents, but they didn't tell her about her little sisters."

A hint of a spark came into Susanna's eyes, her expression growing more normal. Still, she shook her head. "It is some sort of mistake. I'm sorry, but you're wrong. I have no sisters."

The words hit Chloe like a slap. At least Susanna wasn't jumping to the instant conclusion that this was all a scam, the way she had when Seth had told her. Maybe a woman raised Amish wouldn't think that way.

"Lydia found out quite by accident. Her adoptive parents told her the whole story then. Relatives and friends had rushed to the place out in Ohio where the accident happened. We three were in different hospitals, and I guess there was a lot of confusion. In the midst of that, our Englisch grandmother, our mother's mother, took me away." She tried to keep her voice clear of bitterness. "She never told me the truth about my family."

Susanna's gaze finally focused on Chloe's face. Maybe she was starting to take it in. "How did you learn this story, then?"

All she could do now was to forge ahead and hope for the best. "Once Lydia knew the truth, her first thought was to find us. An Englisch neighbor of hers, Seth Miller, offered to help locate me. He's the one who came to Philadelphia to tell me."

"You're telling me that is why Lydia came to my shop that first time? Because she believed I was her sister?"

Chloe nodded, uneasily aware that their actions in befriending Susanna might be considered stalking in some circles. But well meant, after all. "Not just believed, Susanna. The bishop in Pleasant Valley confirmed everything. He told her where to find you."

Susanna set her cup on the table, as if buying time. "Then

why didn't she tell me this herself that first time? Why have you both been lying to me?"

"Not lying," Chloe protested, knowing it was feeble. "We were just trying to get to know you. We felt we shouldn't disrupt your life when your mother was so ill."

Anger flared in Susanna's face. "So you didn't say anything when I could still ask my mamm about it. Instead you've left me with questions that can never be answered."

"I . . . I'm sorry if we did wrong. I know how upsetting it was for Lydia and for me to learn the truth. We wanted to find the right time."

Judging by the expression on Susanna's face, this hadn't been it. She should never have let herself be carried away by her impulsiveness. She should have waited and talked to Lydia first. Seth had been right, little though she wanted to admit it.

Chloe took a step closer to Susanna, longing to touch her but not daring. "I just wanted you to know that you have a family who want to help you. That's all."

Susanna wrapped her arms around herself in a protective gesture. "I don't want help from strangers." Her voice was tight, and she shook her head. "I can't talk about this any longer. Please leave."

A dozen things she might say darted through Chloe's mind. None of them would do any good. She'd failed.

Blinking to hold back the tears that wanted to spill over, Chloe fled.

The only way Nate could keep his mother from stopping back at the shop that afternoon was to promise he'd go himself to assure Susanna that she was all right. So, having seen Mamm tucked up in her chair at home with the newspaper and her mending basket, Nate set off to pay yet another visit to Plain Gifts.

Not that he felt it was necessary, but doing as Mamm said gave him the opportunity to point out to Susanna that he'd been right all along. It was past time for Mamm to come to her senses, give up the shop, and let him take care of her.

He'd make it clear to Susanna that changes were coming, and she'd best accept that fact. He'd been taken off guard by Susanna's resistance when he'd first brought up the subject. Not this time.

But all thoughts of his mission flew out of his mind when he stepped inside the shop. Susanna stood on a step stool, apparently trying to reach the baskets hung above the display shelves. She turned at the sound of the bell, teetering awkwardly as she grabbed a shelf for balance.

Nate rushed over, reaching out automatically, and was rather surprised to find his hands encircling her slim waist. "You shouldn't be climbing up there." He reverted to scolding to hide the awkwardness of the moment as he lifted her down. "It's dangerous."

"Only if I'm surprised." Her creamy skin flushed with embarrassment.

At his touching her? Or because she'd displayed her disability in front of him?

Nate took a step back, brushing against a stack of quilted pot holders and knocking some of them over. As usual, he felt like a bull in a china shop when he was here.

"I'm sorry I startled you," he said, mindful that he wanted to explain matters to Susanna, not wrangle with her.

"No, it's my fault." She glanced down, brushing off her

spotless apron—so she wouldn't have to look at him, most likely.

The action didn't keep him from looking at her, though. Her flawless skin was still flushed a delicate pink. She had a heart-shaped face and a little dimple in her cheek. Funny that he'd never looked at her so closely before, maybe because she made such a habit of effacing herself.

Except when challenged, he reminded himself, thinking of her reaction to his plans for his mother. Still, after what had happened today, Susanna would have to agree that he knew best.

"How is your mother?" she asked before he could speak. "She didn't have to go to the hospital, did she?"

Her obvious concern made him want to reassure her. "No, nothing was said about the hospital. The doctor ran a couple of tests, but he seems sure she'll be fine. She's just supposed to take it a little slow until she's adjusted to the new medicine."

Relief filled Susanna's deep blue eyes. "I'm so glad. It was wonderful kind of you to stop by and tell me."

Nate found himself smiling. "It was the only way I could keep my mother from coming herself, as you might have guessed."

Susanna's answering smile displayed the dimple even more. "Dora has a will of her own, that's certain-sure."

Now was the moment to say what he'd come to say. But before he could, she'd gone on. "Give her my love, and tell her not to worry about the shop. I'll handle everything until she comes back."

If she came back, he thought. Susanna, seeming to assume he was leaving, turned to straighten the stool, as if preparing to climb it.

"You're not going up there again." He grasped the stool and pulled it out of reach. "That's too dangerous for you."

"My limp doesn't make me helpless." The glint in her eyes said this was another topic on which she had a strong opinion. Why had he never seen this side of Susanna before?

"The stool is too rickety for anyone to be standing on." He took refuge in a half truth. "I'll bring over a good step stool from the store. Meantime, tell me what you want, and I'll get it for you."

Susanna pressed her lips together for a second, and then she nodded. "Denke, Nate. The baskets, if you would, please. I have a customer coming in to pick up a pillow she'd ordered made."

He handed down the baskets one at a time. "What does that have to do with baskets?"

"It happens we know this particular customer loves baskets. These are new ones we've gotten in, and if I put them on the counter where I'll be ringing up the pillow . . ."

"You'll likely make another sale." He was interested in her sales technique in spite of himself. "That's clever. Not sure it would work for my bulk goods, though."

She nodded, arranging the baskets along the counter. "Folks come to you for things they have to have, like food. Our customers are more likely to buy something for a gift or just because it appeals to them."

He was letting himself be distracted again from his purpose, but it was interesting. "You deal with more Englisch, I guess. Like the woman who was here this morning when Mamm took sick. She wasn't a local, was she?"

It was a casual question, and he wasn't prepared for the

response it got. Susanna paled, her eyes seeming to grow darker as he looked at her.

"Chloe . . . Chloe recently moved in down the street." She put her hand to her lips, as if to hide some emotion.

Nate stood for a moment, frowning a little. Whatever troubled Susanna wasn't his business. He should say what he'd come to say and get out.

On the other hand, he knew how much his mother cared for her young partner. And Susanna looked so vulnerable that he couldn't just ignore how upset she was.

"Something troubles you about the woman," he said carefully. A disgruntled customer? A shoplifter? "You may not want to talk about it, but if there's a problem, I'll help if I can."

For a moment he could see her struggling to hold back. Then she let out a shaky breath. "I guess I could stand to tell someone about it. I can't trouble your mamm with it now, and there isn't . . ."

She let that die out, but he could guess the rest. Susanna was oddly isolated for an Amish woman, with no family nearby, no spouse, no girlhood friends to rely on.

"Whatever it is, I can at least listen." He leaned against the counter, waiting.

"Denke." She pressed her hand against her forehead. "It's all so odd that I can't quite believe it happened, let alone think what to do about it."

"The woman said something that upset you," he prompted.

"Ja. She said . . . She said she is my sister."

He stared at her, his mind refusing to process it. "She said you are her sister? Are you sure you didn't misunderstand?"

"I almost wish I had." Susanna's voice got a bit stronger, as if deciding to tell him had given her strength. "Her name is Chloe Wentworth. She moved here not long ago, and she's writing some kind of paper about Amish crafts and the people who make them. Your mamm and I have helped her some, letting her take photos of our stock and introducing her to some of the people who make things for us."

"Ja, I remember Mamm mentioning something about it." Mamm had seemed to like the woman, he'd thought.

"Chloe said that she hadn't known very long herself about it. That Lydia Beachy, from over in Pleasant Valley, is also our sister. That our real parents were killed in an accident when we were small, and we were split up and adopted by different families."

He frowned. "Is that the Beachy that has the apple orchard?"

"Ja, Lydia and Adam Beachy. Do you know them?"

"We get apples and cider from them for the store." He frowned, trying to pin down a fragment of memory. "Seems to me I did hear something about an Englisch relative coming to visit them. But still, this seems like a fanciful story, coming out of the blue."

"Chloe said that they waited to tell me because my mamm was so sick." Tears filled her eyes. "But now I can't even ask her if it's true."

"I'm sorry." He patted her arm awkwardly, wanting to stem her tears and not sure how to do it. How would he feel in such a situation? "I guess the thing to ask is whether you really want to find out, or just ignore it."

Susanna blinked back the tears. "At first I wanted to wipe it away. But I can't, can I? I have to know. If my parents kept it from me all these years—well, I have to understand."

Little wonder she'd been upset, with an Englischer she hardly knew coming to her with such a tale. There were troubled people in the world, after all, and he was quite ready to believe this woman was one of them. But Adam and Lydia Beachy wouldn't be involved in anything that wasn't right.

"If you were to go to Lydia Beachy . . ." he began.

Susanna made a pushing-away gesture. "I don't think I can. It was hard enough hearing it from Chloe."

He thought he understood. "You need someone who knows but isn't so involved, ja? What about Bishop Mose?"

"Bishop Mose?" she repeated, looking a bit confused.

"The bishop over in Pleasant Valley," he explained. "You can't tell me this is going on among his people without his knowing about it."

"Chloe did say something about the bishop telling Lydia how to find me. So he must know about it." Susanna rubbed her arms. "It's just . . . ferhoodled, thinking other folks might know something about me that I don't know myself."

Susanna was sounding more controlled, and she looked better, as if talking it over with him had helped her get a hold on the situation. The tears had gone, for now at least.

"Talk to Bishop Mose, that's my advice. You can depend on him to tell you the truth." He hesitated, but discovered that he couldn't leave Susanna's worries so easily. She'd confided in him, and giving her advice meant taking on some responsibility. "I know him. I'll go with you."

"I can't ask you to go to so much trouble. Your store takes up your days."

"Ach, it will do my workers good to be in charge for a few hours." If he was going to do this, he'd do it right. "I'll send one of the girls from the store over to mind your shop tomorrow afternoon, just so Mamm doesn't get any ideas about coming in. And I'll see to a car. Just be ready about one, ja?"

"But . . ." Susanna still looked troubled, but he wasn't sure whether it was over the prospect of learning the truth or spending an afternoon in his company.

"It's the least my mother would expect, ain't so?" He clasped her hand for an instant. "I'll see you tomorrow."

He made a hasty retreat before she could argue. And all the way back to the shop, he wondered how it had happened that instead of giving Susanna an ultimatum about the shop, he'd ended up stuck with going to Pleasant Valley with her.

Chloe bent over a tomato plant, emulating Lydia's actions as she picked plump, red tomatoes for slicing. The aroma teased her senses in a way a store-bought tomato never could.

"Anyway, I'm sorry. I never should have attempted to tell Susanna the truth without having you there."

She'd arrived at Lydia and Adam's farm that afternoon to confess what a mess she'd made of things and had found Lydia in her garden, picking vegetables for supper. The two boys were chasing each other through the apple orchard, followed by Shep, the mixed-breed dog who was devoted to them. The sound of a hammer in the barn gave away Adam's location.

Lydia had been quiet for so long that Chloe had begun to wish she'd yell, or scold, or something. But that wasn't Lydia's way. She finally straightened, stretching her back as if bending over had become more difficult in recent days. The Amish dress and apron might have been designed to hide a woman's pregnancy, but nothing could hide the joy Lydia felt at being pregnant again at last.

"Don't worry yourself so much about it," Lydia said. "It's

done now. It's certain-sure that however we did it, the news would be a shock, I fear."

Chloe nodded, her throat tightening at the thought of Susanna's frozen expression. "Poor Susanna. She seems so alone, and if her partner wants to give up the shop, I don't know what she'll do. I just wanted to help."

"Ach, I know that, and I'm sure Susanna will understand it, someday."

"Someday." Chloe grimaced, pushing a strand of hair behind her ear. "That sounds like a long time."

"It took you a while to get used to the idea, as I recall." Lydia smiled. "You had some funny ideas about the Amish as well, ain't so?"

"Most of those ideas were planted by my grandmother." Chloe shook her head. "But I can't lay all the blame on her. I'm not sure how I could study Pennsylvania folk art and yet remain so ignorant about the Amish culture."

"You're not ignorant now. I heard you talking to the boys in Pennsylvania Dutch."

"Using my few words," Chloe said. "Daniel and David are awfully patient with their aunt." She paused, her hand wrapped around a sun-warm tomato. "I suppose I thought the news might be a little easier for Susanna to accept since she's Amish. Maybe it would have been if it had come from you." Guilt reared its head again.

"There's no easy way to tell someone she's not who she thinks she is." Lydia turned toward the pepper plants, standing like neat little trees in a row. "Just a couple of peppers, and that's enough."

"Let me get them." Chloe stepped over a sprawling winter

squash vine. "My little niece or nephew is probably tired of being squished every time you bend over."

Lydia shook her head at that, but she let Chloe pick the peppers and put them in her basket.

"Do you think I should go and see Susanna?" Lydia asked as they moved toward the edge of the garden.

Chloe hesitated, unsure. "Maybe it would be better to let her get used to the idea for a couple of days. Let her adjust to it, and then we can both go and try again."

Lydia nodded. "Ja, all right. Monday, then. I can get a driver—"

"Don't be silly. I'll come for you." It was a pleasure to be able to provide transportation when Lydia needed it for the places she couldn't easily reach by horse and buggy.

"Denke. That would be kind." At least she'd stopped arguing every time about Chloe driving her. "You'd think those boys would tire out, but it doesn't happen." Lydia glanced toward the orchard where the game, whatever it was, was still going on.

Chloe followed the direction of her gaze. It seemed to satisfy some longing in her just to glance across the pastoral scene. Even the angle of the sun announced the turning of the seasons, and Lydia's garden was a band of bright color across the field, overflowing with pumpkins, winter squash, tomatoes, deep purple eggplants, peppers in every color, and the late crop of lettuce Lydia had planted as the days grew cooler.

Chloe had to laugh at herself. She was starting to think like someone accustomed to the land, instead of a yuppie whose closest approach to a garden used to be a stroll through a city park.

Beyond the lane that led out to the road, the orchard

stretched to the next farm—that belonging to Seth Miller's family. The apple trees were heavy with fruit already starting to ripen. Lydia had promised, or maybe *threatened* was a better word, to teach her to make apple dumplings this fall.

A tall figure moved through the orchard toward them.

"There is Seth coming," Lydia said. "I'll take the vegetables in. I'm certain-sure he's coming to see you, not me." Lydia's eyes danced with mischief.

Chloe tried not to think about the kiss he'd given her earlier, for fear Lydia would read it in her face. "I'm not so sure. I hear he had a crush on you when you were younger."

"Silly boy and girl stuff," Lydia said, laughing. "Go on, now, before Seth thinks he's not wilkom here." She headed off to the house.

It was just a kiss, Chloe repeated as she walked toward the orchard. Just a kiss, that's all.

Before she reached Seth, her nephews spotted her and came running, Shep lagging behind. Daniel and David might not be tired, but Shep's tongue was hanging out.

"Aunt Chloe! Did you come to play ball with us?" Daniel showed her the softball he'd been tossing. At nearly nine, he was more comfortable speaking English than David, who'd just started to learn the language last year.

David gave her a throttling hug. "Please," he said, blue eyes pleading.

"I have to talk to Seth a little first," she said, managing to meet Seth's eyes as he approached. "Then I'll play."

"Then we'll both play," Seth said, catching on. "Okay?"

"Ja, great." Daniel tugged his younger brother's arm when David seemed about to protest. "Komm. We'll finish our chores, and then we can play 'til supper."

David pouted for perhaps thirty seconds. Then he nodded, grinned, and the two boys raced off.

"Must be serious," Seth said. "I don't usually come before your nephews."

Chloe suspected he could see her embarrassment. Any protest at his assumption would lead in a direction she didn't think she wanted to go.

"Let's sit down for a moment." She led the way to the bench Adam had created from the stump of an old tree that had come down in a storm back in the spring. The other apple trees arched over them like the roof of a church, apples glowing yellow and red.

Seth followed her, sitting down and looking warily at her. "Well? What is it?"

"I told Susanna the truth today," she said bluntly. "I shouldn't have, but it just came out."

Somewhat to her surprise, his expression didn't change all that much. She'd expected some sign that he was disappointed in her.

"What happened when you told her?" His tone was carefully neutral.

"It didn't go well. She was shocked, upset, disbelieving." She felt the weight of it dragging her down.

"Pretty much like you were when I told you," Seth said.

She shrugged. "Just about. Isn't this where you remind me that you said this would happen?"

"I don't want to give you a reason to explode," he said, his lips twitching.

"I am not given to exploding," she said, and couldn't help but relax a bit.

Seth shrugged, clasping his hands around his knee. In jeans

and a navy T-shirt, he seemed to fit into his surroundings, but he definitely didn't look Amish. "Maybe it would have been better to wait, but I'm not sure the result would have been any different. It was bound to be a shock. What does Lydia say?"

"Just about the same thing," Chloe admitted, managing a rueful smile. "You know, I'm like Daniel and David, wanting her to say it will be all right."

"Everybody needs to hear that from time to time," Seth said. "It's not a sign of weakness."

"No?" She arched an eyebrow at him.

"No. And while we're on the subject of confessing, there's something I should get off my chest."

He was going to bring up that kiss, and it was the last thing she wanted to talk about. "You don't need to—"

Seth stopped her with a gesture. "Yeah, I do. I'm sorry. I didn't intend to kiss you last night."

Chloe decided to throw caution to the wind. "Why not? I mean, not that I'm saying you should have, but we're both adults. It was only a kiss." A kiss that left her longing for more, but he didn't need to know that.

"Unfortunately, we're not in our usual surroundings, either one of us. How would Lydia react if she heard about it? Or my mother, for that matter?"

"They'd be filling a hope chest for me." He was right, she had to admit. "A casual fling isn't in Lydia's vocabulary."

"Nor my mother's. I'd feel like a sixteen-year-old on his way to his first singing if they knew we . . ."

He hesitated for so long she thought he wouldn't finish. And she certainly wasn't going to help him out. This conversation was like juggling dynamite.

". . . were attracted to each other," he said finally. "If we don't want a lot of unwelcome attention, we have to be discreet."

"Discreet," she repeated the word. "So what exactly does that mean?"

His hand slid over hers where it lay on the bench between them. He began to trace small circles on the back of her hand with his fingertips.

"It means not giving them anything to talk about," he said, but the glint in his eyes seemed to belie the words.

"So no more kisses, you're saying," she said. Dynamite had been the right comparison, judging by how his touch was affecting her just now.

"Right," he murmured. Their gazes collided, and he seemed to lose track of his intent. "Well, except maybe on special occasions. What—"

"Seth, are you holding my aunt Chloe's hand?" Daniel's accusing tone had them pulling apart.

She didn't know about Seth, but Chloe felt ridiculously guilty.

"No, of course not." Seth held up both hands. "See? Now, how about some ball-playing?"

Seth rose, and Chloe followed suit, hoping neither of her nephews noticed how pink her cheeks were.

She loved having a family. She really did. But they certainly could complicate a person's life.

Chapter Four

Susanna hesitated, her hand on the cash box, looking at the teenage girl Nate had brought to the shop to help. "Do you want me to go over it again, Anna Mae?"

There was the faintest toss of the head in response, and something that was probably resentment showed for a moment in the girl's eyes. "You don't need to. I get it fine."

Nate, who'd been waiting with a semblance of patience, gave her a sharp look, and pretty little Anna Mae was suddenly all charm. "Please don't worry, Susanna. I am happy to watch the shop for you, and I'll do just as you've shown me."

"Gut. Denke." There seemed nothing else to say, so Susanna donned her sweater and bonnet.

Anna Mae, perhaps to make up for her momentary annoyance, was exclaiming over the assortment of candles on the counter. Susanna was about to respond when she realized that the chatter was aimed not at her but at Nate.

Well. Did Nate realize that the girl had a crush on him? She didn't suppose Nate missed much.

Anna Mae must be at least twelve or thirteen years younger than Nate. Still, that age gap seemed to work out fine in some marriages. Nate, a widower for so long, couldn't be blamed if he responded to the glowing youth and prettiness of the girl. Next to her, Susanna felt old, awkward, and washed out.

"Are you ready?" Nate said, perhaps preventing himself from adding "finally" at the end of the question. He was probably regretting his offer to take her to Pleasant Valley to see the bishop.

As for her . . . well, now that the time had come, Susanna felt a fierce longing to stay right here where she belonged. But she couldn't, so she'd better put a good face on it.

"Ja, I'm ready." She went resolutely toward the door and the car that waited outside, but she was quailing inside. Did she really want to know the truth about her parentage? And of more immediate concern, what on earth would she find to talk about to Nate during the half-hour drive?

Nate opened the car door for her, and she got in. He slid into the backseat next to her, startling her. She'd thought perhaps he'd ride with the driver up front. He leaned forward, exchanging a few words in English with the stocky, middle-aged Englischer, and then he settled back on the seat as the car pulled from the curb.

Susanna swallowed her panic. Like it or not, she was on her way.

By the time they reached the bridge that spanned the river, Susanna was desperate to break the silence between them. She cleared her throat, afraid her voice was going to come out rusty.

"How is your mamm feeling today? Better, I hope?"

Nate inclined his head toward her. "Ja, a little, I think." He frowned. "I didn't like leaving her alone in the house for a couple of hours, but she chased me out, insisting she is fine and I should stop bothering her."

She could hear Dora saying it in a tone of sheer exasperation. "Surely she will be all right as long as she doesn't exert herself?"

"Ja, but could I count on her to do that?" A faint gleam of amusement showed in his eyes. "Like as not she'll take a notion to clean the windows or redd out the closet."

"Dora would be more sensible." She hoped, at least.

He shook his head. "*Stubborn*, that's the only word for my mamm. I arranged for one of my sisters to drop in this afternoon."

"That won't fool Dora," she said, and then wished she hadn't spoken. She didn't want to enliven this trip with a quarrel.

But Nate surprised her with a sudden grin that seemed to turn him into a different person. That must be how he'd looked when he was younger, before responsibility and sorrow had carved those lines in his face.

"I never have been able to fool Mamm," he said. "But Donna is bringing her kinder, and that will keep my mother happy, for sure."

Something flickered briefly in his eyes as he said the words. Regret, maybe, that he had no kinder? But it certainly wasn't too late for Nate to marry and have a family.

"I suppose your sisters share your concern about your mamm's health."

"I think . . ." He paused, as if changing his mind about what to say. "Perhaps not. But they're busy with their own families and not seeing her every day like I do, and my brother has so much to do on the farm this time of the year. I'm the oldest, so Mamm is my responsibility."

Susanna could only nod, understanding his feelings, even though she feared he sometimes mixed up caring for his mamm with telling her what to do.

"You understand," he said, his voice warming. "After all, you're an only child—" He stopped short, a flush coloring his cheekbones. "I'm sorry. I'm not usually so dumb."

"I keep doing the same thing," she admitted. "I get busy and forget for a moment that supposedly I have sisters. Then the truth crashes down on me again."

"Ja." The word was heavy, as if he'd known the experience. "If you want to talk about it, I'm certain-sure glad to listen. Or would you rather be distracted?"

Nate was being nicer than she'd had reason to expect, and her throat seemed to choke. For an instant she longed to pour out all her doubts and fears. But whatever Nate said, he couldn't want to cope with the emotions of a woman he barely knew.

"Distracted, please. Why don't you tell me about Pleasant Valley?" she asked.

He nodded. "It's a pretty place, I've always thought. The town is smaller than Oyersburg, for sure, but it's very nice, and the valley has fine farmland."

Since they were at the moment driving through some of the farmland, it was natural enough for him to start pointing out various farms. Many of them were dairy farms, often with some sort of secondary business on the property. It was hard for a farm to produce enough income to provide for a family. Up a side road she noticed a typical Amish schoolhouse, white frame with a small playground and ball field.

Nate pointed to a small sign. "That's Joseph Beiler's machine shop. He can fix just about anything, so people say."

"You seem to know everyone," she commented.

Nate shrugged. "I do business with a lot of them. And those I don't, I generally hear about, one way or another."

Natural enough, she supposed. He'd spent his life in Oyersburg and had to be familiar with all the Amish in the area. She hesitated, not sure she wanted to ask the question that hovered on her tongue.

"You said you did business with . . ." She let that trail off, but she suspected Nate knew her thought anyway.

"You're wanting to ask about Lydia and her husband, ain't so?"

She nodded. "I know Lydia a little, from her coming into the shop and bringing Adam's clocks for us to sell. We've talked on several occasions."

Nate darted a look at her. "And what did you think of her, before you heard about her maybe being your sister?"

"I liked her." Maybe that was part of what troubled her. "I thought we were growing to be friends. And now it seems she was hiding something from me all along."

Nate seemed to stiffen, as if her words had hit a sore spot. But what would someone like him have to hide? "That's hard to forgive, ain't so?" His tone was normal enough.

She considered. "I would have said it was hard to understand. I hope I would never be unforgiving."

"You're a gut woman, in that case." But he seemed to draw away from her, as if they weren't in agreement after all. "Well, you asked about Lydia and Adam Beachy. They have an orchard—apples mostly, but some cherries as well. Adam used to work at the camping trailer factory over toward Fisherdale, but he's not doing that now. I guess the orchard and his clock-building and repair are enough."

"Some of that Lydia has mentioned. She obviously loves the orchard."

Nate frowned as if struck by a thought. "It seems to me I heard that the orchard came to them through Lydia's family. That might be something you have a right to know about, if what Chloe Wentworth told you is true."

She nodded, but the ownership of the orchard seemed a small matter with all the other things she had to fret over. A house appeared at the side of the road, then another, and her stomach tightened in protest. They were coming into the town.

"Bishop Mose has a harness shop right on Main Street," Nate said, doing a good job of pretending he didn't sense her stress. "That's Paula Schatz's coffee shop and bakery, and there's Katie's Quilts—you probably know about it."

Susanna nodded, but her gaze was fixed on the small shop with harness and tack in the window. The car pulled up to the curb, and once again Nate leaned forward to speak to the driver. Their words were nothing more than a buzzing in her ears, and she seemed frozen to the seat.

"Here we are." Nate cupped her elbow in his big hand for a moment to help her out. It was the sort of gesture he'd make toward his mother, and there was nothing in it to set up this fluttering inside her.

"You'll soon have answers," he said, his voice a deep rumble in her ears as he steered her up the two steps to the harness shop door.

Susanna managed a nod. *Be brave,* she told herself. She drew in a breath. She would, somehow. But she was very glad she was not alone.

As he guided Susanna into Bishop Mose's harness shop, Nate was a bit surprised that he hadn't been wishing himself out of this situation long since. The time in Susanna's company hadn't been difficult, though he'd been on edge that her emotions would spill over and he wouldn't know what to do.

Still, the sooner Susanna knew the truth about her family, the better. If this story the Englisch woman had told her was true, Susanna would be occupied with a brand-new family. And if she had a family to support her, he was certain-sure it would be easier for her to do what he wanted with the shop.

A glance at Susanna's face told him she was very pale. He could only hope she wasn't going to faint or make a scene. Whatever happened, he'd let himself in for this, and he'd have to see it through.

The smell of the harness shop struck him as he closed the door behind them. Rich scents of leather and neatsfoot oil mingled, telling him where he was even if he were blindfolded. New harnesses hung on the walls, while saddles and bridles were displayed on their own racks. It looked as if the bishop was picking up more business from the Englisch horse people than he used to.

The Englisch couple that was wandering down the aisles didn't look like locals. Tourists, he'd guess, in here only to look, not to buy. He felt their stares as he guided Susanna to the back of the shop.

Here was where much of the work was done. No Amishman

would buy new until the old couldn't be fixed any longer, and Bishop Mose was known for his expertise in mending harnesses. Behind the back counter, several heavy machines for sewing leather were connected to the power source by the heavy belts that ran through a slot in the floor to the cellar below.

The bishop sat at a worktable, bending over a buckle, but he looked up at their approach, his keen eyes moving from Nate's face to Susanna's.

"Nathaniel Gaus. It's been a time since I've seen you in my shop." He stood, laying aside the work and wiping his hands on the heavy apron he wore. His beard, nearly all white now, reached to the middle of his chest, and his face bore as many wrinkles as the leather he worked.

"It's gut to see you, Bishop Mose. I've brought Susanna Bitler to meet you."

The Englischers were staring again at the rapid rattle of Pennsylvania Dutch, and he was irrationally annoyed. He was inured to stares, but Susanna didn't need to be subjected to their curiosity when she was in such a vulnerable state.

Bishop Mose nodded at the introduction, and it was obvious from his expression that he recognized the name. "Ja. Wilkom, Susanna. In a way, I was expecting you might komm to see me at some time."

Since Susanna seemed bereft of speech, Nate figured it was up to him. "Susanna needs some answers. I told her you might be the best person to ask."

"I will do my best." The bishop's face was grave. "Komm. There are chairs on the back porch, and it is warm today. Go and sit, and I'll close the shop and be right with you."

Nate nodded and steered Susanna to the back door. As he went out, he could hear Bishop Mose explaining to his nonbuyers that it was closing time. The woman seemed inclined to argue, but he hustled them out firmly.

The porch ran the width of the shop, and it was furnished with four bentwood rockers and a couple of small tables. The yard stretched to a small stable, and the buggy horse in the adjoining paddock lifted its head to stare at them for a moment before lowering it to crop at the grass. Beyond, a row of trees bordered the small stream that ran parallel to the main road.

Nate settled Susanna in a rocker. "Take off your bonnet and sweater, why don't you? It's pleasant out here." He followed his own advice by removing his hat and dropping it on the nearest table before taking the chair next to her.

Susanna removed her bonnet, smoothing her hair back to her kapp in the automatic gesture women had. The sunlight touching it brought out glints of bronze in the brown, making him remember that the Englisch woman, Chloe Wentworth, had reddish hair.

He studied Susanna's face, looking for a clue to her attitude. She had obeyed him about the bonnet almost automatically, as if it was easier to do it than to argue. She didn't look quite as pale as she had earlier, her skin smooth and even but no longer ashen.

Footsteps sounded, coming toward the porch, and her eyes widened. "This is a mistake." Her fingers dug into the arms of the chair. "I don't want to find out."

Before Nate could come up with an answer, the door opened and Bishop Mose joined them. His keen gaze swept them, and then he pulled up a chair and sat facing them.

"You know, I think I would have recognized you even if I hadn't heard your name, Susanna. You have a look of your mother about you."

Susanna's lips tightened. "Elizabeth Bitler was my mother."

This meeting would be doomed if Susanna were prickly from the start. "I think the bishop meant your birth mother," Nate said.

"Ja, that's so," Bishop Mose agreed. "Elizabeth was your mother, and she was wonderfully devoted to you."

Susanna's expression softened. "Did you know her then?"

"I did. I got to know her during that terrible time of the accident. Do you want to hear about it?"

It was smart that the bishop began with Susanna's love for Elizabeth. She might be more willing to listen. Still, Nate hoped that the bishop might use his influence to reconcile Susanna with her family, and not just because it would make things easier for him with the shop. He hated seeing anyone so alone as Susanna seemed to be.

Susanna hesitated for what seemed a long time. Finally she nodded. "Please."

Bishop Mose leaned back in the rocker. "Ach, well, sometimes it's hard to know where to begin. Your mother . . . your birth mother, that is, was named Diane Wentworth."

Susanna came to attention at the name. "So she really was Englisch, then?"

"Ja. She met your father, Eli Weaver, when he was working out west. Eli's family lived here in Pleasant Valley. Still does. But he had a yen to see a bit more of the world, so he went to Ohio, where he had kin."

That fit together, Nate thought. Susanna and her parents had lived in Ohio before they came to Oyersburg.

"Apparently Diane had left home, and she didn't seem to have anyone. But those two fell in love, and the way I heard it afterward, there was no turning back. Diane decided to become Amish, and by the time they moved back here, she had the language so well that folks who didn't know would have a hard time guessing she'd ever been Englisch."

He paused, as if waiting for Susanna to ask a question, but she remained silent. Nate stirred. It would be more natural for her to be besieging the bishop with questions.

So he asked one himself. "They lived at the orchard where Lydia and her husband live now?"

"Ja, that's true. They had the three little girls—such sweet kinder." The bishop sighed. "Chloe, the baby, was only about a year old when they decided to go to Ohio to the wedding of friends. You were three, and Lydia was five." He paused for a moment. "A truck hit the van they were in."

"Terrible," Nate murmured. Folks sometimes feared driving on the busy roads in buggies, but a motor vehicle could be just as dangerous.

"Everyone was rushed to hospitals. It was hard to identify them, but eventually the police came to me. I went with the family to do what we could. Diane and Eli lingered for a day or two. You kinder were in three different hospitals. I thought a married couple should be with each of you to make decisions. Your father's brother and his wife went with Lydia. Elizabeth and Jonah Bitler, close friends, went with you. But when a cousin and his wife reached the hospital where Chloe was, they found she'd already been taken away by Diane's mother."

The bishop stopped there, maybe to let Susanna take it in. Or maybe because it was difficult for him, remembering such a time.

Susanna stirred, smoothing her hand on her right leg. "I was injured in the accident."

The bishop nodded. "Your leg was badly smashed. You had

other injuries, too. The doctors didn't hold out much hope for you, but Elizabeth never gave up. I always thought it was only Elizabeth's love that brought you through."

Tears shone in Susanna's eyes, but she didn't speak.

"Lydia was badly hurt, as well, with a head injury. Her aunt and uncle were just as devoted to her. She recovered, but she never remembered her life before the accident."

"So they decided to split us up," Susanna said, her voice barely above a whisper.

The bishop nodded. "Lydia's parents wanted her to know the truth, but Elizabeth . . . well, she wanted you to believe she was your mamm. So, in the end, that's how it was. Chloe was out of reach in the Englisch world, and it was agreed that this decision was best for the two of you."

Bishop Mose frowned, staring down at his work-worn hands, slack in his lap. "We don't know the future. We can only act as seems best at the time. If the decision was wrong, at least it was made out of love."

"I understand," Susanna said. "You did the best you could."

That sounded rather final, Nate thought. Wasn't Susanna going to ask the bishop anything? Her seeming lack of interest made Nate uncomfortable.

"Is there anything you want to ask?" he prompted.

"Ja." She fixed her gaze on the bishop. "I understand Lydia found out the truth first. I don't understand why she didn't tell me then."

"I fear you must blame me for that decision," Bishop Mose said. "When Lydia came to me, I already knew how ill your mother was. I thought it might do more harm than good to tell you at such a time. What if it made Elizabeth's last days difficult? I advised Lydia to wait. So if there is fault, it must come to me."

There was an uncomfortable silence. Finally Susanna seemed to realize she had to speak. "I don't blame anyone. I guess it doesn't really matter any longer. Now that I know— well, that's an end to it. I don't have to think about it anymore."

That was so patently false that Nate exchanged glances with the bishop. Susanna was hurt. He could understand that feeling. But didn't she want to know her own sisters?

Bishop Mose looked as if he were carefully sorting through the words he might say. "Nothing that happened was the fault of your sisters," he said finally. "I hope you'll give them a chance to get to know you."

Another long silence passed. Nate was developing an urge to shake Susanna, as if that would make her see things more clearly.

"I . . . I'll think about it," she said.

Bishop Mose nodded, as if that was all he'd expected. "I pray that God will guide your decision. And if you think of any other questions, you will come to me, ain't so?"

"Ja. Denke, Bishop Mose." The words seemed wrung out of her. She got up. Not waiting for either of them, she hurried back into the shop, perhaps hiding her emotions.

It looked as if he and Bishop Mose had done all they could do for the present. Nate rose, pausing to murmur his thanks to Bishop Mose.

The bishop looked troubled. "Be sure she comes to me if she needs to talk about it, ja?"

Nate nodded. "I hope I didn't do wrong in pushing her to see you."

"I'm glad you did. Now, I think, we must wait and trust God to work this tangle out for the best."

Waiting had never been Nate's strong suit—or trust, for that matter. He followed Susanna back through the shop and out the front door.

He didn't speak until they reached the sidewalk, when the vision of what he had hoped for from this meeting started slipping away.

"Komm, Susanna. Aren't you cutting off your nose to spite your face? You have two sisters who want to know you. You can have family to help and support you. What is wrong with taking what is offered?"

Susanna tilted her head to look into his face, and her expression was one he'd never seen before. "Is that why you are being so helpful, Nathaniel? Because you think having this ready-made family will loosen my grip on the shop?"

"No, of course not." He tried to sound offended at the notion. Tried to sound sure of himself.

Unfortunately, he knew in his heart that what she said was true.

If he really intended to cool things off with Chloe, Seth reflected, he probably shouldn't be searching after her on Saturday. He'd been telling himself that his job was, as it had been from the beginning, to serve as Chloe's translator to Amish life, but he had a feeling that excuse was growing thin.

Still, excuses aside, he'd called her. And she'd said she was at the community market, held every Saturday at one of those fraternal lodge buildings that used to be prominent features in small Pennsylvania towns. This particular brick building, right on the main square in Oyersburg, had seen a variety of uses in recent years. The Saturday markets were especially popular, so he'd heard.

The large room on the first floor, once used for fraternal social events, was filled with a bewildering array of vendors. People crowded around tables featuring everything from doll clothes to woven baskets to racks of jams and jellies. Down at the end of the row, a local church group was doing a brisk business in sausage and pepper sandwiches.

He was staring around, trying to spot Chloe in the crowd, when someone tugged on his sleeve.

Chloe smiled at him. "You were so busy looking around, you missed me. This is great, isn't it?"

"Are you saying that as a consumer or as a student of Pennsylvania folk art?" He nodded toward the bag she carried.

"A little of both," she admitted. "I found some handmade jewelry I couldn't resist."

"Not an Amish vendor, then." He took her arm and tugged her aside to avoid a woman pushing a stroller that contained, instead of a baby, several bags of milled flour.

"No, but I've heard there's a stand run by an Amish family that has handspun yarn, and I'd love to find them." She looked around, apparently infected with shopping fever.

"That's probably the Brand family. I'll help you locate them."

Chloe nodded, but as they started down the row of vendors, her expression turned pensive.

"Problems?" he asked, keeping his tone light.

Chloe shook her head. "Not exactly. Lydia and I decided we'd wait a few days before trying to talk to Susanna again. Together, this time."

"You're not still blaming yourself for telling her, are you?"

"I don't see anyone else around to blame, do you?" She shook her head. "Sorry. Lydia refuses to scold me for it, so I guess I have to do it myself."

He pressed her hand, feeling her fingers curl around his. "Try forgiving yourself," he suggested.

She smiled, but with a slight shake of her head. Chloe might sometimes be impulsive, but she also had high standards for herself. He'd seen that in her attention to her work and her family.

"You said you had something to tell me." She paused at a table filled with crocheted baby caps and sweaters, fingering the soft wool as gently as if she touched the baby for whom it was intended.

"Right." He pulled his thoughts away from the pleasure of watching her. "Apparently, if my sources are right, Susanna went to Pleasant Valley to see Bishop Mose yesterday."

Chloe swung toward him, her eyes widening. "She did? Are you sure?"

"Sure as I can be without asking the bishop, and I can hardly do that. Paula Schatz saw her, and she was interested since she knew your mother. She knows Susanna by sight, as well as the man who was with her. Nathaniel Gaus, who runs the bulk foods store here in town."

"That's her partner's son. The one who's so eager for his mother to give up the shop." Chloe's eyes clouded. "I wonder what he was doing there with her."

"I thought you'd be wondering what *she* was doing there," he said.

"I am, of course, but I can figure that out. She'd have gone to Bishop Mose to see if the story I told her was true." He could practically see the wheels turning in her head. "That's a good sign, don't you think? That shows she's interested, and Bishop Mose would surely encourage her to see us. Maybe he'll talk to Lydia about it."

"Maybe," Seth said, doubt shading the word. "But I suspect Bishop Mose has kept a lot of secrets in his time."

"I guess he has." She frowned, and he knew the secret she was thinking about—the secret that had kept her and Lydia apart for so long. She seemed to make an effort to smile. "In any event, thanks for telling me. We can hope it makes our visit to Susanna easier."

He nodded. Whether the bishop's words helped or not, he had a lot of confidence in Lydia's tact. And, though Chloe wouldn't like it, Susanna was more likely to respond to Lydia, who was Amish, than to an Englisch person, no matter how well intended.

He knew that line between Amish and Englisch—he'd been balancing on one side or the other for most of his life, it seemed. It was a difficult place to be.

He touched her arm. "Look, there's the yarn you wanted to find."

"Good." Her face lit. "Don't laugh, but I want to try crocheting a shawl for Lydia's baby."

"Why would I laugh?" He was relieved to see her attention slip into happier channels.

"Because my interest in the hand arts has always been strictly academic." Her lips curved. "I think the last thing I made with my hands was a pot holder when I was about eight. But your mother promised to teach me how to do it, so I want to find the right yarn."

His mother? That startled him. Mamm loved to knit, and

she'd been doing more of that during her slow recovery from a broken hip this past winter. And Chloe had met his mother often enough at Lydia and Adam's, but he hadn't known their friendship had progressed to this stage. Maybe it was just as well that Chloe was already exclaiming over the yarn, so that she didn't notice his surprise.

Sarah Brand leaned over the table, showing Chloe various colors of yarn, while her husband, Samuel, showed a customer what a newly sheared sheep's pelt looked like. He glanced up, greeting Seth cheerfully in Pennsylvania Dutch. The customer moved off, and in a moment Seth and Samuel were deep into reminiscences of their teen years.

Eventually Seth pulled himself, laughing, from the tale of a certain livestock auction and the trouble a bunch of Amish teenage boys could find to get into. He caught Chloe studying him, a slight frown between her brows.

"Sorry. We were just reliving old times. Did you find what you wanted?"

A smile chased away the frown. "Look at this lovely yarn Sarah helped me choose. It's perfect."

He admired the yarn, a delicate shade of yellow suitable, he supposed, for either a boy or a girl. They chatted with the Brands for a few more minutes, and then he and Chloe moved off.

But somehow he felt as if he'd missed a step in the dark. What had been in Chloe's mind when she saw him laughing with Samuel and looked at him that way?

Before he could decide whether to ask, his cell phone rang. He pulled it from his pocket, frowning at the name of the caller.

"The office. I'll have to get someplace quieter to call back.

I hope it doesn't mean another trip next week. I want to go with my mother for her doctor's appointment."

"The commuting you do is getting old, isn't it?" The question sounded casual, but Chloe didn't look at him.

"I guess. Sometimes I think I'd be better off chucking the job entirely and finding something that doesn't demand so much traveling."

Chloe frowned, and there was something he didn't quite understand in her eyes. "Maybe you've started thinking the world out there isn't right for you after all."

"Maybe not," he said, nettled at her tone. "What difference does it make?"

"None at all." Chloe focused on her packages, sliding the smaller bags inside the larger one. "I'd better get home. I have some things to do. Thanks again for letting me know about Bishop Mose."

She gave him a perfunctory smile and headed for the door, leaving him to follow or not.

Seth stared after her. What had just happened? Yes, they'd said they'd have to cool things between them, but this wasn't just cool, it was downright frosty.

CHAPTER FIVE

Susanna stared down at her hands, clasped loosely on the lap of her black dress, and tried to focus on the minister's teaching. John Fischer, the older of the two ministers who served this church district, had a soft, slightly wavering voice, so concentration was called for.

Worship this Sunday morning was held in a large barn on the farm belonging to the Brand family, on the outskirts of Oyersburg. The buggies had been lined up in a long row for nearly three hours now. She had, as usual, been picked up by Dora's eldest daughter and husband for the drive, since their home was closest to hers, and Donna had been quick to offer. She was as forthright and kind as her mother, and Susanna appreciated the way Donna made her feel a part of the family.

Once inside the barn, scrubbed spotless by the Brand family for their yearly turn at hosting worship, the group had separated, with Donna heading for the group of young mothers where her baby and toddler would be at home. Susanna fell into line, and soon they were filing into the barn, men sitting on one side, women on the other, as always.

Susanna sat on one of the backless benches, unmarried women on either side of her. *Young* unmarried women, and it seemed to her they grew younger with each passing year. Next to all their blooming youth she felt far older than her twenty-seven years.

When Mamm was alive, she'd sat with her because there was always the possibility her mother would feel ill and have to leave worship. The first Sunday back without her had been a difficult one. Folks had been kind, many of the women going out of their way to say a word about her mother.

Her mother, Susanna repeated to herself. Mamm was her true mother, not some unknown Englisch woman. Bishop Mose had said that her mamm's love had pulled her through after the accident. Surely that meant more to the relationship of mother and daughter than an accident of birth.

Unfortunately, thinking of Bishop Mose led her right back to the thing that had been troubling her since Friday—her outburst against Nate. Her words had been true, she was certain-sure, but they had not been kind, and after Nate had gone to all the trouble of taking her to see the bishop. Mamm would be ashamed of her.

The preaching ended, and she slid to her knees for the prayer, knowing she had to ask forgiveness. Not just from God, but from Nate, as well. She could not let their disagreement fester in silence.

Making up her mind to apologize to Nate was one thing—finding an opportunity to do it quite another. When the service ended, there was a bustle of movement and talk as women headed for the kitchen to help with the food while the men began converting the backless benches used in worship into the tables at which they'd eat.

Susanna could see Nate easily enough on the men's side, hefting a bench with ease. His height and his light blond hair made him stand out. But he was surrounded by other men still, and there'd certainly be no chance of a quiet apology until later.

Church Sunday wound through its usual routine. By the time everyone had been fed and the food cleared away, most people were ready to sit and chat, letting the kinder play. The men would most likely be talking about the weather, the crops, the need for more rain, the likelihood of an early frost, and such things.

Susanna joined Dora and Donna, who'd found seats in the shade of an oak tree with Donna's two little ones. Baby Joshua was sound asleep on a blanket, and Susanna had to smile at the intensity of his sleep—arms and legs sprawled, plump cheeks rosy, rosebud mouth moving once in a while as if he were nursing.

"That one will fall asleep anywhere, anytime," Dora said, seeing the direction of Susanna's gaze. "But little Barbie is so lively she hates to give up and shut her eyes, no matter how tired she is."

Donna had been attempting to get the two-year-old to rest on her lap, but Barbie wiggled fretfully until her mother let her slip to the ground. She toddled first to her grandmother, then to Susanna, making the fussy noises that showed her need for a nap.

"Here, Barbie." Susanna drew the little girl against her skirt. "Why don't I make babies in a cradle for you, all right?"

She spread a handkerchief out on her lap, folded it into a

triangle, and began rolling the ends in to make the babies. A quick twitch of the pointed end turned it inside out, becoming a cradle if you had enough imagination, and she let it swing between her hands.

Barbie seized it, entranced. "Bopplis," she announced.

"That's right, two of them. Maybe you should sit down on the blanket next to your bruder and rock them to sleep."

Barbie plopped herself down, and in five minutes she'd fallen asleep, the handkerchief cradle clasped in her pudgy hands.

"Gut job," Donna said softly, eyes crinkling. She had the same coloring as Nate, except that where he was ruddy, her face was freckled, making her look even younger than she was. "You have a gift for kinder, Susanna."

Susanna smiled and nodded, trying to ignore the pain in her heart at the thought of the children she most likely wouldn't have.

"Look at Nate," Donna said. "He's another one who's gut with the kinder."

She nodded toward her brother, who was tossing a young boy high in the air, causing giggles they could hear from where they sat. Nate's head was tilted back, and he was laughing just as much as the child.

"Who is the little boy?" It wasn't one of Dora's grandchildren. Susanna knew all of them.

"That's Mary Ann's little nephew." Donna shook her head, face solemn. "Such a shame, her dying so young before the two of them had a chance to start a family. If Nate had a couple of kinder of his own, he might have married again by now instead of turning into a grumpy old bachelor."

"Your brother is not grumpy," Dora said, her tone a bit tart. "And he's only two years older than you are."

Donna didn't seem overly impressed by her mother's opinion, but she didn't argue. She rose, tiptoeing around the sleeping children. "I'll get us lemonade and some cookies. You sit still, Mamm." She scurried off.

Dora shook her head. "I wish they'd stop acting as if I'm helpless."

"I'm sure Donna doesn't think so." Pacifying Dora about her children's attitudes was becoming a habit with Susanna.

"Actually, I'm glad Donna left us for a moment, because I wanted to ask about your visit to Bishop Mose." Dora leaned toward her, concern in her face. "Nate told me what happened with Chloe. I hope you're not upset that he did so. He seemed to think you were satisfied with the answers you got, but I wanted to be sure he wasn't just seeing what he expected."

It sounded as if Nate hadn't mentioned their dispute, and Susanna gave wordless thanks. She wouldn't want Dora to think they were quarreling. Or know what the quarrel was about, for that matter.

"Nate was wonderful kind to take me," she said, which was true enough. As to his motives . . . well, the least said the better. "Bishop Mose explained how it happened that the children were separated, and he certainly knew all about me. So I have to accept that the story is true, hard as it is to believe."

"And?" Dora's shrewd gaze zeroed in on her face. "How are you feeling about it?"

Trust Dora never to beat around the bush, even if sometimes a person might wish she would.

"I . . . I'm not sure." That was honest, if not very satisfactory. "I suppose I should be happy to learn I have sisters, but . . ." Susanna let that trail off, not sure how to describe what she was feeling.

"You can't love two strangers like sisters all at once," Dora said. "Not even if you wanted to."

"That's exactly right," she said, relieved that Dora understood. "Everyone seems to think I should rush into getting to know them, but I'm not sure I'm ready. They may be my sisters by blood, but that doesn't mean we'll automatically have feelings for each other."

"Ja, it wouldn't be easy." Dora seemed to mull it over. "Since the two of them have known for a time, they've had a chance to get used to the idea. It must have been a shock for them, as well, when they first heard. If they care about you, they'll give you the time you need."

"Nate seemed to think I'd be eager to get to know them," she said cautiously, wondering if he'd voiced his opinion to his mother.

"Ach, what does Nate know about the way women think? I wouldn't let Donna get away with criticizing him, good as he's always been to his sisters, but she was right in one thing. He is starting to act like an old bachelor."

Susanna had to smile at Dora's tone. "He's young, still. I'm sure there are plenty of women who'd be interested in him." Involuntarily, Anna Mae's pert face popped into her mind.

"Plenty that are willing to chase him, that's certain-sure," Dora said. "As for him being willing to be caught—well, that's another story."

"Folks say that he loved Mary Ann so much that he doesn't want to put anyone in her place." Susanna hoped she wasn't saying too much. Dora had never talked so openly before about her son.

A shadow seemed to cross Dora's face. She was silent for a moment, and then she made a dismissive gesture with one hand. "Folks will say anything," she said. "You can't believe half of it."

"I expect that's true," Susanna murmured, not sure what was in Dora's mind.

"Ach, well, I shouldn't be jabbering on about his business. We were talking about you, not him." She reached out to pat Susanna's hand. "You take all the time you need to adjust to this news. Don't let anyone rush you."

"Denke." It warmed her heart, knowing that Dora understood and supported her.

"And if you wouldn't mind, just get Nate's attention and tell him I'll be ready to leave in about half an hour."

"Ja, of course." Susanna stood, using one hand on the chair for balance as she always did. "I'll let him know."

And while she was at it, she would do her apologizing. Everything else aside, she couldn't be on bad terms with her partner's son.

Nate must have realized she was coming to see him, because he turned away from the folks he was talking to and walked quickly to meet her.

"Is Mamm getting tired?" He glanced toward his mother, a slight frown wrinkling his forehead.

"Not tired, exactly, but she wanted you to know that she'll be ready to go in about half an hour." Susanna took a breath, praying for the right words. "I . . . I'm glad to have a chance to speak with you, Nate."

"Ja?" His gaze rested on her face, and she forced herself to meet his eyes. She had the sense that he knew what she wanted already but wasn't inclined to make it easy for her.

"I spoke out of turn on Friday, and I'm sorry." Get the apology out, and the rest should be easier. "It was wonderful kind of you to arrange for my visit to Bishop Mose, and I repaid you poorly by biting your head off the way I did."

Nate's reserved expression eased, and something that might have been amusement seemed to tug at his lips. "There I was thinking you were always such a quiet little thing. I didn't know you had such a temper."

"I don't usually let it get the better of me."

"Maybe you should let it loose once in a while. We wouldn't want you to explode like an unvented pressure cooker, ain't so?" The laughter in his voice invited her to join him.

"I . . . I guess not." She wasn't sure how to deal with his teasing. "Anyway, I'm sorry you were the target."

"Maybe you had a point. Maybe I was thinking that having kin here would make you think differently about the shop." His expression grew more serious, and he studied her face so closely that she could feel the blood rise beneath the skin. "I don't want to be on bad terms with you, Susanna. All I can say is that I'll make every effort to settle this business of the shop in a way that satisfies all of us. I can't say fairer than that, ja?"

Susanna nodded. What else could she do? But she didn't feel particularly reassured. After all, Nate's idea of fair might be nothing like hers. Still, it was the best response she was going to get just now, so she'd have to accept it.

Sunday evening was time for Chloe's weekly phone call to her grandmother. She pulled out her cell phone and sat down in the corner of the sofa, sensing a deep reluctance to make the call.

She loved her grandmother. After all, Gran had been the only mother figure she'd ever known. But the revelation that

Chloe had two sisters her grandmother had kept secret all those years had put a wedge between them, and Gran's subsequent implacable opposition to Chloe's efforts to become acquainted with Lydia and Susanna had turned the wedge into a chasm.

Chloe didn't understand, maybe would never understand, her grandmother's attitude. Lydia and Susanna were just as much Margaret Wentworth's granddaughters as she was, but Gran had wiped them out of her life as if they'd never existed.

Lydia apparently didn't have any problem forgiving her grandmother's attitude, but then the concept of forgiving if you would be forgiven was an integral part of Amish faith. Chloe was having far more trouble eliminating her resentment.

Still, she was trying, and making her weekly phone call was part of her effort. Each time she talked with her grandmother, she tried to open Gran's heart. Maybe one day she'd succeed.

Chloe hit the number and prepared to be conciliatory, even if it killed her. "Hello, Gran. How are you?"

"Fine, as always. Where are you?"

Chloe pressed down the annoyance the question always roused. It was as if Gran conveniently forgot Chloe's decision to move to Oyersburg for a few months.

"I'm in my little cottage in Oyersburg." She kept her tone pleasant.

"I hoped you had gotten tired of this whim of yours by now."

There wasn't a hint of bending in Gran's attitude. Chloe could picture her sitting very upright in the Queen Anne chair that was her favorite, every white curl in place, touching the pearls she always wore.

Maybe ignoring the negative was the best course. "I was

able to interview two new craftspeople for the paper I'm writing, and I got some excellent photographs. I've been thinking that I might be able to work up several journal articles, in addition to the research project."

"I suppose it's important that you move on professionally." Gran's tone was grudging, but her comment was a step up from her usual attitude about Chloe's work. "Are you still seeing that man?"

"Seth Miller," Chloe said, striving for patience. Gran knew the name perfectly well. "We're . . . friends." That was as good a description as any, she supposed.

Gran gave a ladylike snort. "He wouldn't go to so much trouble for you if all he wanted was friendship. He's smart enough to know which side his bread is buttered on." She brought out the old cliché with an air that said it proved she was correct in her assumptions about someone she barely knew.

"Seth is successful in his own right," Chloe contented herself with saying. The fact that Seth wasn't interested in her prospective inheritance was one thing she was absolutely sure of in their relationship.

Maybe the only thing. All those hints he'd been dropping—about his obligations to his family, about being tired of the travel his job required—were they preliminary to a decision to return to the Amish?

"Chloe? Are you still there?"

Chloe cleared her mind with an effort. "I'm here. I went out to Lydia and Adam's place for supper today."

"I'm not interested." Gran's reply was automatic.

"I played board games with Daniel and David, since it was raining. Daniel beat me two times out of three."

"I'm not interested," Gran repeated.

Chloe's control slipped. How could Gran not want to know about her two bright, beautiful great-grandchildren?

"Then I suppose you're not interested to know that I told Susanna that we're her sisters."

Silence for a moment. Then . . . "How did she take it?"

Chloe's heart gave a lurch at the sign of weakening. "She was confused, of course. Upset."

"Maybe you should have left well enough alone."

"She had to know the truth, Gran. Just as I did. Lydia and I plan to talk with her again tomorrow."

"I see." Gran's tone had hardened. "When are you coming home?" The question was almost an accusation.

"Not for a while," Chloe hedged. Maybe she ought to drive down to see her grandmother for a few days—

"It seems to me that in your enthusiasm for your new family you're happy to forget the one you already have."

Before Chloe could respond, her grandmother ended the call. She sat holding the phone between her hands, feeling as if she'd been slapped.

By the time she'd picked up Lydia and was driving back toward Oyersburg the next day, Chloe found she was able to think of her grandmother without feeling her stomach clench. She was trying to do her best for both sides of her family, and it wasn't fair for Gran to make her feel like a tennis ball being batted between them.

"Did you call your grandmother last night?" Lydia asked, almost as if she'd been following Chloe's thoughts.

"Yes. She's well." Chloe hesitated, using the narrow bridge

that crossed the Susquehanna as a reason to concentrate on her driving for a moment.

She didn't want to give Lydia false hope that their mutual grandmother was coming around, but she felt the need to say something encouraging.

"I told her about playing board games with Daniel and David. Honestly, those two are so smart they could beat me every time if I didn't have a little luck."

"They're used to the games, that's all it is," Lydia said, with the typical Amish unwillingness to brag about her sons. "You shouldn't feel as if you have to play with them all the time."

"I enjoy it." Chloe smiled, thinking of Daniel's intent expression as he studied the board. "I love having nephews."

"And they're wonderful glad to have you as an aunt." Lydia seemed to be studying Chloe's face as they neared the outskirts of Oyersburg. "I think you're not telling me something about your talk with your grandmother, ain't so?"

Chloe shrugged ruefully. "You see right through me, don't you? The truth is that she made me feel as if I'm ignoring her." *In favor of you.* The words were unspoken, but Lydia probably guessed those, too.

"We would miss you if you went away," Lydia said. "But maybe you should pay her a visit. Old people get lonely."

Chloe didn't think Gran had ever suffered from loneliness, but maybe that was doing her a disservice. Gran had been trained from birth to hide her emotions, so that now it was second nature. Chloe sometimes wondered if all that suppression had robbed Gran of the ability to feel at all.

"I suppose so, but chances are it's just a ploy to get me back there, and if so, it'll end in another argument when I try to leave."

"The only way you'll know is to go and see for yourself, ain't so? Just don't stay away too long. We'll miss you. And I know someone else who will miss you, too."

"If you're talking about Seth . . ." She needed to air her concerns about Seth to someone, but she wasn't sure Lydia was the right person.

"Ja, of course, who else? Even Adam has noticed how much attention he pays to you, and my husband is not the noticing kind when it comes to romance." There was a thread of laughter in Lydia's voice.

"Maybe Seth just feels responsible for me, because he's the one who found me for you." But if that were true, how did she explain the chemistry that sparked each time he touched her? Or the sizzle of that kiss?

"We both know better than that." Lydia hesitated. "If you don't want to talk about Seth, I understand. I just can't help wanting you to be as happy in love as I am."

"You're a lucky woman," Chloe said, buying time to think.

"I am, that's certain-sure." Lydia smoothed her hand over her belly in that protective gesture that seemed common to all pregnant women. "But you can be, as well, with the right man."

That really was the point. "Is Seth right for me? I can't help wondering if he'll . . ." She let that trail off, not sure she wanted to verbalize the rest of it.

"If he will what?" Lydia leaned toward her, as if conscious that they were running out of time for this conversation. They'd be at the shop in another few minutes.

"If he's thinking of becoming Amish again." There, it was out.

Lydia reached out to touch her arm. "I don't know what is

in Seth's mind. A few months ago I'd have said such a decision was impossible, and I still think it unlikely. But if he did, would that mean you couldn't love him?"

Chloe could hear the unspoken longing in her sister's voice, and it startled her that she'd never realized what was in Lydia's heart until now. Lydia wanted to see her back in the faith and life into which she'd been born.

Chloe's throat went tight at the thought of hurting her sister, but she had to speak the truth. Falsehoods had caused enough damage in their lives already.

"I might love him, but I couldn't marry him." She fought to keep her voice even. "That would mean becoming Amish."

"Is that such a bad thing? Our mother did it."

"She must have been a very special person." Tears stung Chloe's eyes, and she blinked them back. "I admire you and the family very much, Lydia, but I know I could never be like you. I'm sorry."

"Ach, don't be sorry." Lydia squeezed her hand and sat back in the seat, watching as Chloe pulled into a parking space a short distance from Susanna's store. "We love you as you are, and we're not trying to change you."

Chloe's tension began to seep away. Lydia had said possibly the best thing anyone could hear from someone they loved. "Thank you," she said softly. She turned off the ignition and blotted away a tear that had escaped.

"Okay, that's enough emotion for one day. We'd better figure out what we're going to say to Susanna."

Lydia smiled. "You Englisch, always wanting to plan things out in advance," she teased. "Why not just see what Susanna is saying and feeling, and go from there?"

"Okay." She opened the door, stepping out into the street. "We'll do it your way. If I start moving too fast, you'll have to step on my foot or something to warn me."

"You'll know." Lydia joined her on the sidewalk, and if there was anything incongruous about the two of them being so different and yet so alike in some ways, it didn't seem to bother her. "All we can do is pray the way I did that first day I came to Oyersburg to meet my Englisch little sister. That God will open her heart to let us in."

Chloe nodded, and together they walked to Susanna's shop.

CHAPTER SIX

Susanna was giving the shop's wooden toys a polish in preparation for creating a new display. Much as she appreciated keeping her hands busy, unfortunately the chore gave her mind too much time to wander. Worrying about the future ran counter to her beliefs, but she seemed unable to stop.

It was a relief to hear the bell jingle. She turned, smiling to greet a customer, and her heart gave an unaccustomed jolt. It was Lydia and Chloe. *Her sisters.*

No matter how many times she repeated that to herself, it didn't seem real. Surely she should feel something when she saw her blood kin, shouldn't she?

Lydia looked much as usual with her maroon dress and matching apron, the black bonnet over her kapp hiding her hair. Instead of her usual blue jeans, Chloe wore a pair of tan trousers with a deep green sweater, green earrings dangling from her earlobes. It seemed so unlikely that they could be sisters, and yet seeing them side by side, she couldn't help but see similarities in their faces. And similar to hers? She wasn't ready to look for that yet.

"Lydia, Chloe." She nodded, not sure what to say.

"It's gut to see you, Susanna." Lydia's voice was as soft and friendly as ever as she came to where Susanna had been working at the counter. "All this time it's wondered me how to tell you, but now you know, and I'm glad."

It was impossible to doubt anything Lydia said—sincerity shone in her eyes. She was the same person Susanna had known for months, and yet she was different.

"I talked to Bishop Mose," Susanna said abruptly. She'd best get this out quickly, before they started trying to convince her again. "He confirmed that the story Chloe told me was the truth."

"Ja, we heard you had been to see him," Lydia said. "Not from the bishop," she added quickly. "He would not discuss your business with anyone else."

"No, I don't suppose he would." Something that might have been anger flickered through her, startling her. She didn't get angry, did she? "He knew all along."

"You're thinking he should have told us. It seemed to me he regretted agreeing to the idea to begin with, but your mamm . . ." Lydia hesitated, as if not sure whether she should go on.

Susanna picked up a small wooden locomotive and began polishing it with unnecessary force. "Go on and say it. You're blaming my mother for all the secrecy."

"Nobody's doing that." Chloe sounded as if she'd been quiet for as long as she could stand. "After all, my grandmother . . . our grandmother . . . was just as determined that I would never know." With one of her quick movements, she snatched the cloth from Susanna's hand. "Please, Susanna. Talk to us."

"I . . . I have work to do." It was a pitiful excuse, and all three of them knew it. She felt outnumbered. This relationship was being pushed on her whether she wanted it or not.

"We'll help, ja?" Lydia removed her bonnet as she spoke, smoothing her brown hair back under her kapp. "Many hands make light work."

"My mamm always said that." The memory pierced Susanna's heart, softening her response to them. "You didn't know her. She was the sweetest person in the world. She would never have done anything wrong."

"I don't suppose any of them thought it was wrong." Chloe picked up one of the carved wooden dogs, straightening the bow around its neck.

"My adoptive mother, your aunt Anna, told me that your mamm had had several miscarriages and had begun to despair of ever having a child." Lydia hesitated. "I don't know if you ever knew that about her."

Susanna shook her head, trying to wrap her mind around the fact that she had not only sisters, but also an aunt who had known something about Mamm that she hadn't.

"I asked her once why I didn't have any brothers or sisters. She said that God had sent them only one child, but that I made them as happy as if they'd had a dozen." She flushed a little, wondering if that sounded like bragging. "I didn't mean—"

"Ach, I know what you mean." Lydia's smile broke through. "Mothers are like that, that's certain-sure. Anyone else might think my two boys very ordinary, but to me they're the most special kinder in the world."

"They are special," Chloe declared. "Daniel is so smart and serious, and David makes me laugh every time I talk to him." She grinned. "I guess I'm a prejudiced aunt."

An aunt. That was another new role for Susanna, but at least it was one that appealed to her. To have some claim to the kinder, to have a special relationship with them . . . that would be worth a great deal, maybe even taking on a lot of new relatives with them.

"They sound like dear kinder," she said.

"We would like you to come to supper and meet them," Lydia said, sounding as if she were feeling her way. "They're excited at the idea of having another aunt."

"So they know?" Again Susanna had the sense that things were moving too fast.

"Ja, well, once Chloe and I found each other, it was hard to keep the news from going around Pleasant Valley." Lydia's tone was apologetic. "It would be different in a bigger town like Oyersburg, I suppose, but everyone knows everyone in Pleasant Valley. Some of the older people knew our birth parents well, you see."

That must have made the situation difficult for Lydia, living there and feeling as if everyone was aware of her business. At least in Oyersburg no one knew except Dora and Nate.

Susanna realized she'd been polishing the locomotive so hard it was a wonder she hadn't rubbed the paint off. She set it down, trying to frame the words that would show Lydia and Chloe how she felt.

"Bishop Mose pointed out that none of the secrecy was your fault." She looked up to find both Lydia and Chloe watching her so intently that they seemed to be touching her. "I know that's true, but . . ." Susanna's breath caught in her throat. "I can't suddenly start feeling like a sister, even if I am. It's just . . . not possible."

"I understand," Lydia said, but regret filled her voice. "Once I'd learned the truth, I realized that if we'd known about each other all along, you and I would have been friends, or maybe like cousins, all this time. We'd have written to each other and shared things about our lives. Maybe . . . maybe we could start there and see how it goes, ja?"

Susanna hesitated. It was reasonable, she supposed, but somehow it still felt disloyal to Mamm. She glanced at Chloe, noting that her normally lively face was serious.

"Was that how you and Chloe started getting acquainted?" she asked, trying to imagine how that would work with an Englisch person.

Chloe's smile returned. "I was pretty tough, actually. I threw Seth Miller out of my office when he came to tell me the truth about my parents and sisters. And when Lydia finally got me to come to Pleasant Valley, I got into a fight with Adam and went storming home again."

"Really?" Susanna tried to imagine herself quarreling with Lydia's husband, the man who made the lovely clocks she sold. She couldn't. That would never be her way.

"Yes, well . . ." Chloe paused, and Susanna had a sense she was struggling. "I was raised very differently, you know. My grandmother . . . our grandmother . . . always felt that the Amish had lured our mother away. She couldn't accept any other explanation."

Susanna considered this unknown grandmother. "That must make her very unhappy, ain't so?"

Chloe's green eyes seemed to darken. "Probably so, although I don't think she'd admit it."

The hurt in her voice touched Susanna's heart. "It's hard for you, too, ja?"

Chloe nodded. "For a time I thought I could just go back home and forget about Lydia, but I couldn't. As difficult as it is to change the way I think about my family, I wouldn't go back to not knowing for anything."

I'm not you. That was what Susanna wanted to say, but those words would be unkind. "I know you meant it for the best when you told me."

Chloe looked rueful. "I shouldn't have blurted it out the way I did. I realize that now. Obviously I'm not very good at keeping secrets."

Lydia and Chloe were both looking at her as if they expected something—more than she could give, she suspected.

When she didn't respond, they exchanged glances. "We would like to be friends," Lydia said, as carefully as if her words were breakable. "Is that all right with you?"

Susanna was swept with a longing to refuse—to try to pretend none of this had happened. Chloe had said she'd tried that, and it hadn't worked. It probably wouldn't for her, either. Once a secret was out of the box, it could never be stuffed back in again.

She felt as if she were taking a giant step into the dark. "Ja," she said. "Friends."

Seth set the clean supper dishes back in his mamm's kitchen cabinets, well aware of the protest in Mamm's gaze. Never mind that her son had been Englisch for the better part of ten years; to her mind washing up after supper was women's work.

He grinned at her. "I know what you're thinking, but I like

sharing the chores with you and Jessie. It gives us a chance to visit."

Mamm's expression lightened. "Ja, well, as long as you enjoy it. You know we love having you here."

"I know." Guilt flickered. He hadn't yet told her that his boss wanted him in San Francisco next week for an extended stay as he worked with a new client.

Mamm would insist they'd be fine without him. But with his mother's slow recovery from her hip surgery and his sister's recent diagnosis of bipolar disorder, he couldn't shrug off his responsibilities as easily as he used to.

Jessie, busy sweeping the wide wooden boards of the kitchen floor, paused when she reached the door, and looked out. "I see Chloe's over at Lydia and Adam's again. It seems like she's there all the time."

There was a discontented note in Jessie's voice that had Seth exchanging worried glances with his mother. Despite the hope that Jessie was doing better on her new medication, he sometimes felt as if they were walking on eggshells around her, always afraid she'd lash out over some imagined slight.

"Chloe is Lydia's sister, for all she was raised Englisch," Mamm said mildly.

"I heard she was driving Lydia over to Oyersburg today so they could visit with Susanna," he added, hoping to send the conversation in a different direction. "She probably brought Lydia home and stayed for supper." He held the screen door so that Jessie could sweep a few crumbs outside. "Your Englisch bruder is always coming to supper, too, ja?"

Jessie usually smiled when he reverted to the Pennsylvania Dutch he hadn't spoken in years, and she did now.

"Ach, we can never get rid of you when Mamm is cooking, ain't so?"

"If you'd eaten as many restaurant meals as I have, you'd know why." He stood at the screen door, looking across Adam and Lydia's orchard, the trees heavy with fruit, toward their house.

Chloe's blue compact car was parked in her usual spot by the oak tree. It had rained earlier, but now the setting sun slanted across the valley, giving it a haze of gold.

He was still uneasy about the way he and Chloe had parted on Saturday. What was going on with her? He knew she was worried about the situation with Susanna, but that didn't explain her coolness to him.

Trying to understand women was a futile act, he sometimes thought. Why couldn't Chloe just come out with whatever was bugging her? Was he supposed to guess?

"Seth." Mamm said his name with a tone that suggested she'd tried more than once to get his attention. "I said, if you're going to walk over to Lydia's, you can take a loaf of the nut bread I made this afternoon."

Why not? Why not go over there, corner Chloe, and get some answers?

"Sure, Mamm. I'd be glad to. You want me to pick up some apples from them, too?"

"If they have any to spare, you might bring a bag back with you." Mamm started to reach for her change purse, and he shook his head.

"I'll take care of it."

"Ja, Mamm, he'll probably eat most of the pie anyway," Jessie said, surprising him. It was a sign of progress, he thought, that she could tease him. Maybe the little sister he'd left behind when he bolted for the Englisch world was finally seeing him as her brother.

Mamm handed him the wrapped loaf of nut bread. "Give them my love, ja?"

He nodded. "Will do." He'd taken a step toward the door when he glanced toward Jessie and saw the disappointment in her face. He hadn't asked her to go along, and he knew how much it meant to her to be included.

"You coming, Jessie?" he asked, as if it was a matter of course that she would.

"Ja, sure." Her face lightened, the sparkle back in her blue eyes.

They headed toward the orchard together, and he matched his long stride to his sister's shorter one. Not that Jessie was all that little any longer. She was in her early twenties now, and most of her friends were married. How much did her still being unmarried have to do with the depression that sometimes seized her in such a grip? He'd been struggling to understand the medical implications of her problems, but the personal were even more important.

Jessie was pert, smart, and pretty, with those big blue eyes and her lively expression. But her problems seemed to have separated her from the other young people her age, and that had to be painful.

They had reached the orchard, and the grass was wet underfoot.

Jessie took a deep breath. "Smells wonderful gut, ain't so?"

After the rain, the air seemed perfumed by the fruit all around them. "Smells like autumn, I think. All that time I was away, if I passed a fruit stand and smelled that aroma, I remembered this place in the fall."

"You've missed it." Jessie darted a sidelong look at him.

"I have," he admitted. "But I don't need to anymore, do I? I'm here now."

Daniel and David, who'd been lingering near the wagon filled with baskets of apples, came dashing to meet them. "We sold three baskets of apples all by ourselves today," Daniel burst out.

"I helped put them in the lady's car," David added, eager not to be left out. "She said we were gut helpers and gave each of us a quarter."

"That was sehr kind of her," Jessie said, smiling at them.

"What did you do with the quarters?" Seth tapped the top of David's straw hat that was exactly like the one his daad wore.

"Gave them to Mammi," Daniel said promptly.

Of course. Everyone, even the little ones, learned to work for their families. Lydia would have showed the boys that she valued their quarters just as much as she did the checks Adam received for his handcrafted clocks. It was a good way of teaching children Amish values.

The boys, happy with Jessie's show of interest, were tugging her by the hands, wanting to show her something about the way they'd arranged the baskets of apples. Laughing, she let herself be led away, and the sound of the laugh warmed Seth's heart. If only Jessie could always be that way—open and happy.

Adam was sorting apples on the long picnic table in the backyard. Seth walked over to join him. Better not make it too obvious that he'd come because he wanted to see Chloe.

"Looks like you've got a couple of eager salesmen manning the apple stand." He nodded to the boys.

Adam's wary look vanished in a smile. "The boys like to

sell the apples, that's certain-sure. They're not so gut at sorting, but at least David has stopped taking a bite out of every one he fancies."

Seth laughed. David was definitely what the Amish would call a schnicklefritz, a mischievous child. "You must be having a job getting the picking done with all the rain we've been having."

"You're right about that." Adam's hands moved quickly through the apples as he talked. "The ground's pretty well saturated, and I heard talk in town that a storm is moving up the coast, all set to bring us even more."

"Guess I did hear something about that on the weather." Seth glanced around at a sound on the porch, hoping he wasn't being too obvious. Sure enough, Chloe appeared, but Lydia was with her.

It looked as if he'd miscalculated. It was all very well to come over here intending to have it out with Chloe, but there were just too many people around.

He handed the wrapped loaf to Lydia. "From my mamm, with her love."

"How kind of her." Lydia cradled the package against her. "You must take some apples back for her."

"She did say she'd like to buy a basket if you have enough to spare." Seth tried to catch Chloe's eye, but she seemed to be looking everywhere except at him.

"Ach, we're not taking money from our neighbor for a few apples," Adam said. "I'll make up a basket. I know what she likes."

"Did I hear you two talking about all the rain when we came out?" Lydia asked, her forehead wrinkling.

"Ja, I was telling Seth what I told you, about how there might be a storm coming up the coast with heavy rain."

"I thought rain was good for the orchard," Chloe said, apparently responding to the concern on Lydia's face.

"Not if it keeps us from doing the picking when we need to," Lydia said.

"And a storm could break branches, as heavy as they are with the fruit," Adam added. He glanced at Chloe. "You'd best keep an eye on that creek behind your place. It floods awful easy."

"The cottage sits well above the water," Chloe said. "I can't imagine it would get that high."

For a moment Adam looked as if he'd dispute the point, but then he turned away and began filling another basket. Adam was reluctant to argue with his Englisch sister-in-law, Seth suspected. He was only too aware of how much it hurt Lydia to see those she loved disagreeing.

"I'm going to need a few more baskets." Adam glanced toward Lydia.

"I'll get them—" she began, but Seth, seeing his opportunity, cut her off.

"I'll do it," he said. "In the barn, are they? Chloe can help me."

Before she could come up with an excuse, he seized Chloe's hand and propelled her toward the barn.

Fortunately she was either too smart or too polite to make a scene. Once they disappeared from view of the others behind the barn doors, she yanked her arm free and faced him, obviously seething.

"What's going on?" she demanded. "You practically shanghaied me to get me out here."

"That's just what I want to ask you. What's going on?"

"I don't know what you're talking about." With her hands

on her hips and her green eyes shooting sparks, Chloe looked ready for battle.

"You. Me." He flung out his hands, frustrated. "You care to explain what happened on Saturday? One minute we're having a good time together, and the next you're looking at me like I'm something you scraped off the bottom of your shoe."

Her color heightened, but her gaze slid away from his. "I didn't do any such thing."

"Come on, Chloe. At least be honest with me. The temperature in the room dropped from mild and sunny to frigid in a matter of minutes, and you know it."

Chloe shook her head, but not as if she disagreed with him. It was more as if she was arguing with herself. "I didn't mean to come across that way. I just thought . . ." She let that trail off, and she turned slightly away from him. "We agreed to move slowly, didn't we? Because of family and . . ." Her gesture seemed to take in the world. Or maybe just the Amish portion of it.

"We did," he said, feeling his way, trying to understand what she seemed unwilling to clarify. "But I didn't think that meant coming to a complete halt. Come on, Chloe. Something happened to make you act that way, and I don't know what. Tell me. You owe me that much, at least."

"I owe you a lot," she said, a spark of the anger back in her face. "My relationship with my sister, for instance. Do you think you need to remind me?"

"That's not what I meant, and you know it." She seemed to be deliberately misunderstanding him. "I'm talking about us. You and me, totally separate from families."

"That's the whole point." The words burst out of her. "Don't you see that? Our relationship, whatever it is, doesn't exist in a vacuum. And just lately I've been getting the impression that you're reconsidering where you belong. Which are you, Amish or Englisch?"

He felt as if she'd thrown a bucket of cold water in his face. He was still groping for an answer when she spoke again.

"You aren't sure, are you? Every time you talk about what you owe your family and how much you love being here, I get the feeling that you're thinking about becoming Amish again."

He hadn't been, not consciously, but the moment he heard the words he knew that possibility had been in the back of his mind all along. He studied her face.

"I don't know, and that's as honest as I can be about it. But is that so bad? I thought you'd gotten over your prejudice toward the Amish."

"It's not a question of prejudice." The pain was evident in her voice. "You ought to know that by now. But I'm not remotely willing to commit to that way of life for myself. And until you decide if you are, it's better if we call a halt."

With that she was gone, leaving him to collect the baskets and wonder what it was he really wanted.

Chloe walked up the street toward Susanna's shop the next day, glad the rain seemed to be over for the moment. She wasn't sure what kind of reception she'd get from Susanna, but worrying about her was at least a change from fretting over her relationship with Seth. She'd done far too much of that last night, lying in bed unable to sleep, listening to the creek pour over the rocks.

Trading that for her concern about her relationship with Susanna was rather like exchanging a sore throat for a sprained wrist. They both hurt, but it seemed a person could only concentrate on one at a time.

Chloe had been impatient with Lydia's slow approach to Susanna, but she had to admit that it seemed more effective than her tactics had been. Maybe Lydia understood Susanna better because they were both Amish, while she was an outsider. She couldn't hope to compete in that area.

Still, she'd been the one Susanna had confided in about the threat to her shop. They'd been friends then, and despite what had happened since, she had to believe that that basic friendship was still intact. And if so, she was determined to build on it. She was going in the shop, and she wouldn't come out until she'd made some positive forward progress with her sister.

The usual assortment of items was displayed on the porch. Two milk cans, decorated with painted hex signs, stood next to a fanciful bird house, designed to look like an Amish barn. It must be a struggle for Susanna to haul all this stuff in every evening and put it out again every morning. She touched a bentwood rocking chair, setting it gently rocking. If she hung around until closing, she could help.

Susanna was busy with a customer when Chloe entered the shop, so Chloe didn't approach them. Instead she paused to admire the handcrafted toy display. A row of faceless Amish dolls called to her, and she picked up one.

If their parents hadn't died in that freak accident on an Ohio highway, she'd probably have one of these tucked away someplace. It would be a battered, much-loved remnant of a happy childhood. If Lydia's baby proved to be the longed-for girl, she could get one for her new niece.

With an exchange of pleasantries, the customer said her good-byes and left the shop, a well-filled bag hanging from her arm. Chloe faced Susanna, trusting her expression showed confidence.

"I hope I'm still welcome to carry on with my project." She gestured with the camera bag that she carried slung over her shoulder.

"Of course." Susanna seemed to make an effort to produce a smile. "You're well, I hope. And Lydia—she wasn't too upset after we talked yesterday?"

Taking that as an invitation to visit, Chloe set her camera bag on the counter. "I don't think so. Lydia seems to have the gift of taking things as they come. That's probably what makes her such a good mother."

"The little boys." Susanna's smile had a touch of wistfulness. "I would like to meet them, one day."

"Anytime you say," Chloe responded, reminding herself that Lydia would be telling her to go slowly. "When you're ready, Lydia would love it."

"I would be a little nervous," Susanna said with a sudden burst of honesty. "I never thought to have any nieces or nephews. What if they don't like me?"

Chloe had to laugh. "You're exactly the way I was, the first time I was going to meet them. What would they think of me? But they're just as loving as their mamm is, and they'll be delighted to have another aunt."

This was good. They were talking, sharing their feelings, with no lingering awkwardness over her having blurted out the secret.

"I wanted to ask you . . ." Susanna seemed to run out of words, and a small wrinkle had appeared between her eyes.

"What? You can ask me anything."

Susanna nodded, apparently accepting her words at face value. "When you told me about our relationship—why did you decide to do it then?"

She hadn't expected that question, and for a moment she couldn't think how to answer. "Well, I suppose it was because you'd told me about your problems with Dora's son about the shop. I wanted you to know that you had family that would be on your side."

"I didn't want to think it was because you felt sorry for me." Susanna's intent gaze wouldn't be satisfied with less than the truth.

"Not sorry for you, no. Just . . . hurting, because you seemed so alone." Chloe managed a smile. "I'm not an expert, but I think that's what sisters do. They hurt for each other."

Susanna's eyes shone with sudden tears. "Denke," she murmured.

Chloe's heart leaped. For once it appeared she'd said the right thing. Now if she could just follow up correctly—

"If you decide you want to buy out Dora's share of the shop, I'd like to help you."

She knew the answer even before Susanna spoke, reading it in the instinctive shake of Susanna's head.

"No. I could not take your money."

"But it would only be fair." She should probably shut up, but she longed to explain. "I'm not rich, by any means, but I did receive some money from my grandfather when he died. He was your grandfather, too, and I'm sure if he'd gotten to know you, he'd have made provisions for you."

Susanna's heart-shaped face was an image of distress. "Please don't, Chloe. I know you mean well, but I can't."

Once again, it seemed she'd rushed ahead of herself in her eagerness to help. Well, if Susanna wouldn't accept financial help from her, there might be another way.

"All right." She reached across the counter to pat Susanna's hand. "I won't bring up the subject again, but I can't help worrying about it. The shop means so much to you. It wouldn't be right for you to have to give it up. Dora's son must be the most inconsiderate man on earth."

"He's not that. He's very kind and caring of his mother. I'm sure he just doesn't realize how difficult the financial side is right now for me. Everything will work out." But the words rang hollow.

"Have you considered a business loan from a bank?" Chloe made an effort to keep her tone casual. "That's done all the time in situations like these. Unless it's against the rules for Amish to borrow money, that is."

Once again, she'd bumped up against something she didn't know about her sisters' beliefs.

"No, it's not forbidden. Amish do borrow sometimes, for new equipment and the like." Susanna actually seemed to be mulling over her words. "But I wouldn't begin to know how to do such a thing."

"I'd be happy to help, if you want to try." Chloe had to fight to control her eagerness. "I can't tell you the number of forms I've filled out in my life. I could stop by the bank today and see what's involved in making a loan application."

Susanna seemed to teeter on the edge of hope. "If I could do that . . . of course, I'd need to find out what Dora would consider a fair price." A shadow crossed her face. "And her son."

Yes, the son. Well, now that she was finally making progress with Susanna, Chloe was not about to let Nate Gaus mess things up. If he tried, he'd have to deal with her.

CHAPTER SEVEN

*N*ate had been telling himself there was no need for him to stop by the shop to see Susanna. No need at all. He could easily have left a message on the business phone to tell her his mother wouldn't be in this afternoon.

So why was he approaching the gift shop? It annoyed him that he didn't have an immediate answer to that question. He always knew his own mind. Anyone would say that about him.

He was trying to be fair about this situation, as he'd told Susanna he would. Still, it was time to come to a conclusion about the business.

This should be a simple enough matter—settle things with Susanna, and then tell Mamm what they'd decided. He tried to ignore the little voice in the back of his mind that insisted it wouldn't be that easy.

He stepped inside, pausing for a moment by the door to let his vision adjust after the bright sunshine outside. At first he thought the shop was empty, and then he realized Susanna was at the back counter with another woman—the Englisch woman who'd been here the day Mamm took sick. The one who was, oddly enough, Susanna's sister.

He walked toward them. Maybe the Englischer would take the hint and leave if he said he had to talk to Susanna. He glanced at her and discovered she was glaring at him with obvious dislike.

Switching his gaze, he greeted Susanna. "Susanna." He nodded to her. "How are you?"

"Fine," she said automatically. He thought she looked a little surprised, maybe even unsettled, at the sight of him. Then she glanced toward the Englisch woman. "You remember Chloe Wentworth, my . . . my sister."

So. He hadn't thought Susanna was ready to claim the woman as her sister. It seemed he'd been wrong.

"Is Dora having a problem? Why are . . ." Susanna let that trail off, probably thinking it rude to ask him why he was here.

"Mamm won't be in this afternoon. She wanted me to let you know." There, that was his ostensible purpose for coming.

"She's not ill? She seemed fine at church." The worry in Susanna's face threw him off stride. Her love for his mother was obvious, and it had to be figured into the discussion they must have.

"I'm afraid she had another bad dizzy spell late yesterday." He glanced at Chloe, hoping she'd accept that this was a private matter.

She didn't show any signs of moving, however. She leaned against a table filled with baskets, her arms crossed.

"Oh, no." Susanna's eyes were dark with distress. "I hoped the change in medication would put an end to the dizziness. She must feel frustrated."

That was exactly what his mother felt. She couldn't accept anything that prevented her from doing what she thought she should.

"Ja, that's it," he said. "We called the doctor's office, and he wants to do some more tests. So we don't have any answers yet."

"Please tell her not to worry about the shop," Susanna said. "I'll take care of everything. She must concentrate on getting better, ain't so?"

He nodded, glad she'd given him this opening. "It seems to me that we—you and I—should come to some conclusion about the future of the shop. Then Mamm can stop worrying about what's happening here when she should be thinking about herself."

Susanna frowned. "She wouldn't like to think we were making decisions that should be hers."

Each time he thought he was making headway, he ran up against the same roadblock. Susanna was as stubborn about protecting his mother as Mamm was about looking after her.

"Not making decisions for Mamm," he said, trying to sound persuasive and to ignore the other woman glaring at him. "It's just a matter of showing her that she doesn't have to feel guilty about giving up the shop. Changes will be easier to take if Mamm knows we all agree on what will happen, ain't so?"

Persuasion didn't seem to be working. Susanna's gaze was doubting, while Chloe's was outright hostile. Well, he had no choice but to forge ahead.

"It seems to me the first question is whether you want to sell the shop outright if Mamm can't go on with it."

Susanna's face set firmly, making her appear momentarily older than her years. "No."

That was blunt and decided. Well, better to know than wonder. Still, had she really thought this through?

"You're sure you don't want to go back home to Ohio?"

Susanna looked almost surprised at the question. "This is my home now."

Did she mean Oyersburg or the shop? He didn't know, and maybe she didn't, either.

"Well, then, the logical thing is for you to buy out my mother, ain't so?"

"I suppose so." She seemed to lose some color. "How much are you thinking her share of the shop is worth?"

Nate glanced around, hoping the women couldn't tell that he was at a loss, an unusual thing for him when it came to business. He'd been so sure that after thinking it over, Susanna would have decided that they should sell the shop outright. Setting a price that way would be simpler than trying to establish an appropriate cost for Mamm's share.

"There is the value of the stock, in addition to the value of an established business, to consider."

"What about the amount my father put up for my half of the business? Wouldn't that be fair?"

Her question startled him. He hadn't thought she'd have an opinion already. "That's true, but the shop has far more stock now than it did then," he pointed out. "You've been on the verge of running out of space for the past year or so."

"The increase in the number of craftspeople the shop represents and the amount of the stock they carry is due in large part to my sister's effort." Chloe's interruption seemed to startle Susanna as much as it did him. "You can't simply divide that in half."

"But I . . ." Susanna began.

"My mother's reputation and knowledge made the shop what it is," he countered, glaring at Chloe.

"My sister's vision and efforts expanded it far beyond the original concept." Chloe came right back at him, and he thought she was enjoying this battle.

He wasn't. "This is a matter for Susanna to decide." *Not you.*

"And for your mother," Chloe retorted. "Maybe we should get an independent valuation of the stock."

"Amish don't bring outsiders into their business decisions," he snapped.

"Stop, both of you."

Susanna's decided voice had both him and Chloe swinging to look at her. Emotion had brought a pink flush to her cheeks, and he was startled at how pretty she was with a bit of animation in her expression.

"I won't have quarreling about the business Dora and I built together."

"No, of course it's not right," he said, regretting that he'd let the woman egg him into a battle. "I apologize, Susanna." He took a breath, trying to come up with a reasonable way to deal with this situation. "Suppose you think it over and decide on an amount you think is fair. I will check through the tax records and do the same. Is that acceptable to you?"

Susanna nodded.

"We'll talk about it later, after we've both had a chance to prepare," he said. And he could only hope they'd be able to do it without her sister.

By Tuesday afternoon, Seth was feeling a little stir-crazy. He'd been cooped up in his small furnished apartment by a steady downpour that had started before dawn. All this rain was courtesy of Tropical Storm Leo, which had worked its way up the East Coast during the past few days.

The apartment was an improvement over the motel where he'd stayed when he'd first begun to spend so much time here, but it still wasn't suited for extended periods indoors. It made him feel like a gerbil in a cage.

He'd been trying to concentrate on his latest project, but his thoughts kept straying to Chloe and her outrageous suggestion that he was leaning toward becoming Amish again. The trouble was that maybe the idea was less fantastic than it seemed.

Was he really considering joining the church? Reversing the action he'd taken years ago when he'd jumped the fence to the outside world?

People did, of course. It was common enough not even to cause much comment when a young man left the community before baptism, stayed in the Englisch world for a couple of years, and then came home, much to his parents' relief. It even happened with young Amish women, though much less often.

He ran his fingers through his hair. That wasn't remotely his situation. He'd been away more than ten years, and he'd built a successful career in a technological field that was about as far as it could be from Amish life. Six months ago he'd have laughed at the suggestion that he'd ever give that up.

He wasn't laughing now. Seth paced to the window and stared out at the rain. Maybe these thoughts had been building up ever since he'd moved his base of operations back here in January, when the situation with Jessie had reached a crisis and his mother, still in a rehab facility after she'd broken her hip, had been unable to cope.

At first the change had been a matter of necessity. He couldn't ignore his family's needs, and they couldn't be farmed out to someone else. He'd had to deal with them. But gradually, as winter turned to spring and then summer, he'd found himself adapting to the slower pace and rediscovering the forgotten joys of a quieter, simpler life.

Unfortunately his job, flexible though it was, demanded speed, busyness, movement. It called for teleconferences in the middle of the night and flying off across the country at a moment's notice.

This last was the source of his current stress. It had begun simply enough, with a conversation with his boss over the new project. Steve was a friend as well as a boss.

As a friend, he understood Seth's reluctance to commit to a lengthy stay in San Francisco at this time. As the head of the company, he had to make decisions that were best for business. He'd made it clear that as valuable as Seth was to them, if his heart wasn't in the work any longer, maybe he should consider making a change.

Seth's lips twisted. Steve had no idea just how great a change Seth was thinking of.

Could he do it? Could he give up the technology he loved? And if he did, what about Chloe?

He'd accused her of being prejudiced, but maybe the truth was that she simply knew where she belonged, unlike him.

Frustrated with the direction of his thinking, Seth grabbed the remote and switched on the television. Even a steady dose of political chatter was preferable to his thoughts.

But the news networks weren't preoccupied with the latest Washington chatter. Instead, they were focused on the storm.

Hurricane Leo, the news reporter announced, weakening now to a tropical storm, was still packing a powerful punch in terms of the rain it was pouring on the vulnerable areas of the northeast.

Seth watched, riveted, as the most endangered areas were outlined. The entire Susquehanna River basin was in the worst flood threat zone.

He flipped to one of the local channels, to find that it had given up normal programming to focus on the storm. Water was inching toward the top of the flood walls in Wilkes-Barre, volunteers were asked to report for sandbagging, and every downriver town was in danger.

Including Oyersburg. Chloe. The creeks would flood first, before pouring into the river. The whole lower end of Oyersburg was vulnerable, including Chloe's cottage, with the creek on one side and the river on the other. And Chloe was blithely ignorant of just how bad it could get.

Snatching up his phone, Seth hit her number even as he yanked a hooded water-resistant jacket from the closet. The call went straight to voice mail. Praying that meant someone else was already calling a warning to her, he left a message, telling her to get out as quickly as possible. Grabbing his keys, he hastened to the door.

The rain drenched him the instant he stepped outside. Ducking his head, he ran for the car, slid in, and spun out of the parking lot. The rain pounded the roof of the car, so loudly he could hardly think. Only one thing was clear—he had to reach Oyersburg and get Chloe out of that cottage. She had no idea how fast the creek could come up or just how dangerous it could be.

Muscles tensed as he gripped the steering wheel. There was a vivid picture in his mind of a flood that had hit when he was a teenager. He'd been among the group of Amish who'd spent days in Oyersburg helping with the cleanup. It seemed he could still smell the mud they'd shoveled out of basements. And that had been minor, as floods went. People still talked about the big one in 1972 that had devastated up-river towns.

And Susanna—he'd forgotten about Susanna in his anxiety over Chloe. Her shop was in the flood-prone area, too. Still, she'd lived in Oyersburg long enough to be aware, and no doubt her partner's family would be there to help her.

The windshield wipers worked furiously, but visibility was still terrible. He found he was leaning forward, as if another inch or two might make him see more clearly. The wind had power lines swaying. A branch flew across the road, striking the hood and skittering off again.

Seth's apartment was in a complex near the interstate, about equidistant from Pleasant Valley and Oyersburg. Pleasant Valley would probably see some stream flooding, but Mamm and Jessie would be all right—there was nothing near enough to endanger them.

Not daring to take his eyes from what he could see of the road, he felt for his cell phone and tried Chloe's number again. Still straight to voice mail. *Where are you, Chloe? Are you safe?*

Flashing red lights ahead alerted him, and he slowed to a crawl as he approached. He stared, appalled, at the water flowing freely around the edges of the bridge over a creek so small he didn't usually even notice it was there.

A yellow-slickered figure approached his window. He lowered it, getting a splash of cold water in his face.

"Where you trying to get to, sir?" The kid looked barely old enough to be out of school, his thin face tense with the importance of his job. He'd be volunteer fire police, probably, more used to directing traffic at parades than dealing with a flood.

"Oyersburg. No chance of getting across here?"

"Nope. Creek's eating the ground away on this side. They're saying the bridge will go for sure this time. Your best bet's to go round by Jefferson." The crack of a branch breaking punctuated his words, and he glanced toward it, looking scared for a moment before getting his emotions under control. "The bridge there's a little higher. You know the way?"

"Yeah. Thanks."

Seth was already turning the car as he punched the button to shut the window, tires squealing on the wet, leaf-covered road. Jefferson was a good ten miles out of his way, and there was no guarantee he wouldn't find the bridge closed when he got there. He did a quick search of his mental map and came up empty. It would be even farther if he took the interstate, and there was every possibility the exit there would be closed.

He snapped on the radio as he sped along the back road and found the local station in Oyersburg. They'd obviously switched to emergency mode, as the announcers gave up playing pop music to read off strings of closings and warnings that would only be comprehensible to people who knew the area. Apparently people were calling the station, reporting on a flooded street here or a bridge closing there. The local radio station was a lifeline at a time like this.

Listening to the string of reports, Seth felt cold fear growing. This was going to be bad—he was familiar enough with the Susquehanna River Basin to know it. The Hurricane Agnes flood in 1972 had supposedly been a hundred-year storm, but it sounded as if the next big one was arriving ahead of schedule.

Jefferson was hardly more than a hamlet. Seth slowed as he went through. Slicker-clad volunteers were evacuating families from the houses closest to the overflowing creek, loading belongings into pickups and people into cars. One family trudged along the road, probably heading for a neighbor's house, the father carrying a toddler while the mother clung to the hands of two little girls.

Seth reached the bridge and braked. Maybe they were too busy with evacuations to post a man here. A yellow DANGER sign leaned drunkenly against a sawhorse, but it didn't block the bridge. Still—

His breath caught when he took a good look. The water, brown with mud and impossibly high, surged within inches of the bridge deck. Tree limbs, brush, logs, and unidentifiable debris floated downstream. Already they were piling up against the bridge, adding their weight to the force of the water. The bridge would go; the only question was how soon.

If he didn't get across now . . .

With a silent prayer, he stepped on the accelerator. He thought he heard a shout from behind him as he shot forward. His tires hit the bridge deck, and he felt it shudder, tremble, sway—

Then he was over. He sped up the hill on the opposite side, risking a glance in the rearview mirror. A massive tree stump hit the bridge. With a groan that he could hear even with the windows shut, the bridge broke apart, letting the stream flow on triumphantly.

Clenching his teeth, he sped on. Surely, by this time, Chloe would have realized the danger. But he couldn't take that for granted. He had to see for himself. And what that said about his feelings for Chloe—well, he wasn't ready to admit.

Curled up in the corner of the living room sofa, Chloe grimaced at the computer open on the coffee table in front of her. She'd had good intentions of getting work done this rainy day, but it seemed everyone she knew had decided to call her.

So she didn't get much work done. She'd had a nice long chat with Kendra, her closest friend and colleague at the museum from which she was technically on leave. Kendra had, as usual, been full of humorous gossip about the ins and outs of museum life, and they'd chatted endlessly about anything and everything.

With one exception. Chloe hadn't mentioned Seth, and Kendra, with unusual tact for her, had respected that omission.

Chloe had still been smiling from Kendra's call when the phone sounded again, but Brad Maitland's voice had wiped the amusement from her face. Brad, a close family friend and a favorite of her grandmother's, had been a sort of honorary uncle to her most of her life.

Brad had sounded grave, but then, when didn't Brad sound that way? He was concerned about her grandmother, he'd said. She seemed to be failing, and he thought it was time Chloe came home. His tone had conjured up images of her imperious grandmother frail and weak, calling for her.

She'd nearly said she'd drive back at once, but she was only too aware that Gran wasn't above using Brad for her own ends. She'd get a second opinion before she raced back to Philadelphia.

Her call to the house in Chestnut Hill was answered, as Chloe had hoped, by Nora, the housekeeper.

"Chloe, it's nice to hear your voice." Nora had known her since she was a baby and considered Chloe as much hers as Gran's. "Are you having a good time? Are you eating enough?"

Chloe laughed at the familiar question. A spray of rain hit the window on the side of the cottage, loud enough to distract her for an instant. "I'm eating fine. My sister makes sure of it. How are you?"

"Can't complain," she said. "But you'll want to talk to your grandmother."

"Not yet," Chloe said quickly. "How is she? Dr. Maitland called to say she wasn't well. What's wrong?"

"I wouldn't say she's sick, exactly." Nora's tone was cautious, reminding Chloe that, after all, Gram paid her salary, and it was to Gran that Nora's first allegiance went. "Just a little more broody than normal."

Chloe heard an imperious voice in the background, demanding to know to whom Nora was speaking. Nora responded soothingly, and in a moment Chloe's grandmother came on the call.

"Chloe? Why were you talking to Nora?"

"Just asking how she is," Chloe said. "And more to the point, how are you? Brad Maitland called to say I should come home, implying you were 'failing,' as he put it. You didn't by any chance put him up to that, did you?"

"Failing?" Gran sounded outraged. "Nonsense. I'm perfectly fine."

Oddly enough, that troubled Chloe. If her grandmother was attempting to manipulate her, she'd surely be more likely to plead illness.

"I'm glad to hear it. I was worried."

"There's no need to be." Gran's tone was tart. "Not that I wouldn't be happy to see you give up this foolishness and come home where you belong."

"Gran . . ." Did she really have to go over her reasons for being here again?

"Yes, I know, you're writing a professional paper. But you could do that anywhere."

"Susanna is helping me," she said mildly, vaguely aware of an unusual level of noise from outside her cottage. "I'm settled here now. But I am thinking of coming for a short visit. Lydia suggested it," she added.

Silence for a moment. "How is she?" Gran's tone was grudging, but at least she asked the question.

"She's blooming. Expecting another baby this winter, and they're hoping for a girl this time."

"And the other one? Susanna?" Gran asked the question in an offhand tone that didn't fool Chloe.

"Doing better, I think. She's getting used to the idea of having sisters."

"Since they're doing so well, there's no reason you can't come home." That sounded more like Gran.

"I said I'd come for a short visit," Chloe said, trying to hang on to her patience. "Maybe toward the end of the week for two or three days."

"Two or three days?" Gran's voice rose.

The noise, like a muffled roar, seemed to be coming from behind the cottage. She rose, carrying the phone, and walked toward the door that led onto the deck.

"I think—"

Her voice died as she looked out the back. The creek—the little stream that normally trickled musically over the rocks—had become a sullen, swollen brown torrent, slapping at the deck. The sound she'd heard was the roar of water, and it was amplified a hundred times, it seemed, when she slid the glass door open.

"I have to go, Gran," she said quickly. "I'll call you later." She snapped off before her grandmother could protest and stuffed the phone in her pocket.

This was incredible. She could only stare, mesmerized, at the scene. Adam had mentioned something about the creek flooding, but she'd never imagined it could be anything like this.

She'd better get the deck furniture inside if she didn't want to see it floating away. She stepped out onto the deck, feeling the boards beneath her feet vibrate to the roar of the water. She took another step, reaching for the nearest chair. The deck groaned.

"Chloe!" The slam of the front door punctuated the word, and Seth raced through the house toward her. "Get inside. Quick."

"As soon as I get the chairs—"

An alarming crack cut off her voice. The deck swayed, the movement almost reluctant. And then the floor was collapsing under her, crumbling into bits, taking her with it—

Seth grabbed her arm, his fingers biting into her skin. Water, shockingly cold, swallowed her feet, pulling at her, dragging her away.

But Seth was stronger. He hung on to her arm, and she realized he was clutching the door frame with his other hand, stretching out over the chasm that had opened in front of him.

"Jump!" he cried, and even as he yanked, she leaped toward him. He grabbed her, both arms around her as they toppled back into the kitchen.

For a moment all she could do was bury her face in his jacket, while a wave of thankfulness for his presence warmed her. She turned back toward the door just in time to see the deck, with an agonized shriek, break away from the house and crumble into the creek.

Seth's hands were strong on her arms. "What were you doing? A couple of deck chairs aren't worth your life. Why haven't you been answering your phone? I tried to call and warn you."

The barrage of questions was angry, but under the anger, Chloe could feel his fear. For her.

"I'm sorry. I didn't realize. The owner's going to be so upset. The whole deck is gone." She still didn't quite believe it even though she'd seen it.

"The deck's the least of it," Seth said, dragging her toward the front door. "Come on. You have to get out of here. The house might be next."

"It couldn't . . . could it?" The depth of his concern was beginning to sink in.

"It could. Don't you listen to the radio? This whole end of town is advised to evacuate. Let's go."

She held back, pulling against him. "All right, but at least let me get my computer, my work . . . and what about my clothes?"

"Right." Seth took a breath, seeming to settle himself. "I'll get the computer and papers. You go pack a bag. But hurry. I don't want to be here when the water starts coming in that back door."

It was hard to believe that could happen, but a few minutes ago she'd have said it was impossible for the deck to be swept away. Rushing into the bedroom, she grabbed a suitcase and began throwing things into it.

Necessities for a few days, toiletries . . . surely she wouldn't be gone longer than that. She snapped the suitcase closed. The rain would stop, the creek would go down, and things would return to normal.

"Let's go." Seth appeared in the bedroom doorway and took the suitcase from her hand. "I already put the computer and briefcase in your car. Once the car reaches the top of the hill it should be safe."

Protesting that she wanted to take another look around would probably be futile. She followed him out, snapping the lock on the door. She moved out onto the sidewalk and stopped, shocked at the sight that met her eyes.

Up and down either side of the street, people were working for the most part in a silence that was more frightening than shouts would have been. Some loaded furniture and household goods into trucks and vans; others seemed to be carrying things up to the second floors of houses. All these people couldn't just be the street's residents. It looked as if half the town was here.

She pulled the hood of her jacket up against the pelting rain and turned to Seth. "It really is serous, isn't it?"

He grinned at her, his face rain-wet. "You're finally catching on. Now let's go help your sister."

Susanna. Fear pierced Chloe's heart. Susanna's shop was just as vulnerable as the cottage was. They had to help her.

CHAPTER EIGHT

*S*usanna's throat was tight with anxiety as she stacked quilted place mats into a box. The water was rising. Incredible as it seemed, the shop was actually in danger of flooding. All her earlier worries over whether she could buy the shop faded away to nothing in comparison. If what folks were saying was true, there might not be a shop left to buy.

"I'll put these upstairs, ja?" Dora's daughter Donna was at her elbow, carrying a stack of paintings she'd taken from the walls.

Susanna nodded, feeling as if her thoughts were spinning out of control. "I think they should be safe there. I don't know where else to put them."

Donna hoisted the stack and headed for the steps. "Surely they'll be all right on the second floor. I can't believe the flooding will be as bad as they're saying."

Susanna couldn't, either. "Best not to take a chance. It's wonderful kind of all of you to komm help."

Donna had arrived a half hour ago. She'd rounded up several other women from the church district, and they'd been boxing and carrying ever since.

"What would my mamm say if I didn't?" Donna said, her freckled face breaking into her easy smile. "It was all we could do to keep her from coming, too."

"I'm wonderful glad she didn't." Susanna shuddered at the thought of having Dora here to worry about, too.

"I convinced her it made more sense for her to watch the kinder while I came to help." Donna started up the stairs, edging around another woman coming down. "Not that she can't outwork all of us when she's feeling herself."

"That's all the candles boxed up, Susanna," Mary Lapp, one of Donna's friends, called across the room to her. "What should I do next?"

Susanna looked around the crowded shop, overcome by a sense of helplessness. Usually she loved the cozy clutter of the place, but now she was faced with moving it or perhaps losing it.

She forced herself to focus. What would be damaged most by the water if it got into the first floor?

"I think the hooked rugs should go next," she said, nodding to the colorful pile. "They're heavy, so don't try to take too many at once."

The woman nodded, moving immediately to the task.

And speaking of heavy, she'd certainly loaded this box up, but she couldn't waste time taking things back out, not with so much to do. She lifted it in her arms and headed for the stairs, her back aching from the effort.

Mary paused, a bundle of rugs in her arms, looking out the window. "Looks like they're sandbagging the house across the street," she said.

"Sandbags won't do much gut, from what I've heard," Donna said, coming back down for another load. "You can stop fire, but you can't stop water."

Susanna pushed herself on, not wanting any of the women to think she couldn't do her share because of her limp. She heard the door open, turned to look, and missed a step, coming down hard on her knees.

In a moment Nate was next to her, shoving the box aside to help her up. "Are you all right?" His voice was gruff.

"I'm fine." She could feel the color coming up in her cheeks. "I wasn't looking where I was going is all."

"You shouldn't be carrying anything this heavy," he scolded, as if she were a child or an elderly person. "Donna, you shouldn't be letting Susanna do the heavy carrying."

Donna looked stricken. "Ach, I'm sorry, Susanna. Let me take it."

"I'm fine," she said, embarrassed at having attention called to her disability. "I can manage."

"There's no need." Nate lifted the box as if it were a feather. "What's in here? Fabric? Better not to put it upstairs then."

"Why not?" Embarrassment made her voice tart. "The water surely won't be that high."

"No, but if even a little gets in the ground floor, the damp will go up through the walls." He turned, heading back down with the box, which forced her to follow him. "I've got the store truck and driver outside, and I brought a couple of other boys to help."

"That's wonderful gut of you—" she began, but he didn't seem to be listening.

"Thomas, Matthew, start loading the truck. Anything that can be harmed by the water or damp should go. As soon as the sisters have a box loaded, you take it."

The two teenage boys who'd followed him in nodded and set to work carrying boxes out the door. Both were Amish, and Susanna had seen them working at Nate's store, although she couldn't have put first names to them. An older man, Englisch, who was probably the driver Nate had brought, went outside to help load. In a moment, it seemed everything was moving at twice the speed it had been.

"I hadn't even thought about the damp getting into things." She wiped her hands on her apron, suddenly aware of how disheveled she must look. "There's more stock upstairs that we didn't even have on display. If we have to move all that, as well—"

"We'll do the downstairs first, ja?" Nate said. "Then, if we have time, we can bring things down from upstairs." He touched her arm lightly. "Don't worry."

She seemed to feel stronger for his touch, which was ferhoodled. "It will be as God wills," she said. But surely it wasn't wrong to hope the shop would be spared.

"All we can do is our best," he said. Stacking up two boxes, he lifted them. "There's enough space in my storeroom for all of it, and everything will be safe there."

Before she could find the words to thank him, Nate was already out the door.

"My brother's bossy," Donna said. "But he means well."

"I know." Susanna flushed. "I mean, I know he means well . . ."

Donna laughed. "And he's bossy. You're too polite to say so, but I'm his sister, so I can."

The door swung open again, this time to admit Chloe and Seth Miller. Chloe's beautiful hair was bedraggled, and it looked as if her jeans were wet to the knees.

"Chloe, what happened? Are you all right?" Susanna hurried to clasp her sister's hand, realizing it was the first time she'd done so.

"I'd be floating down the river by now if Seth hadn't come along." Chloe looked cheerful for someone who'd had such a near miss. "The creek took the deck right off the back of the cottage."

There were murmured exclamations from the others.

"Thank the gut Lord you're safe. Maybe you should see a doctor—"

"I'm perfectly all right. We've come to help. Just tell us what to do."

"I see Nate brought a truck," Seth said. "We have both cars out front, too, so we can load things in them."

Susanna would protest, but she was too thankful. Besides, of course Chloe wanted to help. They were kin, after all.

One of the boys, either Thomas or Matthew, she wasn't sure which, came to pick up another box. "I heard the creek bridge up at Summerdale is gone." His eyes were wide, and Susanna realized there was fear mixed with his excitement. "Someone said the new flood walls upstream will send all the water down to us and swallow up the town."

"Well, we'll send you out on a raft, then." Nate put a reassuring hand on the boy's shoulder. "If there's anything that moves faster than the water, it's gossip. Go on, now." He gave him a gentle shove toward the door.

"He's afraid," Susanna said softly. "Do you think that's true? About the flood walls making it worse for us?"

"Probably." Nate looked grim for a moment. "Everything has consequences, ja?"

Yes, everything did. She wasn't sure how her little shop, precious as it was to her, weighed in the balance of all that might be lost.

"Susanna, if you have a broom or something else with a long handle, I could use it to get the baskets off the hooks." Chloe nodded toward the array of egg baskets that hung from hooks in the ceiling.

"Ja, I'll get it for you." She was only a few steps from the basement door. She pulled it open and reached for the broom that was usually propped on the landing. It wasn't there. And then she saw it, floating in the water that was already up to the top step.

She slammed the door shut, as if that would keep it out, and swung around. Nate, seeing her face, was there in a moment.

"What is it?"

"The cellar's filled with water right to the top step. We should get people out—" She stopped, her voice choking at the thought of all that remained to do.

Nate took a quick look and then slammed the door shut, just as she had. His expression was grim.

"Take your last load out now. We have to go."

"A little longer—" Chloe began, but her words were cut off by the sound of a siren out in the street.

The driver poked his head in the door. "Police are ordering us out. Telling everyone to get to higher ground now. The creek's rising faster than anyone thought it could."

There was a murmur of dismay, but no one argued. Grabbing what they could carry, people headed out the door.

Susanna looked at what was left—what would surely be lost—and felt as if her heart was breaking. "I'll just get a few more—"

"No, Susanna." Nate's voice was kind, but his grasp on her arm was firm. "We must go. All of us."

She pulled back against his grip for an instant, her vision

blurring so that she couldn't see his face clearly. Chloe came, putting her arm around Susanna's waist.

"It'll be all right," Chloe murmured. "Come on."

Susanna nodded. They were right. It was just so hard.

She stepped out onto the porch, automatically locking the door. How futile a gesture was locking up if she was going to lose everything?

The others were squeezing into the two cars and the truck. Susanna glanced down toward the lower end of the street and her breath caught. The street was submerged already, the current washing across it fast and powerful.

Nate touched her arm. "Look." He was pointing toward the river, usually only a glint of water through the trees. Now it advanced across the fields, turning them into a rippling mirror. A shudder went through her. Surely this was what the world must have looked like to Noah just before it vanished under the waters.

A loud crack had all of them turning to look upstream at the creek. The red covered bridge, the subject of so many photos and paintings, cracked again as something they couldn't see struck it from upstream. Almost in slow motion it lifted from its foundation and broke away. For a few minutes it seemed to hold together, floating downstream like an ark. Then it hit the tree line and began to crumple apart, just like Susanna's life.

Chloe put another box on the stack in the storage area at Nate's store and straightened, rubbing her back. She'd have said she was in good shape, but a few hours of lifting and carrying had her muscles protesting.

She probably wasn't the only one. The large rectangular room was filling up as people, some in Plain dress, some Englisch, stacked things wherever they could. Not just the contents of the shop, she realized as a couple of men passed her carrying a table between them. Nate must have offered storage room to others who had to evacuate. People were working quickly, racing the clock to beat the rising water.

Susanna paused in sorting the contents of a box to give her a wan smile. Chloe's heart lurched. Her sister's face was bleak, and she looked exhausted. Still, Chloe knew better than to try to get her to take a break. She'd already tried, as had Donna, but Susanna was quietly stubborn. She listened to what anyone had to say and then went her own way without fuss.

Movement near the door caught Chloe's eye. Nate and Seth stood there, deep in conversation it seemed, and it struck her that there was something very similar in the way they stood and in their gestures, as if being Plain had set its mark upon them no matter how far away they strayed.

That was what she feared, she knew—that Seth was being drawn inevitably back to the life he'd once known. Caring for him could only lead to heartbreak.

The conversation seemed to come to an end. Seth nodded, grabbing a slicker from a stack of them that Nate had unearthed from someplace, and headed out the door. Without stopping to think, Chloe hurried across the room.

Nate had disappeared by the time she reached the door, so she couldn't ask him where Seth was going. She snatched up a slicker and stepped out into the night.

The pelting rain forced her to pause long enough to yank on the slicker. Luck was with her—Seth had stopped to fasten his at the intersection of the store parking lot and the street.

"Seth!" She ran after him, half afraid he'd vanish into the storm before she could reach him.

But he heard her, because he turned, stopped, and waited for her to catch up with him.

"Where are you going?" She pulled the hood up as she spoke, despite the fact that her hair was soaked already.

"They're calling for volunteers to help with the evacuation." Seth's face was grim. "It's bad, Chloe. Worse than anyone expected. Nate's heading down to the south end of town. They're going door to door, trying to get people to leave. I thought I'd go back to the creek and see what help they need there."

"I'll go with you." She snapped the slicker up around her neck.

She could see the reluctance in his face. "Don't you think you'd better stay here with your sister?"

"There's nothing else I can do for her." She managed a smile. "I'm an able-bodied volunteer, right?"

His face relaxed into the smile that always charmed her. "Right. Let's go."

He started walking, and she fell into step beside him. The noise of the rain on the slicker set up an echo that was somehow disorienting, as if she'd wandered into an alien world. Maybe she had. They were all facing something completely out of their normal realm.

"You said they were evacuating the south end of town?" She made it a question as she tried to orient herself to directions. Susanna's shop was at the east end, she knew, where Main Street sloped down a fairly steep incline to run parallel to the creek.

"Right. The south side is down toward the river, where the park is."

She remembered from her first visit to Oyersburg, when she'd met Seth at the park and admired its charming setting along the river. "I thought the idea was that using the flood plain as a park set up a buffer for the town."

"It normally would. Not this time. If the river crests as high as they're predicting . . ." He hesitated. "I hate to say it, but by the time this is over, we could end up with nearly half the town underwater."

Chloe found she was creating a mental map of the town and seeing it in a whole new way. The normally placid river ran along the southern edge of town, while the creek slanted across the east end to join the river just past the end of town. So many people and buildings were in danger—for a moment the task of saving them seemed impossible.

Common sense asserted itself. Nobody could do everything. She and Seth just had to do what they could. Others were working as well.

They turned a corner and started down the hill. Chloe's breath caught. "The whole east end is dark."

"Power's off," Seth said. "The rest of the town will probably go off before long, as well. And then, well, who knows how long it will take to get power restored. Days, maybe weeks."

Ahead of them Chloe spotted what seemed to be a staging area at an intersection, where emergency lights were blinking. It took a moment to realize what she was seeing, and when she did she reached, half-consciously, for Seth's hand. Beyond the intersection the street had turned into a river. The dire predictions had been right. The whole lower end of town was underwater, including the cottage she was renting and Susanna's shop.

They approached the hub of activity. A couple of canopies

had been set up, and EMTs were loading someone onto a stretcher and into an ambulance.

Seth nudged her. "Looks like the guy in charge is over there. Let's see what we can do."

The person in charge proved to be a man who must have been in his sixties and had a brisk, decided manner. At their offer of help, he looked them over appraisingly.

"Either of you know how to run a motorboat?"

"I do." The words were out of Chloe's mouth before she considered what she might be letting herself in for.

"Okay." He pointed. "There she is. If you don't think you can handle her, say so now."

Chloe took a quick look at the boat pulled up where the water lapped against the street, forming an improbable landing place. "No problem. My grandfather used to have something similar. I can manage. What do we do?"

The lines in the man's face seemed to deepen. "Bring out anyone you can. Just mind the current. It's stronger than you think. Don't overload your boat. And watch out for any floating debris." He handed Seth a battery-powered floodlight. "Good luck."

Seth stared at her for a moment, and she suspected he was considering whether or not to try to talk her out of doing it.

"I'm in it now," she said. "I won't back out."

"Get in," Seth said. "I'll push off."

It made sense, so she didn't argue. She took a moment to be sure she was familiar with the boat, and then started it up. It took three tries before the motor caught, and she was aware of Seth's gaze on her.

"I really do know how to run a boat," she said once he'd

pushed them into deeper water and scrambled in. "You might check the locker for any life vests, just in case."

Seth yanked the locker open, emerging with a pair of orange vests. "Here you go." He tossed one toward her. "If we get hit by a log, we'd better be sure we'll float."

She nodded, swinging the vest around her. Impossible to fasten it and steer at the same time, so Seth reached over and pulled the straps tight for her before putting his own on.

He settled on the seat, switching on the torch. "So how did you learn so much about boats?"

Chloe strained to see, making her way slowly. Again she felt that sense of disorientation. She shouldn't be taking a boat down Main Street.

"It was Granddad's favorite activity," she said. "He'd rather be out on the river in a boat than doing the social rounds my grandmother thought was so important."

"You liked to go with him." Seth spoke above the sound of the motor.

"Those were the best times." She smiled despite the situation. Maybe it was better to be remembering lazy afternoons on the water than worrying about what lay ahead. "We were supposed to be fishing, but mostly we just drifted and talked."

Those conversations, her sense that someone understood her without judging or correcting, had helped her grow into the person she was. When Granddad died, a big piece of her heart seemed to be taken away.

As they moved out of range of the flashing lights, Seth played the torch across the water. She'd already been adjusting automatically to the current, but the beam of light showed it up plainly. It was moving fast—faster than she would have believed possible. Fortunately much of the debris was getting hung up on houses and trees, giving them a relatively safe way ahead.

"You okay?" Seth called.

"So far so good." She focused, straining to stay in the middle of what had been the street.

Another boat loomed out of the dark, dangerously low in the water. As it neared she saw what seemed to be an entire family huddled into the small space. The driver gave her a thumbs-up sign as they passed, which cheered her insensibly. He was getting his load to safety; so would they.

Seth's light moved slowly and then stopped, focusing on the front of Susanna's shop. Chloe winced. The water was well above porch level already.

Seth didn't comment, and neither did she. What was the point? A lot of people were going to lose things that were important to them tonight. She just prayed it wouldn't be someone's life.

"Look, there. Someone's signaling us." Seth moved the beam, and it picked up a porch, someone on it blinking a feeble flashlight.

"Okay, got it." She turned toward the porch, trying to adjust for the current and watch for floating tree limbs. A huge one went past, big enough to capsize their small boat if it hit them dead on.

Chloe gritted her teeth. This was harder than she'd dreamed. What had she been thinking, volunteering for this job? She should have left it to someone else. But there hadn't been anyone else.

Just hold it steady. Granddad's voice seemed to echo in her heart, warm with his love. *You can do it. I know you can.*

He'd always believed in her, and somehow that love and belief still strengthened her. Her face was already wet with rain—no one would notice a few tears mixed in.

She guided the boat toward the porch, slowing as she reached it. Seth leaned out, grabbing the porch post and looping a line around it.

"I'll climb out and help them in," he said. "Try to keep it as steady as you can."

She nodded, getting her first look at the people on the porch—a woman in her thirties, probably, an elderly woman wrapped in a blanket and leaning on a cane, and two young children. Her heart sank. How on earth was Seth going to get them safely into the boat?

He was already out, stepping easily onto the partly submerged porch step. She grabbed a line secured to the stern and tossed it to him. "Loop it around the post and hand me the end. I'll pull the boat in closer."

He nodded, flipping the rope around and using it to pull the rear of the boat closer before handing it back to her. He turned to the kids, who were pressing forward even as their mother tried to hold them back. "You folks need a ride?"

"We should have left earlier." The woman's voice verged on tears. "I didn't think it was going to get so bad."

The woman had that in common with plenty of other people, including Chloe. Maybe that was the natural reaction to being plunged into a catastrophe.

"It's okay. You're not the only ones. The important thing now is to get you out." Seth's voice was calm and soothing. "I'm going to try lifting the kids in first. Then maybe you can help me with . . ." He hesitated, nodding at the older woman, who seemed to shrink inside her blanket.

"My mother," the woman supplied. She seemed to take a breath, pushing wet hair back from her face. "Okay. Let's do it."

Seth seemed to assess the two children quickly, and then he picked up the older one, a boy of about eight. "I'm going to lift you in, and then you can steady your sister while I put her in, okay?"

The boy nodded, his eyes wide in a white face. "I can do it. I'm not scared."

"Good man," Seth said.

In a single fluid movement he swung the boy across the gap and into the boat. Chloe wanted to reach out to help, but with one hand controlling the boat and the other grasping the rope, there was nothing she could do except pray.

The boy was as good as his word. He sat down quickly, leaving room next to him for his sister, and then he nodded to Seth.

The little girl showed a tendency to cling to her mother. Seth scooped her up and moved her to the boat before she could form the protest Chloe could see in her little face.

"It's okay," she said, hoping to comfort the child as the boy pushed her onto the seat. "You listen to your brother, and your mom and grandma will be with you in a second." She hoped. Prayed. The rope bit into her hand, and she tried to ignore the pain.

Seth consulted with the woman. "I'm thinking with one of us on either side, we can lift her in. Just be careful on the step—the current is wicked."

She nodded, but the older woman drew back. "I can't." Her voice rose to a wail. "I can't. I'll just stay here."

"You can't stay." Seth's voice was calm even as Chloe longed to shout at the woman. "The house might go, and then what would you do? Come, now. Your grandkids did it. You can, too." He was maneuvering her forward as he spoke, to the edge of the porch.

Chloe held her breath. If the woman struggled, the three of them could end up in the water. How could she save them? In this current—

Before panic could take hold, Seth nodded to the younger woman. Together they lifted, and in an instant the older woman had collapsed into the boat and was gathering her grandchildren into her arms.

Thank you, Chloe murmured. *Thank you.*

Seth helped the woman in, untied the line, and stepped into the boat. Chloe let go of the rope she held and turned the boat upstream.

"Our neighbors," the woman said. "In the next house. They didn't get out yet, either."

Chloe exchanged looks with Seth. She didn't want to leave anyone behind, but it was impossible. They'd never make it if they loaded the boat any heavier.

"We'll come back for them," Seth said quickly. "I promise we will."

Would they be able to keep that promise? Chloe concentrated on the next step. Get this load to safety. That was all she could do now, and it was taking all her strength and skill to maneuver the vessel against the current. *Please.* She realized she was praying again. *Please.*

Seth knelt in the prow, sweeping the water ahead with the beam of light, ready to warn her of any obstacles. Slowly, fighting against the current and the heavy load, the boat began to make headway. At last she felt the keel brush bottom, and volunteers rushed into the water to carry their passengers to safety.

"Thank you." Crying, the woman pressed Chloe's hand. "Thank you."

"It's okay. Take care."

The grandmother was already being looked at by paramedics, while volunteers wrapped blankets around the children. Chloe recognized Nate's sister among them, handing out blankets with a cheerful smile.

"Okay?" Seth raised an eyebrow at Chloe.

"Okay." She nodded toward the volunteers. "We're seeing the best of people, aren't we? Strangers helping each other like family."

"I suspect we really are all family in a situation like this one." He reached out to clasp her wet hand with his.

Warmth flowed through Chloe, erasing her fatigue and fear. She looked at Seth's face and it seemed to come into sharp focus, as familiar as if she knew every inch of it intimately. Her breath caught.

It was all very well to tell herself that she shouldn't get involved with this man. But it was already too late. She cared for him, maybe even loved him. And what was she going to do about it?

CHAPTER NINE

*N*ate stood at the storeroom door, water dripping from his slicker, as the last of the food for the emergency shelter was loaded into the truck. Fatigue dragged at him when he stood still, so he'd best get moving again. The next few days would demand all his strength.

As he turned to leave, he heard someone calling his name and saw Susanna hurrying toward him. Her limp was more pronounced than ever, and his heart twisted.

"You should be taking a break, Susanna." He suspected she wouldn't want to hear that, especially from him.

"Later," she said, dismissing the idea with a quick gesture. "Do you know where Chloe is? I can't find her."

"I think she went with Seth to help down at the creek." He tried not to think about how bad it might be down there.

"I must go and find her. I don't want her doing anything foolish because of me." Her blue eyes were dark with worry, and she reached for the door handle.

Nate planted his hand on the door to keep her from opening it. "Chloe is well able to take care of herself, it seems to me." He didn't mean that to sound like an insult, but the flare of anger in Susanna's eyes told him she took it that way.

"Chloe is my little sister," she said.

He stared at her. Did she realize how much affection was revealed by those simple words?

"I know." He forced himself to patience. Nothing would be served by letting Susanna rush off into the dark after Chloe. "Chloe is doing what she must. We all have to do so tonight, ain't so?"

The truth in what he said seemed to get through to her. She nodded. "At least Seth is with her. Chloe listens to him, I think." Seeming to shake away her worry, she focused on him. "I thought you had gone to help people get out of those houses down by the river."

"I did, but there's a need for food over at the shelter they're setting up. They don't know how many people to expect, but they'll have to be fed. I said I'll take what I can over from the store. We have the truck loaded, and I must go."

"I'll come, too," Susanna said quickly. "I can help with the cooking, at least."

"You don't need to." The strength of his desire to protect her startled him. Taking care of Susanna was what Mamm would expect, wasn't it? "You've worked so hard already."

"There's nothing more I can do here," she said. "I want to be useful."

"Susanna . . ." He tried to find the words that would dissuade her.

"We all have to do what we must tonight." She repeated his words back to him with a hint of a smile.

"Ja, all right, I know when I'm beaten." He grabbed a slicker and held it for her to slip on.

The slicker was too big for her, and he fitted it over her shoulders as best he could, drawing the collar close around her. She reached up to fasten it, and their hands became entangled.

Susanna looked up at him, her eyes wide and startled. His breath seemed to be stuck in his throat, and he didn't want to let go of her hands. If only—

Nate stepped back so quickly he bumped into the door frame. "That will keep you dry."

He plunged out into the rain, welcoming the cold on his face. What had he been thinking? He didn't have feelings for Susanna. He didn't intend to have feelings for anyone. How could longing ambush him that way?

The driver was already behind the wheel of the truck, ready to go. Nate pulled open the door on the passenger side and helped Susanna in, making an effort to touch nothing but the smooth wet fabric of the slicker.

It didn't help. He was still far too aware of her as he crowded into the seat next to her.

He cleared his throat. "Sorry it's so tight. It's only a couple of blocks."

The emergency shelter had been set up in the old consistory building on the square. A large, square old place, it served the community in a variety of ways as it housed the Saturday market, the Christmas festival, and various concerts and events throughout the year. More important right now, it provided the storage necessary for cots and other emergency supplies. The question in his mind was whether anyone had planned for a flood as bad as this one promised to be.

"How was it down by the river?" Susanna braced herself

with a hand against the dashboard to keep from swaying against him as they rounded a corner.

"Water's over the park already." The driver seemed to think the question was directed at him. "I doubt much will be left."

"Surely the pavilions will be all right." She looked questioningly at Nate. The park had been built by the efforts of the community, and it was dear to the hearts of most folks in town.

"They'll be safe, I think," he said, hoping he was right. "I'm afraid the playground won't make it, though." Along with many of his neighbors, he'd helped to build the playground. He didn't want to see it float away, but better the playground than someone's home.

They'd reached the building already and the driver pulled the truck up by the side door that led to the kitchen. "Komm." Nate slid out and helped Susanna down. "I'll see you settled with a job if you're sure—"

"I'm sure," she said.

Inside, the large kitchen was warm and dry. Urns of coffee lined a counter, and a couple of women were putting out boxes of donuts. Most likely the local donut shop had donated its stock before closing. Through a pass-through in the kitchen wall he could see people setting up cots.

"Over here." He touched Susanna's elbow and led her to the brisk, middle-aged woman who was obviously directing activities.

"Julia?"

She turned at the sound of his voice, her worried face relaxing in a smile. "I heard you were coming with supplies. I can't thank you enough."

"It's nothing," he replied. "Here is Susanna Bitler, ready to help in the kitchen. Susanna, this is Mrs. Taylor, from the Red Cross."

"Julia, please." She shook Susanna's hand. "I'm always glad to have a volunteer who knows her way around a kitchen."

Susanna nodded, returning the woman's smile with more poise than he'd have expected. Still, running the shop would have made her more comfortable with outsiders than many Amish women might be.

With Susanna safely in Julia's hands, Nate turned his attention to getting the truck unloaded. A couple of older Englisch men who'd been setting up cots in the large room on the other side of the kitchen pass-through came to help, and soon they had a line of people passing boxes and bags from the truck to the kitchen. They worked in silence, for the most part, without the friendly banter that normally accompanied this kind of chore. He suspected everyone had the same thought: How bad was it going to get?

When the truck had been unloaded and all the supplies stacked on a counter or stored in the pantry, Nate looked around for Susanna. He found her at the restaurant-sized stove, stirring something in a large kettle. She looked perfectly composed, her face focused on the task at hand despite the fact that she must be worried sick over what she stood to lose. He admired her fortitude.

It was only polite to let her know he was leaving, right? He crossed to her.

"Making soup?"

She glanced up, nodding. "Julia says people will want something hot. I'm wonderful glad the stove is gas. I wouldn't know what to do with electric."

"It'll stay on when the power goes off, too. I should start rounding up some lamps and lanterns. You'll need those before the night is over, I'm afraid."

Susanna didn't look unduly upset at the thought of the power going off, Nate thought. She might not realize how helpless many Englisch were when they couldn't flip a switch for light and heat.

Julia's voice sounded over the hum of conversation in the kitchen. "The first evacuees are coming in. Get ready, everyone."

"Poor things," Susanna murmured.

Nate followed the direction of her gaze. Through the passthrough, he could see the first bedraggled group arriving. They looked . . . shocked, he realized. As if they couldn't quite believe this was happening to them.

"We'll have to pray their homes are still there when this is over," Nate said, reminding himself too late that the first-floor apartment Susanna had shared with her mother was in the danger zone. But Susanna hadn't even mentioned that—all her concern had been for the shop.

"Ja," she said softly. "I know the contents of a house are just things, but if it's someone's home, those things are precious."

"I guess I'm not as attached to my home as a woman might be, but I think I understand. Maybe if Mary Ann had lived—" He stopped, not liking where that sentence was going.

"I'm sorry." Susanna's eyes were filled with pain at the thought of his loss. "You must still grieve for what might have been."

The empathy in her voice shamed him, reminding him of

her own loss. He was swept with impatience for the pretense he'd lived with for so long.

"Even if she'd lived, Mary Ann wouldn't have turned our house into a home."

Susanna's eyes widened in shock, but it was no more than he felt himself. Why had he blurted that out to Susanna, of all people?

He froze, irresolute. Then he shook his head sharply.

"Forget what I said," he ordered, and left the kitchen before he could make things any worse.

With the dawn came a slacking off of the rain. Seth leaned against a truck, wondering if the other workers were as exhausted as he was. Probably, but they were making an effort not to show it. This corner had been an impromptu landing spot last night, and the water still lapped at the street, but more quietly now.

Two workers were putting up barricades where Main Street began its slope down toward the creek. The last of the ambulances had gone off an hour ago, probably called to some other area. A few trucks remained, along with the makeshift tent that sheltered the work area where coffee and blankets were dispensed.

Chloe was smiling as she stood exchanging a few words with Nate's sister. Donna was packing up blankets and coffee thermos jugs, and Chloe began helping her.

But Chloe's movements were slow, and she rubbed her shoulder as if it ached. One way or another, he had to convince her to get some rest.

He walked over to where the women were working, his sneakers squelching with every step. He'd given up on trying to stay dry hours earlier. It just wasn't possible.

"Good to see the sun come up," he said, nodding to Donna.

"Ja, for sure." Her freckled face was drawn with fatigue, but she had a ready smile.

"At least now we'll be able to see what we're doing." Chloe's pallor tugged at his heart. "When was it that the power went out; did anyone notice?"

"Around three, I think." He'd glanced at his watch at some point, surprised to find it was still working. As far as he could tell, the whole town was out, making the misery even more acute for people already driven from their homes.

"You got everyone out," Donna said, loading a box of blankets into the back of a pickup. "That's the important thing."

Someone attracted her attention and she turned away, leaving Seth alone with Chloe.

He touched her arm. "You okay?"

"Yes." She smiled. "You?"

"I might have been more tired sometime in my life, but I don't remember it," he said.

A car horn blared, drawing everyone's attention. It was Dave Hartman, the emergency coordinator.

He made a sweeping gesture, signaling them to come closer. People began moving toward him, feet dragging.

"We got everyone out of this end of town," he said, taking off his safety helmet to run a hand through wet gray hair. "Good work, folks. Police are putting up barricades to keep everyone out until it's safe to get back in."

"You got any guesses as to when that will be?" one of the men asked.

"Your idea is as good as mine." Dave nodded to the lower end of town, covered now by swift-moving brown water. "We should get an update from county officials in an hour or so. From what I've heard so far, the river's not even going to crest until late tomorrow, and they're talking a record high."

A low groan greeted the words. These people probably knew better than Seth did what that meant.

"We've done it before, we can do it again," Hartman said. "Meantime, go home and get some sleep."

"That's if we still have a bed," someone else said with black humor, and a rueful laugh ran through the crowd.

"Right." Hartman put his helmet back on, the gesture weary. "There's more to do, if you're up to it after you rest. Report in either to the office on Main Street or to the temporary trailer on Market Street." He raised his hand in what might almost have been a benediction. "Get some rest. You need it."

The group dispersed slowly. Seth turned to Chloe. The way she was sagging, a slight breeze would knock her over.

"You heard the man. We need to crash."

She looked at him blankly. "Where? My bed is underwater."

A good question. Seth tried to force his sluggish brain to function. Susanna's place was down in the flood zone, like Chloe's.

Dave came over to them. "You folks have a place to stay?"

Chloe gestured helplessly at the water.

"Yeah, that's what I figured. No problem. You can come home with me."

"We can't impose—" Chloe began, but he cut her off.

"Listen, there's nothing my wife likes more than a houseful of people to take care of. She's probably cooking breakfast for half the neighborhood right now. She'd be the first one to say you should stay with us."

"We might get rooms at a motel," Seth said, reluctant to move in on strangers.

"Either closed or full," Dave said. "Come on. You can follow me."

With a glance at him, Chloe nodded. "All right. Thank you. But I have to make sure my sister's all right first."

Dave nodded. "Okay, here's my address." He pulled a soggy card from an inside pocket. "I'll call my wife and tell her to expect you. Don't let us down now."

Still cheerful, he tramped off.

"I'm sure Susanna is fine . . ." Seth began.

Chloe shook her head. "I have to see for myself."

Well, he wouldn't expect anything else. "Our cars are at Nate's store," he reminded her. "Someone there will know where she is. With Dora, I'd think."

Chloe nodded, and they started plodding up the street side by side. They hadn't gone more than half a block before an SUV pulled up next to them. The woman driving leaned across to the window.

"Hop in. I'll take you where you need to go."

Seth would have protested, but he suspected Chloe's strength wasn't going to hold up much longer. He nodded, and they climbed in the back. "Gaus's store," he said.

The woman nodded and pulled out. "There's a cooler back there with juice and soda," she said. "Help yourself."

"Thanks." Seth was too tired to ask who she was or where

she was going with the drinks. He pulled out a couple of small bottles of orange juice and handed one to Chloe.

In a few minutes, the woman swung into the parking lot at the store. "Stay safe," she said. Before they could even thank her, she'd driven off.

"Random acts of kindness," Chloe said, and he nodded. They'd probably never know who the woman was, any more than the people they'd brought out of the flooded houses would know them. It didn't matter.

The door to the storeroom was unlocked, and when Seth opened it, he found several people still at work, sorting supplies that were probably destined for the shelter. He hailed the nearest person—a vaguely familiar-looking Amish woman. He didn't realize who she was until Chloe spoke.

"Dora, is Susanna still here?"

She shook her head, eyeing Chloe with a certain amount of wariness. "She's at the shelter. She and my son took some foodstuffs over, and she stayed to help."

"Is she all right?" Chloe's voice wavered slightly.

Maybe Dora heard it because her look softened. "Most likely she thinks she's better off busy than worrying."

"I'm sorry. Your shop . . ."

"It will be as God wills." The phrase of acceptance had always annoyed Seth when he was young, but it had begun to make a bit more sense.

"We'll head over there, then," he said.

Dora caught Chloe's hand. "Tell her she's to stay with me, ja? And you, as well, if you need a place."

"That's kind of you." Chloe blinked at the unexpected offer. "I already have a place, but I'll tell her. And I'll try to get her to take a break."

Dora nodded. "Maybe she'll listen to you, ain't so? She hasn't listened to anyone else."

"I don't know about that, but I'll try." Chloe looked doubtful.

They went back out into the rain, but at least it was a gentle drizzle and not a downpour any longer. A small thing to be grateful for. "We can take my car."

Chloe started to protest, but Seth kept talking as he steered her toward his vehicle. "There's no point in trying to park two cars at the shelter. The lot's bound to be crowded."

"You don't have to come." Chloe's mouth was set in a stubborn line.

"Maybe not, but I am. And once you're sure Susanna is okay, you're going to get some rest."

"I'm fine." But at least she made no more objections about letting him drive to the shelter.

"Sure you're fine." He slid into the driver's seat and started the car. "That's why you're rubbing your shoulder and swaying on your feet."

Caught in the act of massaging her shoulder, Chloe didn't bother to argue. "Muscle strain, that's all," she said. "Putting down the river with Granddad was a little different from what we did last night."

"I don't know about you, but I'd just as soon not have to put in a night like that one again."

"I suppose a lot of people are thinking that same thought," she said. She pushed damp hair off her face. "I just realized— Lydia is probably worried sick about us. If only she had a phone—"

Chloe stopped herself. She tried to be sensitive to the Amish beliefs of her sisters, but he suspected she found it difficult at a time like this one.

"Once we're settled, I'll call my mamm's phone shanty and leave a message. She'll make sure Lydia knows what's happening."

"Good." Chloe relaxed against the headrest with a sigh.

"Here we are." He pulled into the parking lot. As he'd imagined, it was nearly full. He found a spot, and in a moment they were approaching the double front doors of the square brick building.

"This used to be the lodge hall of a fraternal organization." He pulled the door open. "They were once big in towns like Oyersburg, but most of the buildings have been put to other uses."

Chloe didn't seem to be listening, and he could hardly blame her. Besides, she'd been here for the Saturday market. He wasn't leading a sightseeing trip, but he had the feeling that if he didn't keep his mind busy, he'd fall asleep on his feet like a horse.

They emerged into a center hallway, and a hum of noise came from the big room to the left where most of the stalls had been set up for the market. Now one end contained cots, and the other long tables and chairs. Several children were sound asleep in their makeshift beds, but it looked as if most of the adults were too keyed up or too worried to sleep. They gathered in small groups, talking, or simply sat, staring into space. The scent of coffee and pancakes wafted from the far end of the room.

"The kitchen," he said, touching Chloe's arm. "That's where Susanna will be, most likely."

She nodded, and they worked their way through the crowd toward the kitchen, not talking. Seth studied Chloe, alert for any sign that exhaustion was overtaking her.

But she somehow kept putting one foot in front of the other. He'd seen Chloe in a lot of roles since they'd met—the serious scholar, the reluctant sister, the determined idealist. Tonight he'd seen her turn that stubborn determination of hers to a fierce need to help others no matter the cost to herself, and his admiration had increased with every hour that passed. Chloe might still struggle with her difficult heritage, but she knew how to set that aside to do the job in front of her.

His feelings had clarified a little during this long night. Admiration. Attraction. And something more? He didn't know, but he wanted to find out.

Chloe pushed open the swinging door to the kitchen, with him right behind her. She stood for a moment, scanning the figures moving purposefully around the room.

"There." He touched her arm. "By the stove."

Susanna, an oversized white apron over her deep blue dress, stood at the mammoth gas range. She was flipping pancakes with a practiced hand while sausages sizzled in a cast iron fry pan.

The aroma hit Seth, making him dizzy. How long had it been since they'd eaten? Time had telescoped and stretched like a child's rubber toy since he'd rushed toward Oyersburg to find Chloe.

"Susanna." Chloe hurried toward her, narrowly missing a collision with a gray-haired man carrying a tray full of serving platters. "Are you okay?"

Susanna's face blossomed into a smile when she saw Chloe. "Ja, for sure. What about you? When I heard you'd gone back down to the creek— Ach, you shouldn't scare me so bad."

Susanna was talking like a big sister, her tone loving and scolding all at once. Some of the fatigue seeped from Chloe's face when she heard it.

"We had a busy night." Her gesture included Seth. "Looks like you have, too."

"There's plenty to do, that's certain-sure." Susanna turned back to her pancakes, lifting them to a platter waiting warmed on the back of the stove. "What am I thinking? Do you want some breakfast? There's plenty."

"Sounds great," Seth said before Chloe could speak. She might not think she needed food right now, but he knew better.

The woman working the next set of burners reached across to take the spatula from Susanna. "You go and eat with your friends, dear. And then you'd better get some rest."

"I'm not tired," Susanna said, but her drawn face gave the lie to the words. These sisters were a stubborn bunch, it seemed, Seth thought.

"Yes, you are." The woman included them in her smile. "You all look like you need food and rest, so take it. We'll want you able to work the next few days, not dead on your feet." She waved them away with the spatula.

Seth ushered Chloe and Susanna away before they could argue, guiding them to a corner of the kitchen where some of the other volunteers were snatching a meal. "Sit." He pushed them into chairs. "I'll get the food."

But another volunteer was there before he could move, setting laden plates in front of them. Someone else pushed a carafe of coffee toward him, but Seth shook his head. He'd had enough coffee during the night to last him.

The first bite of pancakes and sausage was bliss. He looked toward Chloe to be sure she was eating.

She wasn't. She had her arms around Susanna, hugging her, and they both had tears in their eyes.

It seemed the emergency had broken through some part, at least, of the barrier between Chloe and her sister. Could he say the same about Chloe and himself? He didn't know.

CHAPTER TEN

Susanna struggled awake, coming vaguely to an awareness of something very much wrong. What . . . ?

Memory flooded back as she opened her eyes. She was lying in a double bed. The large, square room was sparsely furnished as was typical of an Amish house. A wooden chest of drawers, a row of pegs on the wall for clothing, a bookshelf. A rocking chair sat next to a small table by the window.

She stared at the window but could make nothing of the grayness beyond. It could be any time from dawn to dusk. How long had she been asleep?

Pushing back the double-wedding-ring quilt, Susanna slid her feet to the floor, her bare toes encountering a hooked rug. The white nightgown she wore fell around her in waves. Obviously it was one of Dora's.

She pushed disheveled hair back from her face. She had a vague memory of Nate guiding her staggering steps up to the spare bedroom at some point, and embarrassment heated her cheeks. What must he think of her, unable even to walk upstairs by herself?

Hand on the bedside table for support, she stood, relieved to discover that her legs held her up. Her limp was bad enough, but she really hated it when someone saw her stumble, the invariable result when she'd taxed her body beyond its limits as she had in the past twenty-four hours.

A memory slid into her mind as if it had been jarred loose by the events of the past day. Herself at six or seven, curled up in her small bed, wrapping the pillow around her ears to shut out the sound of her parents' voices in the next room.

"I'm chust saying maybe it's better for Susanna to know the truth about herself from us." Her father had sounded as if it took all his strength to hang on to his patience. *"Then we don't have to worry about her finding out by accident."*

"No!" Mamm's voice had risen, frightening her. *"I won't have it."*

"But when she marries . . ."

"She won't marry, you know that. She's not like other girls." Mamm's voice had been strong and determined. *"No one else wants her. But we do. She's ours, and I won't have you telling her otherwise."*

Susanna realized she was gripping the edge of the table so hard that her fingers hurt. She forced herself to release her grip, rubbing her hand automatically.

The memory must have been buried very deep. She certainly hadn't thought of it in years, but now it might have happened yesterday. In light of what she knew now, it was clear that Daad had wanted to tell her the truth about her parentage.

Mamm had won that argument, obviously. If she'd ever

known how her words would one day hurt Susanna, she'd never have spoken them.

No one else wants her.

Pushing the thought away, she moved to the rocking chair, where someone had laid out clothes for her to wear. Maybe Mamm had been right, at least about the not marrying part. But someone did want her—Dora, her sisters.

The memory replayed in her mind of those moments when she and Chloe had held each other close. Susanna wasn't even sure who had initiated the hug, but it had seemed so right. It had *been* right. In that moment she had felt their relationship, deep in her bones. It was as if her heart and Chloe's heart had called to each other in that moment. Whether she and Chloe and Lydia knew one another or not, they were sisters.

As for marrying—well, even without marriage, her life could be fulfilling, as long as she had the shop. Fighting down a wave of panic, she pulled the nightgown off over her head. Get dressed, that was the first thing. And then find someone who could tell her what had happened to the shop.

Dressing quickly, Susanna realized that the soft blue dress must belong to one of Nate's sisters. It fit fairly well except that it hung a bit long on her. She found the straight pins to fasten the front of the dress lying on the table and slipped them in place with the ease of long practice. The shoes were her own, obviously cleaned and dried to be ready for her.

Now for her hair, and then she could go. She brushed it out, tackling the tangles with energy. Normally she'd have put her hair in a single thick braid before climbing into bed, but she'd probably fallen asleep before she could start.

A knock at the door told her Dora must have heard her steps

and known she was awake. "I'm awake—" She swung the door open, losing her words when she saw that it was Nate, not Dora.

"I . . . I thought it was your mamm." She knew her cheeks were pink at facing Nate fresh from bed with her hair hanging halfway down her back.

"She wanted me to tell you to come and have something to eat." If Nate was embarrassed as well, he hid it better. "Don't hurry. Mamm just always wants to feed people."

"I know. Denke, Nate." Gathering her scrambled thoughts, she began to ask him about the shop, but he was already starting down the stairs.

Closing the door, Susanna hurried with her hair. She wrapped it into a bun, securing it with hairpins, and setting the prayer covering in place. This one looked new, and she guessed either Dora or one of her daughters might have made it but not worn it yet. Giving it to her was a kind gesture.

As she went out of the room, she spared a thought for her own things, many of them maybe underwater by now. She had little that couldn't be replaced, but Daad's family Bible and the quilts her mamm had made would be a loss. Still, her apartment sat a bit higher than the shop. Maybe those things she treasured would be spared. If not . . . many folks were losing far more than that, she feared.

Taking a quick look around the upstairs, she gripped the banister. Five bedrooms, it seemed. Nate had probably hoped to fill them with kinder.

Apparently the room she'd been in was the largest one. His, maybe? If so, Nate shouldn't have given up his room to her.

Mingled aromas testifying to cooking and baking drew her to the kitchen, along with the chatter of female voices. Dora and her two daughters bustled about, using what seemed to be every available pot and pan, while Donna's young children played with blocks in a corner out of the way.

"Here's Susanna," Donna said.

Rachel, her younger sister, smiled at Susanna. "Did we wake you with all our noise?"

"Ach, I'm certain-sure you should have slept longer." Dora came to give her a quick hug. "How do you feel?"

"Fine, I'm fine." It seemed to Susanna that she'd been saying that often lately. "What's happening? It looks as if you're planning to feed the whole town."

"Not quite that," Dora said, "but it comes close. With the electricity off and the stores closed, there'll be plenty of hungry mouths to feed."

"Since we don't rely on electric like the Englisch, we'll fix what we can here." Donna set a steaming bowl of vegetable soup on the table and gestured Susanna to a chair.

"I can help—" she began, but Dora pushed her gently to a seat.

"Eat first," she said. "Then you'll have the strength to cope with whatever comes next."

Rachel bent to take two shoofly pies from the oven, the heat bringing a flush to her cheerful round face. "You'll have a wedge of this once it cools," she said. "It will fill up the empty corners."

Donna sniffed with mock disapproval. "Dry-bottom shoofly pie. Whoever heard of the like in this house?"

"My Stephen likes it this way," Rachel said. She was married less than a year, and obviously taking pleasure in making the pie the way her husband preferred. "You're just jealous."

"What do I have to be jealous about?" Donna snapped a tea towel at her sister. "I use Mamm's recipe."

"Girls, stop your chatter and let Susanna eat in peace." Dora

157

smiled fondly at her daughters, obviously knowing that all their fratching was done in fun.

A spoonful of the hot soup seemed to warm Susanna all the way down. "What's the news? Have you heard anything?"

The women were suddenly so quiet that the sound of the toy blocks was like a clap of thunder. Dora sat at the table, her face tightening.

"Nate went to check on things an hour ago. He says the creek is going down, so that's gut. But it's an awful mess with water still in the street, and the police aren't letting anyone go closer. They say it's too dangerous."

"But surely, if we could just get a look—"

Dora shook her head. "I know. I feel that way, as well. It's worse for you because your apartment is there, too. But we'll have to be patient until it is safe to go in, like everyone else."

Dora's words were a reminder. Susanna wasn't the only one at risk of losing much. She nodded, feeling a little ashamed of her single-mindedness.

"How bad is the river?"

"They're saying it will crest tonight." Donna glanced at her children, as if to assure herself that they didn't hear or understand. "A record high, so they say."

"The electric is out, and the water plant is flooded so the pipes are shut down." Rachel's brown eyes were solemn. "It's just lucky for us Nate thought ahead and filled plenty of jugs with water."

Something in her voice reminded Susanna that Nate had been as much a father as a big brother to his two younger sisters. Much as she disagreed with Nate at times, Susanna had to admire his dedication to his family.

"Nate says we can't expect anyone to get into town to help until tomorrow, at least," Rachel went on, shivering a little. "I used to read stories like that, about people stranded on a desert island and the like, and think it sounded as if it would be fun. But the real thing isn't fun at all."

"Ja, there are plenty of folks who need help now and will in the days to come." Dora rose. "We must accept what happens as God's will, and do what we can for others."

Every word Dora said was true, but Susanna couldn't help thinking it was very hard to accept what was happening as God's will.

The shop was all she had left now. Surely God wouldn't let that be taken away from her.

Chloe had insisted on helping clean up after the huge lunch Emily Hartman had served when they'd awakened. At the moment she was putting plates into the glass-fronted dish cabinet that took up half of one wall in the kitchen and covertly watching Seth dry the last few cups.

The T-shirt Emily had found for him to wear while she washed his clothes stretched across his broad shoulders, and a strand of wheat-colored hair fell onto his forehead. He looked up, caught Chloe's gaze, and smiled.

Her heart lurched. After what they'd been through together, she was finding Seth very nearly irresistible. She longed to let go of everything that urged caution. What would happen if she did? Warmth seemed to spread through her.

"Feeling better now?" he asked.

Maybe it was best he not know what she was really feeling.

"There's nothing like hot water and a hot meal to get a person feeling human again, is there? How is that working, anyway? I thought the power was off."

"It is." Seth hung the dish towel neatly on the dish rack. "Dave has a generator big enough to power the whole house, and he has a well. He says he can't be in charge of emergency services unless he's prepared for emergencies himself."

"Makes me feel a little guilty, being warm and clean when so many aren't either." She set the last dish in the cabinet and closed the door.

"We'll be better able to help others if we feel better ourselves," Seth said, sounding practical. "By the way, I spoke to my mother just before you came down. She had a message from Lydia, saying they'll be here to help as soon as the bridge is open again."

At some level, Chloe had known that Lydia wouldn't be able to stay away, but it still cheered her to think of seeing her sister. "How is it in Pleasant Valley? Did they get any flooding?"

"Some basement flooding from the creek, that's all. My mother said they've been able to get most houses and stores pumped out today."

Seth carried the cups over and reached above her head to put them in the cabinet where they belonged. Chloe discovered she was holding her breath at his sudden nearness.

She cleared her throat. "Your mother and Jessie are all right, though?"

"They're okay."

Something in his voice told her that wasn't entirely true. She put her hand on his wrist. "Something's bothering you. What is it? Your mother didn't fall, did she?" That was one of his recurrent worries, she knew—that his mother would try to do too much and end up with another broken hip.

He shook his head, his lips twisting slightly. "It's Jessie. She's determined to come with the work crew to help, and Mamm's just as determined to keep her home. They both want me to side with them."

It reminded Chloe uncomfortably of her relationship with her grandmother. "Is there any real reason why Jessie couldn't help? I mean, physically she's fine, isn't she?"

He nodded slowly. "I suppose so. Mamm worries, though. Jessie has what the doctors tactfully call 'impulse control' issues. If she should fly off the handle . . ."

Chloe struggled with her own impulses. Technically it wasn't any of her business, but she couldn't help caring, and she was an old pro at reacting to overprotectiveness. Seth's mother was gentle and loving, but it sometimes seemed to Chloe that her hovering irked Jessie beyond all bearing.

"Maybe one of us could keep an eye on her if she came to help," she said finally. "Or Lydia could. Would that reassure your mother?"

"It might." His hands, braced against the marble countertop, were so taut the muscles stood out like cords. "I spent ten years ignoring my family." His voice was harsh. "I'm still paying for that neglect. If I make the wrong decision, about this or anything else—"

"You won't," Chloe said quickly, hoping that was what he needed to hear. "As long as you're acting out of love, I don't think you can go wrong. And in the end, isn't it up to Jessie? She's old enough to make her own decisions." And learn from her mistakes, the way Chloe had to.

Seth gave a short nod and pushed himself away from the counter. She recognized the signs. He'd let her glimpse his inner tumult, and now he was backing off.

"Speaking of family, have you called your grandmother? She's probably worried. I'm sure the flooding is all over the network news."

"I haven't yet. As a matter of fact, I think my cell phone may be at the bottom of the creek. Or floating its way down the river." She'd discovered it missing sometime in the night, but the loss was minor compared to everything else that was washing away.

Pulling his phone from his pocket, Seth handed it to her. "Use mine." His lips tilted in an ironic smile. "I wouldn't want you to miss a scolding for your negligence."

True enough, Chloe thought as she punched in the familiar number.

The call was answered on the first ring by her grandmother, not the housekeeper, probably a measure of how worried her grandmother was. "Hello? Who is this?" Gran's voice was sharp.

"It's me, Gran. Chloe. I had to borrow a phone, that's why the number is unfamiliar. I called to let you know I'm all right."

"Why didn't you call earlier? Surely you knew I'd be concerned. It's only common courtesy to let people know what's happening—"

"Gran, I'm sorry," Chloe interrupted, hearing the genuine fear beneath the scolding. "I had to leave my house because of the flooding, and I lost my cell phone." Probably best not to say what she'd been doing at the time. "I'm okay, honestly. I'm dry and fed and I've had a couple of hours of sleep, which is more than a lot of people here can say."

"Come home at once. I told you to begin with that this idea of yours was foolish, and now you see the result."

Chloe tried without success to follow that line of reasoning. "I don't think my being here had anything to do with the flood hitting. And even if I wanted to come back to Philadelphia, I couldn't. The roads are closed."

"As soon as they're open, then. Promise me, Chloe." The autocratic voice seemed to waver just a little.

"I can't, Gran." Chloe kept her tone even. "There's too much work to be done here. You've always taught me that it's my duty to help those less fortunate. This time that includes my sister."

Silence for a moment. "Is Susanna safe?"

At least Gran wasn't pretending not to remember her name. "She isn't injured, but her home and her business are both flooded, and it's too soon to know how bad it is." She hesitated, realizing that it was impossible to explain what it was like to someone who hadn't experienced a flood. "She needs me to be with her. As long as I'm needed, I have to stay."

Chloe found she was reliving that moment at the shelter when she and Susanna had suddenly been holding each other. She'd felt a joy that was somehow fierce in its strength. They were sisters, and Susanna was finally realizing it.

Another silence, longer this time, from her grandmother. And then . . .

"I suppose I still find it hard to see you as an adult who can take of herself." Gran's tone was that of someone making a startling discovery. "You'll let me know if there's anything I can do. And stay in touch." This last was delivered in Gran's usual tart tone, and she hung up.

Well. Was it possible her grandmother was actually changing? Chloe handed the phone to Seth.

He looked at her with his eyebrows slightly lifted. "I think that's the firmest I've ever heard you speak to her."

"I finally learned it's the only thing that works with my grandmother. Maybe if my mother had known that, she wouldn't have had to run away from home."

Seth's eyes narrowed. "She wouldn't have become Amish. That's what you mean, isn't it?"

She hesitated, seeing the barriers falling into place between them again. But she couldn't say anything except the truth. "I suppose I do."

Nate paused just inside the door of the shelter, his gaze sweeping the room in search of Susanna. She probably could have taken a break until it was time to cook supper, but most likely she found it easier to forget her worries when she stayed busy here.

The consistory building was more crowded now as additional neighborhoods were evacuated in the face of alarming predictions as to the river's crest. Luckily there was plenty of room, and the sturdy old building was well away from the river. A pair of elderly men played checkers, using a stool for a table between them. Some people slept, while others gathered in small groups, probably sharing the latest predictions.

There were no Amish among the evacuees. Most lived outside town, and those in the danger area would have moved in with family or friends.

Finally Nate spotted Susanna. She was in the far corner of the room, bending over a young Englisch child, trying to get the little girl interested in a toy. The child drew back, finger in her mouth, looking on the verge of tears. Small wonder. Her young life had probably been turned upside down in the past few hours.

"Come on," Susanna coaxed. "Barbie wants to play with you, don't you, Barbie?"

With a jolt he realized that his niece Barbie was there, hidden from his view on the other side of Susanna. Apparently his sister was here working and had brought her along.

Barbie held out a doll to the Englisch girl, giving her a sweet smile that was very like her mother's.

The child didn't accept, but she pointed to Susanna's apron, as if in explanation.

"You think we look different from you, I guess," Susanna said cheerfully. "We wear different clothes, and sometimes we talk differently. But that's just on the outside." She put her hand over her heart. "Inside we want to be friends, and inside is what matters, ja?"

Little Barbie held out the doll again. This time the child took it.

"There, now," Susanna said. "Why don't you build a bed for the baby with those blocks?"

In an instant the kinder were working together, happy despite their differences in language and clothing. If Susanna were being judged on what she was like inside, as she'd said, it occurred to Nate that she was truly beautiful.

He backed away from that thought quickly. It wasn't his business to be thinking about Susanna like that. He had a task ahead of him, and he prayed it wouldn't be as unpleasant as he feared.

He took a step closer, and Susanna turned, seeing him. Her smile slid from her face at his expression.

"Something is wrong. Tell me."

"No, no, nothing." Well, that wasn't true, but at least nothing new. "I came to get you. The creek has gone down enough that the police are letting people into that end of town to have a look."

"We can go into the shop?" She clasped her hands at her breast in a gesture that mingled hope and prayer.

"Not into the buildings, no. They say it's still too dangerous for that. But they'll let owners walk down the street and have a look. We have to wear boots. I brought some from the store. Your sister is waiting in the car to take us there."

Susanna nodded, and he thought she was trying very hard to stay calm. "I'll just need to tell Julia that I'm going."

It took only a moment to let the supervisor know, and then he guided Susanna to the side street where Chloe was double-parked, waiting for them. His mother sat in the front with Chloe, so he and Susanna slid into the back.

"We'll know soon, ja?" His mamm reached over the back of the seat to clasp Susanna's hand.

"We will." Susanna glanced at Chloe. "It's wonderful kind of you to drive us."

"No problem." Chloe pulled out onto Main Street. "I thought you could use some company, and I was free at the moment."

"Where's Seth?" Susanna asked, seeming to bracket the two of them together.

"He was helping move furniture at the middle school, the last I heard."

Nate didn't see anything startling in her response, but he saw Susanna give her sister a sharp glance. She'd apparently heard something he hadn't.

They reached the barricade in a matter of minutes. Chloe parked and turned toward them. "I was told that they'd let in owners and renters in small groups, accompanied by an officer. I'll go and see if they're ready for us yet."

Susanna nodded, her eyes wide with apprehension. He'd like to comfort her, and Mamm as well, but what could he say? They'd have to see for themselves.

He followed Chloe with his gaze as she approached the man in charge, feeling a grudging admiration for her capability. He'd heard from his sister about her work with water rescue. Obviously there was more to Susanna's Englisch sister than he'd at first thought.

A small group of people passed the car, going back up the hill. Several of the women were weeping, and they all wore looks of shock. His mother murmured something soft and sympathetic, her eyes filled with shared grief.

Seeing Chloe returning, he got out and went around to help his mother pull on her boots and get out.

"They're ready for us," Chloe said. "Remember not to touch anything. There's some question of the floodwater being contaminated."

They walked with her to the barricade, where a young officer waited, and started down the street.

It was the first real glimpse Nate had had of the devastation, and it stunned him. Mud and debris filled the street, and several pieces of lawn furniture clung precariously to trees. One house was off its foundation. Still in one piece, it sat tilted diagonally several yards away, looking like a child's dollhouse that had been tipped over. Several porches had been ripped off. A chicken coop, washed from an upstream farm, sat forlornly in the middle of the street.

They came to a halt in front of the house where Susanna rented the first floor.

"It doesn't look too bad. I'll bet some of your clothes and personal belongings are salvageable." Chloe was trying to be cheerful, but she had a point. The yard had been scoured away and the porch hung loose at one side, but the house still stood. Judging by the water marks, the flooding had reached about a foot or two in the first floor.

"You'll be allowed to go in and bring things out once the house has been checked for safety." The officer spoke slowly, as if not sure Susanna understood.

She nodded, turning away, and Nate realized she was yearning toward the shop. That was apparently home, even more than the apartment was.

He didn't have a good feeling about the shop, and his fears were realized once they were close enough to get a look. The creek must have flowed unimpeded across the road and straight into the shop. A deep channel was cut along one side of the building, exposing the foundation. Water must have gotten to the four- or five-foot mark in the first floor. The only good thing he could think to say was that the structure was still standing.

His mother put her hand over her mouth, and he saw that she was holding back tears. "Our poor shop," she murmured. "It's all broken."

He put his arm around her, trying to comfort her, and looked at Susanna.

She took a step toward the shop, shaking off her sister's restraining hand. "No," she said. "No." She lunged forward, startling them, but Nate caught her before she could reach the building, pulling her back gently.

"You can't go inside, remember? There's nothing we can do right now."

She looked up, eyes wide and shocked. But dry. Somehow it might have been easier to deal with her if she'd collapsed in tears.

His mother put her arm around Susanna, and the two of them stood together, looking at what was left of their shop.

"What do we do now?" Susanna said, but not as if she expected an answer.

Mamm hugged her. "Now we rebuild, of course."

It was a fine, hopeful thing to say. Nate wasn't foolish enough to argue now. But looking at the devastation, he had his doubts that rebuilding would ever happen.

Chapter Eleven

Susanna arranged cans of soup on a shelf at the bulk foods store the next day, aware that Anna Mae was watching her with a critical eye. When Susanna had volunteered to help out in the store between her shifts at the shelter, Nate and Dora had both tried to dissuade her.

All their arguments made sense, but Susanna had the feeling that if she didn't stay busy, her whirling thoughts would spin her around like a top. If only she and Dora could get into the shop—

Anna Mae had offered to show her what to do, and she seemed intent on making it clear that she was the knowledgeable one here. Perhaps she'd felt Susanna was too critical the day Anna Mae had watched her shop. Whatever Anna Mae's motive, Susanna had no objection to being the underling. Let Anna Mae have her moment in the sun.

Susanna started another carton of soup. Canned goods had been flying off the shelves since Nate had reopened the store this morning. Small wonder, since most stores in town, with their dependence on electricity, remained closed. The downside was that no one knew how long it would be until trucks started coming in to restock. Nate had been giving so freely to the shelter that his storeroom was emptying quickly.

Nate didn't seem to count the cost of his giving. While she wouldn't have expected any other reaction, Susanna still found that admirable. He could so easily have held some back with the excuse that he had to provide for his own people first, but he hadn't.

An Englischer brushed past her with a laden cart, and Susanna realized she'd been standing in the middle of the aisle, lost in thought. Murmuring an apology, she stepped aside to let him reach the back counter where Anna Mae was checking people out.

Susanna glanced at the contents of the man's cart as he passed her and then looked down the aisle at the canned meats section. Thomas had just restocked that area a short while ago, but now it was empty, and the Englischer's cart was filled to the brim with canned meat and fish.

Frowning, Susanna moved to the counter, her gaze on Anna Mae. The girl was tallying the cans as the man put them on the counter, not seeming to feel that there was anything wrong with his order.

"This shopper has taken all the canned meat we have in stock."

She spoke quietly to Anna Mae in Pennsylvania Dutch, trusting that the Englischer wouldn't understand. He was young, in his twenties maybe . . . not the typical shopper at a bulk foods store.

"So?" Anna Mae smiled at the customer. "Nate will be pleased that I made a big sale."

"I don't think . . ." Susanna began, troubled.

"Why don't you get back to stocking shelves?" Anna Mae's tone was tart. "This is my job."

Maybe Anna Mae was right, but it didn't sit well with Susanna to see someone buying so much that there was nothing left for anyone else. Turning her back on the half-emptied carton, she went in search of Nate.

She found him in the storeroom, pulling a carton from the shelf. At the sight of her, he shoved it back. "Are you ready to take a break?" he asked.

She shook her head. "Perhaps this is none of my business, but it troubled me a little. There's a man . . . a customer . . ." She had difficulty getting the words out. He'd think she was foolish. She shouldn't interfere.

"Ja?" Nate leaned his elbow against the shelf, seeming in no hurry.

"He's cleaned the shelves of all the canned meat and fish you had stocked. Anna Mae says that's fine, but I thought you would want to know."

Nate had straightened before she finished speaking, his brows drawing together in a frown. "You thought right," he said, and strode toward the front of the store.

Susanna lingered behind as Nate reached the counter, indulging in what was probably a futile hope that Anna Mae wouldn't realize she'd fetched him. Still, she was close enough to hear his voice.

"I'll take this customer," he said, gently moving Anna Mae to the side. He eyed the man. "This is all the canned meat we have in the store."

The Englischer shoved his hands into his jacket pockets. "So? It's for sale, and I'm buying it."

"I'm afraid not." Nate's tone was politely regretful. "I can sell you three of each, if you want."

"What do you mean, three? It's none of your business how much I buy." The man's face flushed, but Susanna thought uneasiness was mixed with his anger.

"Not today you can't," Nate said. "I don't know when my next shipment will be in, and this is an emergency situation with so many stores closed."

The customer glared at him for a moment. Then he glanced around the store before leaning on the counter. "Look, I can get a lot more than your price for the stuff in some of the townships. There's a shortage, see? People expect to pay more. Say I split the difference with you. That's fair, right?"

"No." Nate's pleasant expression didn't change, but a steely note came into his voice. "Thomas, you can put this stock back on the shelf, please. This gentleman won't be buying anything today."

"You can't do that—"

Thomas slipped the cart away quickly, leaving him standing there empty-handed. He glared, and Susanna's breath caught in her throat. If he offered violence, what could Nate do?

The moment passed. Maybe the man became aware that everyone in the store, Amish and Englisch alike, was staring at him.

"Dumb Dutchman," he muttered, and flung himself toward the door.

There was silence for a moment. Then an elderly Englischer stepped to the counter. "It seems like emergencies bring out the worst in some people. Glad you didn't let him get away with those shenanigans."

There was a murmur of approval from the other customers,

and Susanna found she was smiling. That is, until she caught Anna Mae's gaze, looking daggers at her.

Well, the girl was young. She would learn. In the meantime, if she wanted to blame Susanna, she could bear it.

Susanna was helping a customer find the powdered milk a few minutes later when she realized Nate was standing behind her. He waited until the woman had moved away, and then he spoke quietly.

"Denke, Susanna. I'm glad you caught what was going on. Anna Mae should have known better."

"Please don't say anything to her," she said quickly. "She was just excited about making a big sale. I think she wanted to impress you."

"Why? I know she's a gut worker already."

Was he deliberately being dense, or didn't he realize the girl had a crush on him?

"Not impress you as a boss. Impress you as a man. You know what I mean."

A spark of humor touched his face, softening his mouth. "I know what you mean, all right, but I could never be interested in someone so young and foolish."

"She won't always be young and foolish," Susanna said, enjoying his rare look of amusement.

"Ja, and I'll still be too old for her, even if I were looking to marry again." His face stilled, and his eyes seemed to darken.

Without doubt, Susanna knew he was thinking of the words he'd let slip about his wife. His gaze was intent on her face, and her breath caught in her throat. For an instant she thought he was going to speak, to say whatever it was he held back about Mary Ann and their marriage.

A shopping cart rattled in the next aisle, seeming to recall him to where they were. With a sudden shake of his head, he turned away, leaving Susanna shaken.

She glanced across the store, trying to pretend nothing had just happened. After all, nothing had. Neither of them had said a word they couldn't have said before a roomful of people. Still . . .

Her gaze reached Anna Mae and stopped. The girl was staring at her again, with dislike so open it was almost a blow.

Susanna dropped her gaze, hoping nothing showed in her face, and began straightening items at random on the shelf. Keeping her hands busy might help her regain her balance.

The outside door opened, and young Thomas ran in. She could see the excitement in his face from where she stood.

"Have you heard?" He spoke loudly enough for the whole store to hear. "The bridge is open!"

A babble of voices greeted his announcement, and relief swept through the room like a warm breeze. The bridge was open, so they were no longer cut off from the outside world. It was the first good news many people had had for days. Maybe the end of their ordeal was in sight.

Seth was heading out of Dave's house when he saw Chloe coming down the stairs. She'd avoided being alone with him since that awkward moment when the chasm of being Amish had opened up between them again. He'd begun to feel as if he were walking a tightrope around her. One wrong move, and it was into the net with him.

He stopped at the bottom of the stairs, waiting for her. "Have you heard the news? The bridge is open. We're not cut off any longer."

Chloe's face brightened and she came the rest of the way down with a skip in her step. "Terrific! Lydia said they'd come as soon as the roads are open."

Her thoughts had gone immediately to the sister she hadn't even known existed six months earlier. She didn't even seem aware of the dichotomy between her obvious love for her Amish sister and her regret at that Amishness.

"It means other help will be arriving from the outside, too. But Dave says, given how widespread the flood damage is, we shouldn't expect too much too soon."

"In other words, we volunteers should get busy, I suppose." She slung her bag over her shoulder. "Off to work. Where are you headed?"

"To help set up a Salvation Army lunch wagon down on Market Street." Seth paused. "You want to come and help?"

Chloe shook her head. "I'm scheduled to work at the shelter today. I'd like to be sure I'll see Lydia when she arrives. I wish she had a cell phone. For that matter, I wish *I* had a cell phone. Until my replacement phone arrives, I feel lost."

He chuckled as they went outside together. "Maybe we're all a little too dependent on our devices."

"You think?" Amusement flashed in her green eyes, but Seth reminded himself that her improved mood probably had more to do with the prospect of seeing her sister than with anything he might say.

"Nate's store seems to be a staging area for the Amish," he said. "I'd guess she and Adam would check there first. You could leave word there that you're at the shelter."

"Good idea." She pulled open her car door. "I'll see you later."

He put a hand on the door. "Maybe you could give me a lift

as far as Market Street. They asked us not to try and park too many cars down there."

Did he imagine her momentary hesitation? Then she nodded toward the passenger's side. "Hop in."

Silence stretched between them for all of a block. Then Chloe made a slight sound of exasperation.

"This is ridiculous. We may as well get this thing out in the open. I know my reaction annoyed you yesterday, but I think it was perfectly natural. If my mother hadn't become Amish, I wouldn't have lost her. Of course I regret it." She glared at him as if daring him to disagree.

Seth held back a sharp answer. Nobody ever argued someone out of feelings—he'd learned that a long time ago.

"How do you know?" He kept his tone neutral.

Chloe blinked, a frown line appearing between her brows. "I . . . well, I know. If she hadn't clashed with Gran so much, if she hadn't left home when she did, she'd never have fallen in love with an Amish man. Therefore she wouldn't have been in the van the day she was killed."

"She wouldn't have had you." He spoke the truth that was so obvious to him. "'What if' is a dangerous game to play, Chloe. There are too many variables. You can't know what your mother's life would have been if she hadn't married your father."

"No, but . . ."

Seth could almost see her sharp intelligence struggling with the belief her grandmother had implanted in her all Chloe's life.

"I suppose she might still have wanted a life that was different from what she'd known," Chloe said. She waited while an army reserves truck rumbled through the intersection. "But

I have a right to wish I'd known her and known my sisters, for that matter. You can't deny that our parting was the direct result of the accident." A flare of anger lit the words. "If our mother had married someone else—"

"You wouldn't be you." He studied the face that had become so familiar over the past months—the stubborn tilt to her jaw, the spark of fire in her green eyes, the tender lips he couldn't help wanting to kiss. "I, for one, would consider that a great loss."

She darted a sharp glance at him, as if wondering if he was making fun of her. "I'm being irrational, that's what you're saying."

"No." He hesitated. How risky was it to say what he really thought? "I'm saying I thought you'd lost your prejudice against the Amish."

"I have," she said instantly. Defensively. "I've accepted that my sisters are Amish. I wouldn't criticize their lifestyles."

"You just disapprove of all their choices. Do you think people don't sense it?" He was pushing too hard, but he couldn't seem to stop himself.

Chloe's lips firmed and she made the turn onto Market Street before she spoke. A water buffalo was parked in front of the library, and people with jugs and bottles were lined up for fresh water.

Chloe made her way around it and drew to the curb in the next block, just short of the barricade that still closed the street down to the river.

As he grasped the door handle, she spoke.

"I've tried to accept the past." Her voice was husky. "It's not so easy."

The sudden vulnerability in her expression made his heart

clench. He wanted to say something that would erase it, but there wasn't anything. This struggle was one Chloe had to fight alone.

It seemed to Nate that the store was like a large pot of stew coming to a boil. All day long people had been in and out, some shopping, some just trying to find out what was going on. The store had always been a hub of activity for the Amish of Oyersburg, but now the circle was growing larger.

Natural enough, he supposed, trying to answer questions, assess his stock, and get through to his usual suppliers. Now that the river had crested, folks were venturing out, checking damage, deciding whether they needed help or should be providing it.

Thomas appeared at his elbow. "Matt Ziegler and his boys are here. They say their farm is fine, and where can they go to help?"

"Wait a minute." Nate scrabbled through the drift of papers on the counter. "We sent some folks down to Hemlock Street, but I don't know how many, and—"

He broke off as a list slid into view, showing neatly who'd asked for help, who'd volunteered, and who had gone where. "Susanna?" He glanced at her, startled. "What gave you this idea?"

"I just thought it might be of help. I didn't mean to interfere."

"It's not interfering. It's just what we need." He ran a pencil down the list. "Ask Matt and his sons to go down to Ninth Street, Thomas. There's water backing up from one of the runs there."

Thomas nodded and darted off, and Nate turned to Susanna.

She was stepping away, already effacing herself as she so often did. Maybe she was more comfortable being an observer, but if so, she knew how to put that to good use.

"You'll find poster board on the shelves above the workbench in the storeroom. Do you think you could make a chart showing this information?"

"Ja, of course, if that would help."

"You know it would." He smiled, liking her assurance. Susanna wasn't as timid as he used to think, especially when it came to something she felt strongly about.

He watched her for a moment as she took the list and hurried off toward the storeroom. It must have been difficult for her to butt into the situation with Anna Mae and the Englischer this morning, but she had done what was right. He suspected she always would.

That air of hers of staying on the sidelines, watching others— was that the result of the injury that had no doubt kept her from a normal life as a child? Or would she always have had that sweet shyness, regardless of circumstance?

One thing was certain-sure—her life recently had been one blow after another, with her mother's illness and death, his own plans for the shop, the discovery that she had family she hadn't known about. And then the flood, threatening the life she'd built here. The fact that she was so quiet about it didn't mean she wasn't feeling it.

Susanna had courage, more than he'd given her credit for in the years he'd known her. Still, surely her new family . . . well, Lydia and her husband, at least . . . could be a comfort and support to her, if only she'd let them. If he could help make that happen, it was the least he could do.

Anna Mae scurried out of the storeroom, brandishing the

inventory sheet he'd sent her off to do. He'd have to know what was needed, assuming he could get through to his suppliers and they could get a shipment to town.

"All finished." She handed it to him with a quick sweep of her lashes and a smile. "It was quite a job with everything moved around to make room for all the stuff that folks have stored in there."

"Denke, Anna Mae," he said absently, running his gaze down the list. Supplies were lower than he'd thought. If the trucks didn't get through soon, they'd be down to what remained in the shop.

"What else can I do for you?" Anna Mae leaned a little closer, her sleeve brushing his.

Nate took a casual step back. Anna Mae's flirting seemed to have accelerated since Susanna had started helping in the store, and it had begun to annoy him.

"You can get back to the register and let your sister have a short break," he said, not looking at her. "I'll be calling my suppliers if anyone needs me."

The store's telephone was in the back hallway, about as inconveniently located as possible, but at least it discouraged his young workers from using it for personal calls. They knew full well that was not allowed, but that didn't stop them from trying. As long as they weren't neglecting their work, he left them alone. He could, vaguely, remember what it was like to be a teenager.

This time his chief supplier answered the phone, but the news was not encouraging. He'd get there when he could, but his own shipments weren't coming in yet. After extracting a promise that the supplier would send a truck to Oyersburg as soon as possible, Nate hung up.

When he reached the front of the store again, he was in time to see a van followed by a couple of cars pull into the parking lot. People began emerging, so many that it seemed impossible they'd all been wedged into the vehicles.

A smile spread over Nate's face as he realized what was happening. The bridge was open. The Amish from Pleasant Valley had arrived to help.

Susanna emerged from the storeroom with the chart he'd asked her to make, and he took her arm and drew her over to the window.

"Look. See anyone familiar?"

Her breath seemed to catch. "Lydia. My . . . My sister."

"That's her husband, Adam, right behind her, and it looks as if they've brought half the church district with them."

"Chloe said she'd come as soon as she could." Susanna glanced up at him, a question in her eyes. "I don't know her very well."

"She's family." He answered what he thought was the question. "Naturally she wants to help, with you affected by the flood."

"Chloe was forced out of her home, too."

He puzzled over that comment. Was she thinking they had come only because of Chloe? Did she find it so hard to accept that her sister's family would jump to help her also?

The group was entering through the front door now, and he nudged Susanna forward. "Don't you think you should go and greet your sister?"

She hung back. "In a moment. I'm sure they're looking for you to tell them what to do."

Shy and stubborn was a difficult combination, Nate decided as he strode toward the group. Susanna was going to need a push or two if she was to build a relationship with her birth family.

And if he did the pushing, she'd no doubt become convinced that as she'd told him once already, he just wanted them to give her an option other than the shop.

Still, somebody had to try.

"Wilkom, wilkom." He couldn't help grinning at the sight of all those willing, well-rested volunteers. They were such a contrast to the tired faces of those who'd been working for what seemed an eternity.

"We're here to help." Adam Beachy spoke up. "As soon as we heard the bridge was open, we headed out."

"You're a wonderful-gut sight. I don't mind telling you, folks here are about worn-out, and the cleanup is just starting."

"It'll be a long haul, judging by the little we've seen so far," Adam said, and several others nodded. "We thought some fresh food might be needed, so there are boxes of fruit and baked goods in the van. Should we bring the food in here?"

"Maybe your driver could take it right to the shelter," Nate suggested. "That's where the greatest need is. Thomas, go with Mr.—?" He paused, looking inquiringly at the older Englisch man who must be one of the drivers.

"Miller, Ben Miller," he said. "Come along, young Thomas. You can guide me to the shelter."

Thomas grinned at the break in the routine, and the two of them headed out.

Nate glanced at Susanna, who still hovered back by the counter as if uncertain what to do. Lydia was watching her with the worried concentration of a mother for a child. He had a feeling it was going to take more than anything he could do to get Susanna adjusted to her new family.

"Susanna has a chart of where workers are needed," he said, deliberately leading the group toward her. She handed the chart to him, her cheeks flushed.

He laid it on the counter, and they bent over it. "You can see where we've sent workers already," he said, pointing. "The west end of town is still closed until they finish inspecting the buildings for safety, but the area toward the river is open."

He took a step back, letting the men crowd around the list, and managed to put himself near Lydia Beachy.

"Go to her," he said softly. "She won't make the first move."

Lydia sent him a look that mingled surprise and gratitude. Then she rounded the counter quickly and held out her hands to Susanna. For a moment Susanna didn't budge. Then she stepped forward into her sister's hug.

Nate turned back to the men. He should be glad. He *was* glad. But it occurred to him that the more Susanna moved into her sisters' lives, the more she might move out of theirs. And he found that thought strangely troubling.

CHAPTER TWELVE

Susanna set the last of the breakfast dishes in the drainer and picked up the towel.

"I'll finish up the drying," Dora said, snatching the towel from her hand. "I can do that, even if the lot of you think I'm worn out and useless." The words were said with a smile, but Susanna could hear beneath them the faint fear that they might be true.

She surrendered the towel. "We know you can work rings around all of us. You just have to give yourself time to get back to normal."

Dora shook her head slightly, her lips pressing together, accentuating the wrinkles that surrounded them. She was discouraged, obviously, and no wonder. Dora wasn't one to take to being idle. It was foolish of Nate to think she'd be happy sitting in her rocking chair.

"So many folks need help right now." Dora shook her head as if chiding herself. "And all I can do is mope around and worry about the shop."

"I know." Susanna put her arm around Dora's waist in a quick hug. "I'm feeling the same, and blaming myself for it, too."

Dora's expression seemed to ease. "We're foolish, the both of us, ain't so? You saved much of the stock, the water has gone back down, and the shop is still standing. Everything will be back to normal in no time."

Susanna nodded, relieved to see her partner's mood improve. "In the meantime, I'll try to make myself useful over at the store."

"Try?" Dora had a little of her usual laughter back in her face. "Nate told me everything you did yesterday. Not that I was surprised. I told him you can do anything you set your mind to."

Susanna was still smiling at this exchange when she crossed the parking lot to the store, but she had a sneaking suspicion that the town's recovery from the disaster might not be as easy as Dora hoped. In the past few days, when Oyersburg had been cut off, none of them had realized the full extent of the flooding.

Towns up and down the valley had been hit, some not as bad, some worse. In each of those towns, people were working and wondering and longing to be back to normal. Looked at that way, the problems seemed overwhelming.

Do the next thing, she lectured herself as she opened the side door to the store. That's all anyone can do.

The store was busy already. Someone, probably Nate, had posted her charts at the front window, and it looked as if the list of those needing help had grown considerably since the previous day. The next thing, she reminded herself.

Nate was deep in conversation with an Englischer who wore

a hard hat and carried a clipboard, two signs of authority in these trying days. With a final word, the man headed out the door. Nate turned, saw her, and came toward her.

He nodded toward the departing figure. "He was from the group that's inspecting the properties down in the west end. He came to let us know that it's safe to go back inside your house and the shop. Not to start work, but just to see how bad it is and bring out a few things."

"That's wonderful-gut news." Susanna could feel a smile blossoming on her face. "I'll get your mamm."

"Wait." Nate grasped her arm to stop her, and as it had before, his hand warmed her right through her sleeve. "We'll have a look first, before taking Mamm in there."

Susanna blinked. "Why? It's her shop, and she was just telling me how much she longs to get back in."

Nate looked like a man struggling to be patient. "She has a lot of years of her life wrapped up in that shop. If it's very bad, I want a chance to prepare her before she sees it."

Nate might be bossy, but Susanna realized he was acting out of love. "I understand. But I don't think your mother will."

His sudden smile lit his face. "I'll take the blame for it, ja?"

"I'll be sure to remind you of it," she said.

The sun was shining as they walked down the hill, and it might have been any early fall day if a person could stop looking at the damage. They weren't alone. Trucks rumbled by, and a group of teenagers carrying buckets and shovels passed them, their laughing voices a contrast to their obvious mission.

"School is still closed, I guess," she said, nodding toward the group.

"At least until the end of the week, I hear. They're still assessing the damage." Nate seemed to be thinking of something else, and he glanced at her inquiringly. "Did you have a chance to visit with Lydia and Adam yesterday?"

"A little." Was he still hopeful that her new family would distract her from the shop? But that was probably unfair of her, and what did it matter anyway? The flood seemed to have swept away lesser troubles. "They want me to come see them on Saturday. I said I'd think about it."

Nate nodded, not speaking.

"Aren't you going to give me your opinion?" she asked, sure he had one.

"I'm afraid to," he said, his lips quirking into a smile she couldn't help but return.

The smile faded as they moved into the flood area. The yellow house on the corner of her block had been knocked off its foundation so that it stood, still intact, several feet away. Just a few days earlier Susanna had seen the owner, a cheerful elderly woman who loved gardening, out tending her chrysanthemums. Now the yard was a sea of mud.

"Can people really come back?" She didn't realize she'd spoken aloud until Nate answered her.

"Some will. And some will give up and move on."

Susanna wanted to pray for the gardener and her flowers, but she wasn't sure what to ask. Was it better to try to struggle through all the rebuilding or to give up? Perhaps it was best to pray as faith taught—that God's will be done.

A Dumpster had already been moved into what was left of the front yard of one house. A man and a couple of teenagers, wearing boots and gloves, dragged saturated carpeting out the front door, struggling to lift it to the Dumpster.

"Wait," Nate said, and went quickly to help. Together they

managed to heave the sopping carpet into the Dumpster, and a moment later he rejoined her.

They neared the house she had called home in recent years. "Your building doesn't look too bad," Nate said. "Do you want to go in and bring out your clothes and such?"

She was trembling inside, but it was not from worries about a few dresses. "I'd rather see the shop first. Maybe we can stop on our way back to get a few things from the apartment."

For a moment it seemed he would argue the point, but then he nodded and moved on. It made sense to do it that way, didn't it? There was no point carrying her belongings down to the shop.

The farther down the block they went, the worse the devastation became. The full force of the flooding creek had swept through the lower end. She glanced down the block toward the cottage Chloe had rented and gasped. There was nothing left but a pile of mud and rubble.

Nate followed the direction of her gaze. "Ja, I heard about your sister's place. But Seth said they took the important things when she got out, so all she lost was some clothes."

"She didn't even mention it to me. And I didn't ask." Guilt swept over Susanna. How could she be so selfish as not to think about what Chloe might have lost?

"Then I guess she's not that upset about it." Nate's tone was practical. "Well, there it is."

The shop stood as they'd last seen it, forlorn and storm-battered. Something inside Susanna was shaking as they approached the door.

"Excuse me."

They both turned at the call to see an Englisch woman leaning out the window of a car. "We have coolers full of sandwiches and drinks in the back for anyone who's ready for something. Please help yourself."

"Thank you. Not just now." Susanna blinked back sudden tears at the sympathy in the woman's voice.

"Guess it's a little early." The man driving leaned across the seat, giving them a sympathetic smile. "We'll come by later, as long as the food holds out." With a wave, he drove on to the next house.

"That was kind."

"People are, for the most part," Nate said. "A crisis brings out the best in some and the worst in others."

She nodded, remembering the man who'd tried to buy them out cheap so he could sell high. "Maybe it just shows what people are really like inside." The thought was vaguely unsettling. What qualities had it brought out in her, besides a tendency to focus selfishly on her own loss?

Well, she was about to find out how bad it was. Susanna took a step to the porch and felt Nate's hand firmly gripping her elbow.

"Careful. Mind where you step. We don't know how weak the boards might be."

The window to the left of the door was gone—not just broken but swept away, frame and all. She was still fumbling for the key when Nate shoved a key in the lock. She'd forgotten he'd have one, of course. He owned the building, after all, even though they always spoke of the shop as theirs.

Taking a steadying breath, Susanna entered the shop. Or what was left of the shop. She looked around in disbelief. It didn't look terribly bad on the outside, but inside . . .

"Could be worse, I guess," Nate said, his boots squishing in the layer of mud on the floor.

"I don't know how." She choked out the words.

The shelves and tables looked as if a giant hand had swept through, knocking and breaking with abandon. The one glass cabinet, where they kept the more fragile items, was smashed beyond repair, and a wall shelf hung drunkenly across the door to the back room. Anything they'd left behind was lost in the mud and debris on the floor, or it had washed out the broken window.

"You were right," she said. "Your mother will be so upset to see it this way."

"Ja." Nate's voice was gruff, and she sensed that he was moved more than he wanted to admit.

"The first day I came in, I loved it." For a moment Susanna seemed to see the shop through those eyes. She'd stood just inside the door, she remembered, overwhelmed and yet welcomed by the color and scent and feel of the place.

"Mamm told me once that when she saw you here that first time, she knew you'd love the shop as much as she did." Nate lifted a table, righting it, making a small sign of order in chaos.

Susanna nodded, lost in memories. "I was wonderful glad when she offered me a job. And when we became partners . . ." She didn't have the words to express how that had felt.

"When Mamm first wanted to start the shop, I was doubtful," Nate said, moving cautiously toward the stairs. "But she had always worked so hard to provide for us kids that I thought she should have her dream."

Susanna followed in Nate's footsteps, thankful for the pair of boots he had provided.

"You were fairly young when your daad died, ain't so?"

Nate paused on a step. "Sixteen. But even before his accident, he didn't—"

Susanna looked up at him, shocked at the bitter note in his voice. "He didn't what?"

Nate's face twisted in a smile that expressed the opposite of humor. "I guess you wouldn't know, not growing up here. My daad was that rare thing, an Amish man who was lazy. Oh, Mamm made excuses for him, but I saw him for what he really was. Bone lazy."

Dora seldom spoke of her late husband, and Susanna had no way of knowing whether Nate's assessment was correct or not. But his feelings were genuine, whether he'd been right in his judgment or not.

She struggled to find the words to respond. "You've more than made up for him, taking care of your mother and sisters the way you have."

She began to see where that bossiness of his had originated. He must have felt from the time he was small that the responsibility for the family lay on his shoulders.

"I tried." They emerged into the room at the top of the stairs, and Nate seemed to shrug off the subject. "Let's have a look for anything we should take out of here."

Susanna nodded, respecting his boundaries. He probably wouldn't have said all that about his father if not for the shock of seeing his mother's dream in such a state.

Susanna brushed her hands on her skirt and opened a drawer in the large cabinet where they stored extra items made of fabric. The holiday-themed place mats and wall hangings seemed as bright as ever, but she could smell the damp filtering into the upstairs already.

"These fabric things should go right away," she said. "But I don't think we can carry them all."

"No, likely not." His gaze passed over the quilted pieces

with little interest. "If you can stack things that should be moved first near the steps, I'll send the boys down to get them today. And I'll have to get a carpenter in as quick as possible."

"We'll need to get the mud out before a carpenter can start work." Her thoughts scrambled through the enormous list of things that had to be done before the shop could reopen. She realized Nate was staring at her. "What?"

He shook his head. "I didn't mean a carpenter to start repairs yet," Nate said. "To give me an opinion on whether the building is salvageable."

Susanna straightened, looking at him blankly. "Salvage-able?" She repeated the word, its syllables leaving a bad taste in her mouth.

Nate's square jaw seemed to harden. "I know it's not what you want to hear, Susanna, or my mother, either. But before I sink money into fixing the building, I have to know whether it's worth fixing."

Logical. Of course it was. But in her heart, it felt like a death knell for her dreams.

Chloe glanced at Susanna as she drove down the winding country road toward Lydia and Adam's place on Saturday afternoon. She'd feared Susanna would change her mind at the last minute about coming, but thank goodness she hadn't. Getting her there was another step forward, and Chloe was in a mood to look for hopeful signs.

"This is pretty country, isn't it?" Chloe hated making stilted conversation about the scenery, but it was better than sitting in silence.

"Lovely. It's good to see something so . . . so untouched."

Susanna gestured at a field of cornstalks turning golden in the fall sunshine.

"That's what I was thinking, too. Maybe we need a little relief from the troubles once in a while." If Chloe was right in what she hoped, Susanna would end this day feeling closer to her family. How could she resist her nephews? Chloe couldn't help smiling at the thought of their little faces.

And she had a lot of respect for Lydia. If anyone could get through Susanna's reserve, it would be Lydia.

"There's the lane." She pointed ahead of them. "I see they have the Apples for Sale sign up." The sign, roughly painted on a piece of plywood, leaned against the fencepost at the end of the lane.

"Lydia spoke of the orchard several times when she came in the shop. Before . . . well, before I knew, I mean." Susanna leaned forward. "She obviously loves it."

Chloe nodded, making the turn. "Our parents lived here, you know, before their deaths. I think Lydia feels the orchard brings her closer to them."

Susanna turned a startled gaze upon her. "I didn't know they lived here. And us, too, I guess. I suppose there's a lot I don't know."

Chloe tamped down her urge to plunge into explanations. For once, she wouldn't jump in without thinking.

"Lydia and I would love to tell you what we know, anytime you'd like to hear it. And Seth's mother has lived next door for ages." She pointed at the house on the far side of the orchard. "She's told me some stories of what she remembers from when we were small."

"Seth's family is Amish, ja?"

"Yes." Seth would probably be here today, and a flicker of apprehension went through her. She couldn't ignore his background when his family was around.

"It's strange, thinking that this was my home once and not remembering it at all." Susanna drew in a breath, and her hands clenched suddenly in her lap.

Chloe looked up the lane and understood. Everyone was outside, it seemed, waiting for them. It must look like a horde of strangers to Susanna.

"I remember the first time I came." She slowed when she saw the two boys racing toward the car. "I felt so overwhelmed because all these strangers knew things about me that I didn't know about myself."

Susanna's hands eased. "That's how I feel, too."

Pulling into her usual spot along the lane, Chloe cut the motor and smiled at Susanna. "It will be fine, I promise. Come and meet them."

She stepped out of the car and braced herself as Daniel and David rushed to her. David's hugs were sometimes so impetuous that he nearly knocked her off her feet.

He threw his arms around her. "Aunt Chloe!"

She hugged him, reaching out to pull David into the embrace as well. "How are you? It's so good to see you."

"We're all right. Did you bring our new aunt?"

Daniel's hand closed on his little brother's shoulder. "Remember what Mamm said. Don't rush at her." He smiled up at Chloe. "Mamm said you were in a flood. Did you get wet?"

"Was it like Noah?" David added. Their blue eyes and smiles were uncannily alike.

"Yes, I got wet. And muddy. But no, it wasn't as bad as Noah's flood." Arms around them, she piloted them around the car to where Susanna was just getting out. "These are Lydia and Adam's boys, Daniel and David."

"We're glad to meet you," Daniel said, his company manner in evidence. As the older one, he was always the most careful about his behavior.

"Can we call you Aunt Susanna?" David added.

Susanna looked a little startled, but she smiled and nodded. "That would be nice."

Lydia had reached them by this time, and she touched Susanna's arm lightly in welcome. Chloe could tell by her expression that she wanted to hug her but was holding back.

"Wilkom to our home, Susanna. Komm, meet the others."

"What is that wonderful smell?" Chloe asked.

"Apple butter." Daniel tugged at her hand. "We're making apple butter today. Komm and see."

Chloe let herself be hauled over to where Adam was feeding a wood fire under an immense copper kettle. A dark, spicy mixture bubbled gently in the kettle, while Seth stirred it with a long wooden paddle.

"Apple butter? Adam, are you sure you want to let Seth do the cooking?"

Adam straightened, grinning at her. "He's not cooking. Just stirring. Everyone has to take a hand at stirring. You can be next."

Seth's mother, Emma, came to greet her. Her warm smile didn't quite erase the worry lines in her forehead. "Are these boys trying to put you to work already?"

"They're trying, but they haven't succeeded yet. How long has this been cooking?"

"Since early this morning," Emma said. "It takes a gut eight hours to make apple butter. And mind you don't let it stick, Seth."

Seth smiled at his mother's chiding. "I won't. Come over here, Chloe. I'll show you how."

With a quick glance to assure herself that Susanna was occupied by Lydia and the children, Chloe let herself be persuaded. *Careful,* she warned herself. *The fire isn't the only source of heat when you're around Seth.*

He put her hands on the paddle, enclosing them in his as he did. "Stir it clockwise, scraping the sides and bottom to be sure it's not sticking."

He was too close, his arms practically around her as they worked the paddle.

"I can manage. Thanks."

The glint in his eyes told her he knew exactly what she was thinking. "Okay." He let go.

Chloe nearly dropped the paddle. The mixture was so thick that the movement was like rowing through molasses.

"Harder than you thought, ja?" Adam said, his eyes twinkling.

"Ja," she said emphatically, making both men laugh.

Funny. When she'd first met him, she'd thought Adam a dour, humorless chauvinist. It was only when she'd gotten to know her sister's husband that she realized what she'd seen that first day was his complete devotion to Lydia and his fear that she would be hurt.

Maybe Adam had grown to like her a bit better with time. She hoped so, but she knew he was still wary of the influence of their Englisch aunt on his children.

"Be sure you get the sides of the kettle." Seth grasped the paddle to help, his hands brushing hers again.

"I never pictured you as a cook." She made an effort to keep the atmosphere light. "How do you know so much about making apple butter?"

"I wouldn't claim to know how much sugar and spices go in. That's for the experts to decide. But everyone has a part in apple-butter making."

He seemed to have a point. Susanna and Lydia were sorting glass jars on the picnic table while his mother measured spices. Seth's sister, Jessie, was supervising the two boys as they trundled a wheelbarrow of wood to the fire. Jessie's blond hair shone in the sunlight, and her blue eyes sparkled when she laughed at something one of the boys said. She looked like the popular image of a young Amish woman, but every day she battled against the bipolar disorder that plagued her.

Adam shoved a last log on the fire. Rising, he said something to Seth in dialect, laughing, and went off to help the boys.

Chloe glanced at Seth, detecting a trace of embarrassment in his expression. "What did Adam say?"

"It was nothing."

"It was something since it made you blush."

"You make me sound like an old maid." He grinned. "Okay, you asked for it. He reminded me of an old saying that courting couples love to stir the apple butter together but they're likely to let it burn."

Now it was her turn to feel her cheeks grow hot. "He . . . was just kidding."

"Sure." His gaze evaded hers, as if he realized they were venturing onto dangerous ground.

Chloe's thoughts scrambled to find something to say. Her gaze landed on Jessie again. "Did your mother come to any decision about letting Jessie assist with the flood relief?" That seemed a safe enough topic.

Seth nodded, frowning slightly. "I'll bring Jessie over to Oyersburg tomorrow to help at the shelter. Are you going to be there? I told Mamm someone would keep an eye on her."

Chloe discovered a reluctance to become responsible for Jessie. But she was the one who'd thought volunteering might be a good idea, wasn't she?

"Sure." She tried to force enthusiasm into her voice. "I'll be glad to show Jessie the ropes."

"Great, thanks. I told Dave Hartman I'd help with tearing stuff out of flooded houses tomorrow. They're supposed to start hauling things away, but nobody's been able to figure out where they're going to put everything."

That was an aspect of the problem that hadn't even occurred to her. Her eyes sought out Susanna again.

"From what Susanna said, she hopes work can start on the shop in a day or two."

"Just let me know when, and I'll be there to help," Seth said. "Is the building in bad shape?"

"Not as bad as some, but bad enough. Susanna said Nate Gaus is bringing someone in to decide whether it's worth rebuilding."

"That's natural enough, I guess. But if it's not, what will your sister do? Move the shop to a different location?"

"She doesn't know." Chloe looked down at the apple butter, which was slowly darkening with each bubble that came sluggishly to the surface and burst. "I want to help her, but I'm not sure she's ready to accept anything from me."

"Give her time." His voice was filled with sympathy. "She'll come around. After all, who could resist you?"

She was spared finding a reply by David and Daniel scurrying over. David leaned precariously over the kettle. "Is it ready yet?"

His brother hauled him back by his suspenders. "Not yet, dummy. Mamm didn't even put the sugar in yet."

Chloe tried giving him the look that seemed so successful when Lydia did it. "Are you supposed to call your brother a dummy?"

"I guess not," Daniel admitted. "I'm sorry, David."

David didn't seem to care, apparently immune to insults. Maybe that was part of being brothers, she supposed.

"Do you know what's the best part of making apple butter, Aunt Chloe?" David said, fixing his round blue eyes on her.

"Eating it?" she guessed.

David grinned, showing the gap where he'd lost his first tooth. "After it's all poured out, we get a piece of bread and scoop up what's left in the pot." He rubbed his tummy. "Yummy."

Laughing, Seth tapped the top of David's straw hat. "You have to wait a bit yet."

The image seemed to imprint itself on Chloe's heart. The man reaching out, the boy laughing up at him, the golden colors of fall around them, the air filled with the aroma of the wood fire and apples. It was a perfect, beautiful slice of life, and she didn't want to lose it.

I want a life that's real. That was what her mother had told a friend, trying to explain the choices she'd made. In this moment, Chloe could almost agree.

CHAPTER THIRTEEN

*F*or Susanna, helping Lydia get the canning jars ready for the apple butter was a soothing, comforting task. The scent of spices, the sun slanting across the grass, even the high voices of the children brought back memories.

"You've done this many times before, ain't so?" Lydia smiled at her, the dimple appearing in her cheek, with the look that was so oddly like her own.

"Every fall for as long as I can remember until we moved to Oyersburg. Daad said we probably shouldn't have a fire burning all day once we lived in town."

She was speaking Pennsylvania Dutch, not Englisch, falling into it quite naturally since she was alone with Lydia. Maybe that added to her sense of familiarity.

"It must have been hard to leave your friends behind to move here." Lydia ran the tip of her forefinger around the glass edge to be sure there were no nicks to spoil the seal.

"In a way, it was." Susanna hated thinking about those difficult days when they realized her mother's cancer had returned. "But Daad and I were both so eager to move Mamm within reach of the specialists that I didn't really have time to think about it."

"She went to the medical center in Danville, ja?"

Susanna nodded. "Daad thought Oyersburg was the best place to settle, since it had an Amish community and was only a little over a half hour's drive to her doctors. And then he passed away just a year later."

"I'm sorry for your loss. It was odd, wasn't it, that his decision brought you back to where you'd started, and you didn't know it?" Lydia glanced at her, sunlight picking out highlights in her light brown hair. A question seemed to hover on her lips. "When you were little, didn't you remember anything about your life before the accident?"

Lydia so obviously wanted her to say she did, making Susanna feel guilty that she didn't. "I'm sorry, I don't. But from what you and Chloe told me, I was only three. I wouldn't, would I?"

"I suppose not. It's just . . . well, I've felt so guilty that I didn't remember my sisters. Mamm says the head injury wiped out those memories forever, so I shouldn't feel bad about it, but I do."

"Your mamm is . . ." Susanna tried to remember what they'd told her, but the story was muddled up in her mind.

"My daad was brothers with our birth father," Lydia said. "When I wonder what our birth father looked like, I just look at him. They were very alike, everyone says."

There would be no photographs of him, of course, and that birth father, as Lydia called him, seemed impossibly remote to Susanna. "If our . . ." She couldn't say *mother*. It was too disloyal. Elizabeth Bitler was her mother.

"Diane was Englisch." Lydia used the first name as if she spoke of a mutual friend. "So of course there were photographs of her. Chloe can show you, if you'd like to see them."

Something in Susanna rebelled at the thought. "Not . . . not yet."

"I understand," Lydia said, her voice soft. "Mamm and Daad— your aunt and uncle—wanted to come today, but they thought it might be too many relatives all at once. They said to say they want to meet you, but not until you're ready." There was a hopeful lilt to her voice.

"Not yet," Susanna said quickly. She felt a flicker of panic at the thought of meeting these strangers who seemed to know more about her than she knew herself. Her response had to hurt Lydia, and Susanna hated that it was so.

Daniel and David ran up to the picnic table, interrupting them before she could say anything else that would cause discomfort.

"Emma is putting the sugar and spices in, Mammi. Is it ready yet?" Daniel looked up at his mother, his blue eyes solemn.

"It has to cook awhile longer. Be patient."

"I hate to be patient," David said, pouting a little.

Lydia touched their small faces lovingly. "Good things take time," she said. "We can't rush them."

The words resonated in Susanna's mind. If Lydia really felt that way, it should make it easier to move slowly. The problem was that she was beginning to feel too much at home here.

"Emma Miller is a gut friend, ain't so?" she said, trying to change the subject.

Lydia nodded, giving in with a smile. "We've been neighbors since we moved here when we were first married. Before that, another relative took care of the place. And before that even, our birth parents lived here. Emma was a gut friend to Diane. She helped her adjust to life here, I think."

"It must have been wonderful hard for her." For the first time, Susanna found herself thinking of her birth mother as a young mother struggling to adapt to Amish ways. "Just the language alone would be challenging."

Lydia nodded. "Emma says she was wonderful quick at learning Pennsylvania Dutch, though. And she taught Diane how to do a lot of things, living so close. She says they used to have a laugh over it when the jelly didn't gel or the biscuits didn't rise."

"Diane must have been lighthearted." Mamm would be more likely to weep if something didn't turn out right, it seemed to Susanna. She'd always been so intent on making everything perfect.

"From all I've been able to find out, she was a happy person. Apparently she had a time of depression after Chloe was born, but that happens to some women."

The mention of depression had Susanna watching Jessie, who was taking a turn stirring the apple butter. "Chloe said something about Jessie having problems that way."

"Jessie's difficulties are much more serious than what our birth mother had." Lydia shook her head slightly. "I've seen her at her worst, and it was frightening. The doctors call it bipolar disorder and some other things I don't remember. It worries poor Emma half to death sometimes."

"Is that why Seth came back?" Of course, he might be hanging around because of Chloe. Anyone could see they were crazy about each other. Anyone but the two of them, it seemed to Susanna.

Lydia nodded, her face troubled. "I finally had to speak to the bishop about some things I'd seen Jessie doing, and he sent for Seth, since Emma was in rehab for her broken hip then. I hated doing it. It seems so wrong, to speak to the bishop about a neighbor."

Susanna touched her hand in an instinctive gesture of comfort. "It sounds as if you did her good in the long run. That's the important thing."

"I guess." Lydia smiled slightly. "That's what I pray, anyway. I know Emma worries about what is to become of her. It doesn't seem likely she'll marry."

Probably not. Lydia couldn't know that she'd struck a blow at Susanna's heart. She would probably never marry, either. Never have a man look at her in the cherishing way Adam looked at Lydia, never laugh at the antics of her kinder, never feel a new baby growing beneath her heart.

"I think we have time before the apple butter is ready to can," Lydia said suddenly. "There's something I want to show you. Will you come to the porch for a moment?"

Susanna nodded, just as glad to be diverted from the path her thoughts had taken. But once they reached the back porch and settled into the two rocking chairs, she noticed something. The others were rather obviously ignoring them. This was not as accidental as it seemed. She felt herself freeze up inside. They had been talking about her—planning something about her.

"Please don't think we were plotting." Lydia seemed to read her thoughts in her expression. She touched the miniature dower chest that sat on the table between them. "I told the others that I wanted to show you this, that's all. They're giving me an opportunity."

"I see." Was that supposed to make her feel better? Still, whatever Lydia planned, she knew Lydia's intentions were good.

"My mamm gave me the little box after I found out the truth about my parents." Lydia's lips pressed together. "It was difficult, knowing they'd held the truth back from me all those years. In some ways I'm still struggling with it."

"I guess you would be." She softened. Lydia hadn't asked to have her life turned upside down with this knowledge any more than she had. "What does the box mean?"

Lydia's fingers caressed the lid. "Our father made this for me when I was a little girl. After the accident, Mamm put some things in it that she thought I might want someday." She smiled wryly. "And then she couldn't give it to me, because she'd agreed to keep the secret."

"Secrets can be harmful," Susanna said slowly, thinking of the things Nate had let slip. He held more secrets, she felt sure of it, and they seemed to be pressing on him, as if they needed to be spoken.

"Ja, they can. Even when people have the best intentions." Lydia lifted the lid of the box. "I have shown this to Chloe, and we both felt you should see it as well." She lifted items out, one at a time, and set them on the table.

"We can't know what this was from," she said, opening a folded paper to disclose a dried flower, so fragile a breath would disintegrate it. "I like to think it was a memory of their love."

Susanna didn't remember them. She couldn't think of them as her parents. Even so, tears prickled behind her eyelids at the sight.

"They didn't have very long together," Susanna said softly.

"Seven years." Lydia folded the paper back over the flower. "But they were happy years, from everything we know. It's harder for Chloe to understand the joy of Plain life, growing up Englisch as she did. But you know."

Lydia was right. She did. There was joy each day in the assurance you were living the way the Lord wanted. That you were in the place He had prepared for you.

"This is a journal our mother wrote in. Not every day, but it seems she did when she had something special she wanted to record." Lydia paused. "There is something toward the end that troubled me, when she said she feared she'd made a mistake in becoming Amish. I wrote to a woman in Ohio who had been her friend, and I've put her answer in the journal for you to read."

She didn't wait for a response, but just left the fat leather book in front of Susanna on the table.

Maybe it would have been natural to reach out and take the book, but she couldn't. She didn't think she wanted to gaze that deeply into the heart and mind of the stranger who had been her mother.

"Mammi, Mammi!" David darted away from his father's restraining hand. "The apple butter is ready."

"In a minute, David." Lydia smiled at Susanna. "Please, take the book with you. Then you can decide if you want to read it or not. It's as much yours as it is mine and Chloe's."

Susanna pressed her lips together. She seemed to stand on the brink. One part of her longed to turn away, to retreat to the safe world in which she knew everything there was to know about herself.

But could she do so? Every day seemed to bring new challenges. Her life was changing at an alarming rate, and nothing she did would stop it.

If she read the journal, maybe she would begin to understand how she'd come to this place. With the sense of stepping off a cliff, Susanna nodded and picked up the book.

Saturday afternoons were always busy in the store, but this was the most hectic Nate had seen in some time. In addition to the shoppers, volunteers moved in and out, checking on assignments. Susanna had made some changes to the boards, so that they now showed how many people had gone to each area and when, making it easier to see where help was most needed.

Thomas passed him, staggering a little under the weight of the cartons of canned goods he was carrying. Nate lifted off the top two boxes and shifted them to the floor in front of the rapidly emptying shelves.

"Denke." The tips of Thomas's ears, visible through his corn-silk hair, reddened, a sure sign the boy was embarrassed. "Anna Mae wanted the shelves refilled right away."

"You're doing fine work, Thomas." The boy was well intentioned, even when he made mistakes, and he was shaping up well. "No need to rush."

Thomas grinned. "That's what Susanna keeps telling me. She says hurrying just gets us rattled."

"Susanna's a wise woman," Nate said. He realized he was scanning the store for Susanna's slim form and pulled himself up short.

Susanna was having a well-earned afternoon off with her family. And no matter how indispensable she'd begun to seem in the present crisis, he should not be spending so much time thinking about her.

Nate glanced at the clock above the door. Nearly noon, and Mamm would be waiting lunch for him. "I'm going to the house for lunch. Thomas, you take charge while I'm out."

Nate's eye caught a flash of resentment on Anna Mae's face, and she flounced away from the counter, heading toward him. Unfortunately the girl had begun to have an inflated image of her ability.

He was going to have to talk to her, but not just now. Quickly, before she could reach him, he went out the side door and headed across the parking lot.

That incident with the Englischer who'd tried to make money off the suffering of others had shown Anna Mae's immaturity. All she'd seen was a big sale. It had taken Susanna to realize something was wrong.

Nate gritted his teeth and reminded himself that he shouldn't think so much about Susanna. For an unmarried man and woman their ages, there could be only one result of growing closer, and marriage was out of the question for him.

Marriage could be fine for the right people. His sisters were happy, as were many of his friends. But he couldn't think of it without hearing Mary Ann telling him she was leaving. Or without thinking of his mother, working herself half to death because his father couldn't be bothered to take on a man's responsibility.

Still, Susanna persisted in intruding into his thoughts. It was amazing that he'd once barely noticed her.

He opened the door to the smell of roasting chicken. Mamm turned from setting a platter on the table to smile at him.

"Gut. I saw you coming and got the meat up."

He moved to the sink to wash. "Mamm, you don't need to make such a big meal every day."

"What else do I have to do, since I can't get into the shop?" Mamm spooned mashed potatoes into a bowl.

He definitely didn't want to get into a discussion of the gift shop with Mamm, not until he'd figured out the best course of action.

"Lots of new volunteers showed up today, maybe because it's Saturday." He sat down, knowing she'd resent it if he tried to help her. "A whole van load of Mennonites came all the way from Ohio. They're going to stay and work for a week."

"That's wonderful fine news." Mamm, apparently satisfied that she had everything on the table, sat down. "We'll have to be sure there's plenty of food for all of them."

Nate bowed his head for the silent prayer. When he'd finished, she passed the platter of chicken.

"What about the shop?" she said, as if continuing a conversation they'd already started. "When can we start work on it?"

He forked off a piece of chicken, trying without success to think of a way to divert her. "Not yet," he said. "I need a little more time to see what all has to be done." And to decide if it was worth repairing at all.

"I don't see what the holdup is." His mother's tone was fretful. "We're losing money all the time we're closed."

"I don't think anyone in Oyersburg is shopping for gifts right now," he pointed out. "They're too busy taking care of things like food and water."

"You're right." A look of compassion filled her face. "So many are in need. I shouldn't be selfish."

"You're never selfish, Mamm. I wasn't meaning such a thing.

But it's better to take a little more time now than to jump in and regret it later, ain't so?"

"I suppose. As long as we're open by the time folks start thinking of Christmas gifts. We were already talking about our displays. Now we'll have to start over."

Nate frowned down at his potatoes and gravy. "You know, Mamm, maybe it's time you were thinking of giving up the shop, after everything that's happened."

"Give it up?" His mother's lips pressed together for a moment. "Nathaniel, you brought that idea up once before, and I told you what I thought of it. I understand you were scared when I had that problem with my blood pressure, but that's all taken care of now."

"You can't be sure—"

"Nonsense. If I can spend six hours straight cooking food for the shelter, I can certain-sure work in the shop."

He looked at her heightened color and knew he'd have to move carefully. "I'm not saying you can't do whatever you feel able to. I'm just saying that maybe the flood is a sign that it's time you took it a little easier."

His mother gave him a look of sheer exasperation. "If you think the Lord would send a flood just to convince me to do what you think is best, you're just plain ferhoodled."

Nate reached across the table to clasp her hand. "I just want to take care of you, Mamm."

"You think I don't know it?" Her voice softened, and she smiled, her face crinkling. "Nate, Nate, you're always trying to take care of everyone, whether they need it or not."

His chest seemed to tighten. "I had to, didn't I?"

"Ja, you did." Pain flickered in her faded blue eyes. "We

won't talk about your daad, ain't so? But your sisters are grown and married now, and your brother and his family are settled on the farm. It's time you thought about your own happiness."

The unexpected turn left him speechless for a moment. "I'm happy enough already."

"Your life is devoted to that store, if you call that happiness." She held his gaze. "Just like Susanna and the shop."

"That's foolishness," he said shortly. *Wasn't it?* "We weren't talking about me. We were talking about the shop and what's to become of it." He took a breath and leaped. "I'm thinking maybe it's not worth it to try and fix up the building."

His mother just stared at him for a long moment, seeming to consider and discard a number of things she might say. "What would you do with it, if not fix it up? You can't leave it the way it is."

"No, but I might sell."

"You can't sell it unless it's cleaned up, at least," she countered.

He hated to admit it, but she was right. "There's a difference between cleaning up from the flood and getting the building ready to open as a gift shop again. Mamm, you don't understand—"

"I understand that you own the building," his mother said flatly. "If you choose to kick your own mother out, I suppose you can."

"I'm not talking about doing any such thing, and you know it." Trying to reason with his mother was like talking to the wall when she was in a stubborn mood.

"Sounds like it to me," she said. "Well, if you won't get in there and help Susanna get the place cleaned up, I guess that means I'll be doing it."

"You can't."

She smiled, not speaking, but he knew what that smile meant.

"All right," he said finally, snapping his fork down on the table. "If you agree to stay away, I'll help Susanna get the place cleaned up. But I'm not making any promises about what happens afterward."

"Denke, Nate. That's what I wanted to hear." His mother turned placidly back to her food.

He suspected he'd been outmaneuvered, and he wasn't even sure how it had happened. But one thing was clear. It was going to be awfully hard not to think of Susanna when he was seeing her every day and every night.

By Monday, Seth had moved from Dave and Emily Hartman's place back to his own apartment, since most of the roads and bridges were opened. He'd been trying to catch up on the work the company paid him for, but he found it difficult to concentrate when there was so much else crying out to be done.

Seth glanced across the front seat of his car. Jessie sat still, her hands clasped in her lap. This would be her first day of helping with flood relief. She'd been unusually quiet all the way to Oyersburg.

"Are you a bit nervous about doing this?"

Jessie stared at her hands and began pleating and unpleating her skirt. Finally she fixed her gaze on his face. "What if I don't know what to do?"

His heart hurt at the insecurity in her voice. "I think you'll be fine. And if you're not sure what to do, there will always be someone to ask."

"Who?"

"I'll be there. Or Susanna. Or Chloe. That makes it okay, doesn't it?"

Her smile flickered, and her hands stopped their restless movement. "Okay." She eyed him. "Now you tell me what's worrying you."

"Nothing." He said it too fast, his voice too casual.

She didn't speak, and he glanced away from the road long enough to see her face. Her expression spoke volumes for her. If he had the right to ask how she was, then he owed her the same level of honesty in return.

"The truth is that I'm not enjoying my work the way I used to." He'd been trying to simplify it to a way Jessie might understand. Maybe he needed to do that in order to understand it himself.

"If you don't like it anymore, why don't you do something else?" Jessie sounded like the little girl who'd once thought her big brother could do anything.

"I've spent a long time getting where I am. I'm not sure I know how to do anything else."

They were coming into Oyersburg, and she stared out the window at muddy streets and damaged houses. "You could come home," she said. "To stay. Mamm would love it. And I would, too."

"Thanks, Jessie. I'm not sure I could go back to being Amish again. But whatever I do, I won't go off and leave you and Mamm again. Promise."

"Is it because of Chloe that you don't think you can come back?"

"Partly, maybe," he admitted.

214

"If Chloe hadn't been taken away when she was a baby, she would be Amish, too."

"Could have been, but she isn't." No, she wasn't any more than he was. Instead, they were neither one thing nor the other, it sometimes seemed. "Look, here's the shelter," he said, relieved to end this conversation.

As soon as he and Jessie stepped inside, he could see the changes a couple of days had made. Most of the cots had been taken away, and the few that remained were set off behind portable screens to give people some privacy.

"Most of the people who slept here at night have found other places to stay," he explained. "The big job now is getting people fed." He gestured toward the long rows of tables and chairs. "People can come in here for meals if they need to, and the workers also make things like sandwiches to take to folks who are cleaning up in the flood area."

Jessie nodded, seeming reassured, and he realized that she might not have understood what she'd have to do. "I can make sandwiches."

"Sure you can." He gave her a reassuring smile. "Mamm says you're a good cook, and that's what they need now."

Jessie seemed to square her shoulders as if ready for a challenge.

He spotted Susanna and Chloe coming toward them, and in a moment Susanna was greeting Jessie in Pennsylvania Dutch. "We're sehr glad you're here, Jessie. If you want to come to the kitchen, I'll help you get started."

Jessie nodded and glanced at Seth.

"I'll probably leave to work somewhere else, but I'll come back to get you around four. Okay?"

"And you can just ask me or Susanna if you need anything," Chloe added.

"Okay." Jessie gave them a smile that lit her face, and she went off toward the kitchen with Susanna.

"She looks better," he said, watching the two of them.

"Jessie wants to be part of things. We all do."

Something in Chloe's voice had him studying her face. "I'm sure that's true, but I meant Susanna."

Chloe blinked. "Oh. Well, yes, I guess she does seem less worried. They're going to start working on the shop this afternoon."

"That's good news," he said. So why did Chloe look as if something was weighing on her?

"What's wrong?" Blunt, he supposed, but he knew her well enough to sense when something was wrong. "I thought you were pleased with how it went yesterday at Lydia's."

"I am. I'm fine." She didn't meet his eyes. "I'm happy that Susanna and Lydia clicked as well as they did."

He raised his eyebrows. "Sounds like you're protesting a bit much."

Annoyance flared in her face and then slowly faded. "I suppose . . . I guess I should have expected it. It's only natural that Lydia and Susanna would have more in common with each other than with me."

He'd wanted her to tell him what was bothering her, but he didn't find an answer to her problem as easily as he had with Jessie. In fact, maybe there wasn't a good answer. He touched her hand in silent sympathy. Chloe, like him, was caught between two worlds, and that could be a painful place to be.

CHAPTER FOURTEEN

*A*re you sure you don't want me to drive you home?" Chloe hesitated in the shop doorway, seeming reluctant to leave without Susanna on Monday afternoon.

"I'm going to work a bit longer." Susanna appreciated Chloe's concern, but she wasn't ready to stop now that they'd finally been able to work at the shop. "You go." She gave her sister a gentle push. "I know you want to check on Jessie. And maybe say good-bye to Seth, ain't so?"

Chloe's lips twitched. "You're getting as bad as Lydia. Don't matchmake."

Warmth spread through Susanna. It was nice having a sister to share a joke with, just knowing there were people who wanted her.

"I'll see you tomorrow." She gave Chloe a quick hug. "Go." She made shooing motions with her hands.

Laughing, Chloe went, and Susanna turned back to the shop. Truth to tell, it was a bit of a relief not to have Chloe and Nate in the same room. Chloe's silent antagonism toward him kept Susanna on alert, afraid she would speak her mind. She hadn't, thank goodness, and Nate probably hadn't even noticed.

The shop looked better already, and she'd stopped feeling queasy at the sight of it. Nate had brought some helpers earlier to shovel mud out, and once she could see the wide wooden floorboards the place had begun to look like the shop to her.

"Not so bad, is it?" Nate stood by the door to the back room, hands on his hips. "The boys did fine in here."

"I'm wonderful glad they could help. And you, too, of course." Nate had been here all afternoon, and she knew it was a sacrifice, with all there was to do at his own store. "I'm sure you have plenty of other things to do, so don't feel you have to stay any longer."

He shook his head and turned to the steps. "Maybe we can get some work done upstairs now, if you're not too tired." He paused, glancing at her.

"I'm not tired," she said quickly. She wouldn't have him thinking she couldn't do her share.

"Gut." He started up the stairs.

Susanna followed, trying to keep her steps even. "I thought the rest of what's stored upstairs would be all right now."

They emerged into the upstairs space and Nate looked around, frowning. "I'm thinking it would be best to pack everything up and move it to the back room of the store. I can send a couple of people with a truck to do the actual moving once it's boxed."

"That's fine, but why do we have to?" It was her turn to frown.

"Damp." He pointed to a stain at the base of the wall. "It

will turn to mold, and it has to be cleaned and treated quickly. No, it's better to move everything."

Her heart sank. "I didn't realize the damage would keep getting worse."

"I'd guess a lot of people are realizing that same thing about now. We've been telling ourselves the worst was over when the water went down, but I'm afraid it isn't." He picked up a box. "Let's get started."

Susanna nodded, grabbing a box from the stack Nate had brought in from the store earlier. She started taking wooden napkin holders from the shelf where they'd been stored.

"I can handle this by myself," she said. "Chloe and Lydia will be here tomorrow, and they'll help."

Nate was bent over a large carton, and he turned his head to look at her. "You're trying very hard to get rid of me, Susanna."

"No, of course I'm not." Was she that obvious? "I just know you have other work to do, that's all."

"Nothing that can't go on without me for a time, at least. I'll stay and take you home, or Mamm will have something to say about it."

Light dawned. "Your mamm made you come and work on the shop today, didn't she?" The corners of her lips tilted. She could just hear how Dora would have lectured him.

He threw up his hands in a gesture of surrender, his face relaxing in a smile. "It was the only way I could keep her from coming herself. But I would have helped anyway," he added.

"I know." No matter how much he'd like to see his mother give up the shop, Susanna felt sure he wouldn't leave it in this state.

"Can I use this to pack things in?" The floor creaked as Nate pulled a chest out from under the eaves.

"Ja, of course." Her heart gave a little thump at the sight of her dower chest. "Your mamm and I thought it would make a nice display piece down in the shop, with linens stacked in it. We just hadn't gotten around to putting it out yet."

Would they ever, now? She tried to brush the thought away but it clung like a persistent spider web.

Nate ran a hand over the smooth maple of the chest, fingering the precise mitering of the corners. "The maker was a real craftsman." He glanced at her with sudden knowledge in his eyes. "This was yours, ain't so?"

She nodded. "My daad made it for my fifteenth birthday. He said every girl should have a dower chest."

"It wonders me that you'd want to have it in the shop, in that case." He opened the lid, his hands careful. "Don't you want it at home?"

"Well, I don't have a home, not right now," she pointed out, hoping that would end the subject.

Nate's gaze didn't waver from her face. "You gave it up long before the flood, it sounds like."

He was persistent. She resigned herself to telling him what he so obviously wanted to know.

"My mother's dower chest is at the house, and we didn't need two of them. I suppose I never really needed one, but my father was such an optimist." She smiled, remembering how Daad had insisted that someone would come courting.

"I don't see what's so optimistic about that," Nate said. "Naturally he thought you'd marry."

She carried an armload of quilted pillow covers over to him, kneeling to put them in the chest. "It didn't work out that way."

"Then the boys in Ohio must have been blind."

The conviction in his voice surprised her. "Not blind. I was just a friend, that's all. They told me all their troubles and asked my advice about other girls. They didn't see me as a woman."

"Like I said, blind."

She tried to smile, but they were getting too close to the heart of her pain. "It was my limp. Sometimes I think that's all folks notice when they look at me."

Nate's hand closed over hers on the edge of the dower chest. She looked up at his face, startled and shaken by the warmth that flowed through her at his touch.

"I promise you, when people get to know you, they don't even see your limp at all." His voice was so deep it seemed to reverberate through her. She couldn't move, couldn't keep her face from betraying the effect he had on her.

And then he was turning away, seeming to catch his breath. He cleared his throat. "You . . . Did you have a nice visit with Lydia and her family on Saturday?"

"Ja, very nice." She averted her face, busying herself with folding the pillow covers. "We made apple butter, and I got to know the little boys." She smiled, thinking of Daniel and David. "They are very sweet."

"Probably enjoyed making the apple butter, ja? I know I did when I was young." Susanna could feel his gaze on her face as he talked, but she refused to look up. "Did you learn more about your birth parents?"

"I wasn't sure I wanted to." She surprised herself with her honesty. "But Lydia had some things that belonged to her . . . our mother . . ." She still found it difficult to say the word. "Lydia wanted me to take a book, kind of a journal, it is, that Diane had written in. I didn't want to hurt Lydia's feelings, so I took it."

"You read it?"

She nodded. "I wasn't going to, but I did." Susanna smoothed her hand over the patchwork pillow cover. "She sounded so young. They loved each other very much. And then it was all over." Her throat grew tight.

He was silent for a moment, as if in respect for her surprising grief. "You can take comfort that even if their time together was short, they were happy in their love."

Nate's voice held sympathy, but there was something more . . . something pained and hard in it. She'd sensed that emotion before, when he spoke of his wife. She studied his face, searching for a clue, feeling as if she was the one who had to comfort him.

"You and Mary Ann . . ." she began, and then she didn't know how to go on.

"Ja." The word was short. Forbidding. When he looked at her it was like a blow. "Have you ever been trapped in a lie, Susanna? Everyone talks about how happy we were, how much we loved each other."

"I'm sorry." She spoke to the feelings, not the words, and she put her hand on his forearm. The muscles were so taut it was like touching metal.

"I thought we were happy." The words burst out as if he couldn't hold them back. "And all the time she was thinking of leaving me. That day she went away, when she was in the accident—she wasn't coming back. No one knows that but me." His gaze seemed to focus on her face. "And now you."

"I would never say anything about it. Ever."

"I know." The muscles of his jaw twitched, and he shook his head almost angrily. "I don't understand why I told you, but maybe that's the answer. You're safe."

Safe. Her heart winced, but she tried to smile. "Like the boys telling me about their loves. They knew I would never speak of it."

The tension in Nate's face seemed to smooth away, to be replaced by something else she couldn't name. He leaned toward her, reaching out to touch her face with his hand.

"I am not like those foolish boys, Susanna. I see you as a woman." His fingers stroked her cheek, warming where they touched. Her breath caught. She seemed to feel that warmth moving right to her heart.

Nate leaned closer until she could see nothing but his face . . . the fine lines, the intensity of his gaze. And then he kissed her.

For an instant she was so startled she froze. And then her lips softened under his. She reached out, clasping his arm to draw him closer, longing, wanting . . . Her thoughts spun dizzyingly.

Nate drew back after an endless moment. Slowly, as if he didn't want to. His face looked as dazed as hers must be.

"I didn't intend . . ." He let that die. "Or maybe I did." A smile tugged at his lips. "I'm not sorry. But I think we should be . . . well, cautious."

She nodded, trying to catch her breath, to make her mind work. *Cautious* was a good word. She needed to think about what had just happened. She had to be sure what she felt before it happened again.

"*The* water is on!" Chloe stared at the water gushing from the tap into the deep steel sink at the shelter. Today was Wednesday, so they'd been close to a week without water in the pipes. It had seemed like forever.

Jessie ran across the kitchen from the pantry to join her in staring, mesmerized, at the stream of water. A bit rusty, true, but it was there.

Chloe grabbed Jessie, spinning her around in a circle in a mad dance. "We have water. No more hauling it from the tankers. No more heating it on the stove."

Jessie laughed, probably as much at Chloe's antics as at the water. "It is a wonderful good sight. It'll make things easier, for sure."

"I don't know when I've been so silly." Chloe leaned on the sink, grinning. "I guess it's just relief." She turned off the tap and watched water circle the drain. "With the water on and electricity restored, we're really getting back to normal."

"Ja?" Some of the animation faded from Jessie's face, and she turned away.

Chloe reached out to clasp her arm. Jessie had been a different person these last few days, working cheerfully at every task that was set before her, never complaining or sulking. Chloe didn't want to see that Jessie change.

"What is it, Jessie? What's wrong?"

The girl hesitated, her face averted. She shrugged. "I guess that means I won't be needed."

There was something lonely about the words that made Chloe's heart clench.

"I'm sure that's not true." She scoured her brain for volunteer jobs Jessie could fill. Nothing involving technology, obviously. "Even after the shelter closes, there will be plenty of work to do helping with the cleanup. I know you're not afraid of hard work."

Jessie's expression eased. "I can clean, that's for sure. And hammer a nail or saw a board."

"There, you see? That's the kind of help Susanna needs now with the shop, and there are probably a hundred more people like her."

"Gut. I mean, not gut that people are in trouble, but gut that I can help. I just want to be useful."

The words had a poignant ring, coming from Jessie. Her condition had isolated her in many ways from the life she'd expected to have.

Seth and his mother were so wary around her, so careful of her. Was all that protection really necessary?

"I think we all want to feel useful," Chloe said. "You know, with the work experience you're getting here, you can probably get a job easily in Pleasant Valley when this is over."

Hope flared in Jessie's face. "Do you think so?"

"Why not?" she said. "You're smart and capable. You can do it."

Jessie's smile broke through, and Chloe realized she was beautiful when her face showed a bit of animation.

"You're right, I can." Still smiling, she turned away. "Denke, Chloe. I'll get back to stocking the pantry."

Chloe watched her go, marveling at the change in her. Maybe all Jessie really needed was someone to believe in her.

Stocking the pantry was definitely a one-woman job, since there wasn't space in there for two. Chloe took a sponge and a bottle of cleaning spray from the sink. She'd better make sure all the tables were clean before they left for the night.

Scrubbing tables wasn't demanding enough to keep her thoughts from wandering. She was going to have to make some decisions soon. The tiny furnished apartment on Main Street her landlord had found for her wasn't very comfortable, and did she really have a reason to stay here in Oyersburg now that Susanna was well on the way to accepting her sisters? There was the flood relief, of course, but beyond that, what next?

The outside door opened and closed. She glanced toward it to see Seth. The lurch in her heart told her that there was one very solid reason why she was having trouble deciding on her future path, and it was striding toward her right now.

She smiled, hoping she didn't look as glad to see him as she felt. "Hi. Have you heard the good news? The water is back on again."

Seth grinned. "I'm sure I never expected to see Ms. Chloe Wentworth of Philadelphia so delighted at the prospect of water coming out of the tap."

"Go ahead, laugh at me." She swatted at him with the damp sponge. "You'd be happy, too, if you'd spent the day trying to cook and clean up using cold water from jugs."

"It's called roughing it," he said, leaning one hip against the edge of the table.

"Yes, well, I never did like summer camp. I wouldn't have made a good pioneer woman. Your little sister can work rings around me."

A shadow dimmed Seth's smile. "Has Jessie been all right today?"

"You worry too much. She's been fine. Do you want me to get her?"

She took a step toward the kitchen, but Seth caught her arm, arresting her motion. Somehow she ended up standing very close to him.

"In a minute," he said, his voice low. "I haven't seen you in days."

"You just saw me yesterday," she protested, discovering that her breath was behaving strangely at his nearness.

"To say hello in passing. I'm talking about being alone together."

She met his gaze and then realized that might not be such a good idea. She couldn't seem to look away. "I thought that was the idea. Remember our bargain? That was your thinking, as I recall."

"Stupid idea," he muttered, close enough that his breath was warm against her cheek. "I'm suggesting we should amend that deal."

This is a bad idea, a little voice in the back of her mind was saying, and she silenced it with a ruthless slap. She didn't want to be sensible, or cautious, or any of those other boring things.

"What did you have in mind?" Her lips were an inch away from his, and something stronger than gravity was pulling them together.

"I'd say—"

"So that's it!" The shrill voice had them spinning apart. Jessie stood in the kitchen doorway, fists clenched.

"Jessie . . ." Seth began, but she swept over him like the tide.

"Acting like you want to be my friend." She advanced on Chloe, fury contorting her face. "Lying to me."

"Jessie, I do want to be your friend. Honestly." Chloe's heart thudded against her ribs.

"No, you don't. You just want to get close to Seth, that's all. No one wants to be my friend."

Jessie raised her fists. Chloe took a step back, bumping into a metal chair and sending it clattering to the floor.

"Jessie, stop it!" Seth's voice commanded. He grasped his sister's wrists. "That's enough. You're being foolish."

"You mean I'm being crazy." Jessie practically spat the words at him. "That's what you think. That's what everyone thinks."

She burst into a storm of hysterical weeping, struggling against his grip.

Appalled, Chloe reached out to help.

"No." Seth's tone stopped her. It was as curt as if she were an interfering stranger. "It's better if you go. Now."

Chloe wanted to argue. Wanted to stay and help. But it seemed obvious that just the sight of her was disturbing Jessie.

"I'm sorry," she said, aware of how feeble that sounded. Chloe backed away, hurried to the kitchen, and sprinted out the back door.

She stopped, grasping the metal railing. Her thoughts reeled. She'd wanted to help, but she'd just made things worse.

And if anything had been needed to show her just how firmly Seth was tied here, this had been it.

Packing up the second floor of her shop with Lydia and Chloe the next day was certainly less fraught with emotion than doing it with Nate, Susanna thought with a sense of relief. Their chatter should stop her from replaying Nate's kiss over and over again, at least.

"I think we should be able to finish this afternoon," Lydia said, straightening and stretching her back. "Is it all right if I use the rest of the space in this dower chest to store these table runners?"

"That's fine." Susanna carefully averted her eyes from the chest. Better that Lydia should do it than that she should.

She hadn't been able to avoid seeing Nate, since she was staying at his house. He had been cheerful and much as usual, while she felt as if she'd been struck dumb in his presence.

Apparently that hadn't been too obvious, though. Dora hadn't commented on it, other than to ask several times if she felt all right.

If only she knew what he was thinking, or more important, what she herself was thinking. Her head seemed a ragbag of memory and emotion.

Chloe was talking nearly as fast as she was packing—too fast, as if, like Susanna, she was trying to keep from hearing her own thoughts.

"Are you sure you should be doing all that bending?" Chloe attempted to take the quilted table runners from Lydia, but Lydia swatted her away, laughing.

"I'm fine. Why are you fussing so much?" Lydia sat down on the floor and began stacking the pieces in the chest.

"You're pregnant. Is it good for you to do so much bending?"

"You're as bad as Adam," Lydia said. "I'm fine and healthy, and it's another three months yet. And whatever you do, don't say anything to Adam about pregnancy."

"Why not?" Chloe countered. She wiped off her hands with the tail of the oversized T-shirt she wore. "If he agrees with me—"

"He'd be embarrassed, that's why. Expected babies aren't talked about in mixed company."

Chloe looked from Lydia to Susanna. "That's so . . . old-fashioned."

"I guess it is, but it's how we do things," Lydia said, as if that finished the matter.

Susanna could see that Chloe was about to burst out, so she spoke quickly. "Amish clothing is supposed to hide pregnancy and give privacy for nursing mothers. All the women know,

229

of course, but we only talk about it to each other. Or between husband and wife, of course."

Chloe seemed to conquer her desire to say something critical. Instead she smiled at Lydia. "If you're supposed to hide your pregnancy, you'd better do something about your face. You're absolutely glowing."

"Happiness can't be hidden, they say." Lydia put her palms to her cheeks. "I've so longed to have another baby, and now it's coming."

"A little girl, maybe?" Susanna asked, mentally sifting through her supply of baby quilts. There was a postage-stamp crib quilt in shades of pink that would be perfect.

"Maybe." Lydia looked at Chloe, mischief sparkling in her eyes. "What about you, Chloe? Have you thought about having babies?"

Chloe's expression seemed to freeze. "I'm not even close to it."

Susanna realized she and Lydia were both staring at their little sister. The discouragement in her tone couldn't be missed.

"I thought Seth . . ." she began, and then thought she shouldn't.

"Seth isn't thinking of romance right now," Chloe said, and the very finality of her tone spoke of pain.

Susanna exchanged looks with Lydia, and they both converged on Chloe.

"What is it, Chloe?" Lydia touched her shoulder with a loving caress. "You can tell us."

Chloe shook her head, and Susanna saw that Chloe . . . tough, modern Chloe . . . was fighting back tears. "We had agreed that we'd take it slowly. But yesterday, when we were alone, I thought . . ." Her voice trailed off miserably. "Jessie saw us embracing, and she just flew off the handle. Screaming and crying—I'd never seen anything like it."

Susanna put her arm around Chloe's waist, feeling her quiver with unshed tears.

"I know." Lydia stroked her hair. "I saw her lose control like that once. It's no wonder you were frightened. I surely was."

"Not frightened. Just shocked. I wanted to help, but Seth wouldn't let me." She shook her head vigorously, hair flying. "He's so obsessed with his responsibilities that he won't let anyone in, even me. And if he should go back to the church—"

Chloe stopped, sucked in a breath, and rubbed her face with her hands. "Enough. He's the worst guy in the world for me, and I'm an idiot for falling for him."

"I don't think it's idiotic to love someone," Lydia said, her voice gentle. "Even if it doesn't work out, it's gut to love. And you have to admire Seth for wanting to take care of his family."

Chloe took a step back, trying to smile. "He's more like Nate than either of them would believe, I guess."

Chloe's mention of Nate's name seemed to echo in Susanna's head. But Chloe didn't suspect anything, surely. She couldn't know about Susanna and Nate. She was just trying to steer them away from her own hurt.

"From what I've seen of Dora, she doesn't want to be taken care of," Lydia said, quietly accepting Chloe's reticence. "What do you think, Susanna?"

"About Nate?" She should never have said his name, because she could feel her cheeks grow hot, and she had to struggle to keep from looking at the dower chest and remembering Nate's hands on it, the expression on his face, the moment when his lips had touched hers.

"About Nate," Lydia repeated, and both she and Chloe stared at her, awareness dawning in their faces.

"Susanna!" Chloe exclaimed, seizing her hands. "You and Nate? I wouldn't have believed it."

"No, no." Susanna shook her head. "I don't think . . . I mean, I'm not sure, and he's not sure . . ." She let that trail off.

What could she do? Admit that she had feelings for him but that she couldn't believe he was really serious about her?

"All right. We won't tease you about it," Lydia said, enveloping Susanna in a hug.

Chloe put her arms around both of them. "But if you want to talk, you have us. That's what sisters are for, you know."

Susanna's throat was tight with unshed tears. She didn't know about Nate, but somehow Lydia and Chloe made it easier to believe that someone might love her for herself alone.

Chapter Fifteen

*N*ate had barely reached the front counter in the store the next morning before Anna Mae came to confront him. He suppressed a flood of exasperation. The girl had been like a kettle coming to a boil for days now, despite everything they all had to keep them busy, and obviously she was now ready to explode.

"I want to talk to you before we open," she said, planting herself in front of him, her pert face challenging.

He began putting fives and tens into the cash register. "Can it wait, Anna Mae? I'm busy."

"I want to get this settled now. I should be the one to be in charge when you're not here. I've worked for you the longest. I know much more about the store than Thomas or Susanna or anyone else."

Nate gave her a sharp look designed to remind Anna Mae that he was the boss. "Susanna isn't employed here," he pointed out. "I appreciate your efforts, Anna Mae. But I am the owner, and I make the decisions based on what I think is best for the store."

Her eyes flashed, and he suspected she was on the brink of saying something that would end in his having to fire her. He gritted his teeth in exasperation. Why did females have to get so emotional about business decisions, anyway?

"Before Susanna started hanging around, you depended on me." Her voice was raised. Thomas, stocking a shelf in the pasta aisle, came to the end to see what was going on, and Susie, Anna Mae's sister, took a few hesitant steps toward them.

Nate tried, and failed, to sympathize with the girl. "You are being foolish, Anna Mae. Susanna is my mother's partner and an experienced businesswoman. It is kind of her to help out in the store when we're so busy."

"She's . . ."

Susie rushed to grab Anna Mae's arm. "Hush. Stop now. You'll get in trouble."

Anna Mae shook the restraining hand off. "Susanna is nothing but a crippled old maid. She—"

"Enough." Nate fought down a flash of pure rage. "You will have to find someplace else to work, Anna Mae."

"You're firing me?" She looked at him in disbelief.

He'd smile, except that there was nothing funny about it. What did the foolish child think would happen when she spoke to her employer that way?

"I will send you your final check for this week."

She stared at him a moment longer, and then she turned and ran out of the shop. Her sister stared after her, and from the expression on her face, she thought she'd be next.

"Susie, you had best see that your sister gets home. Take the rest of the day off. I'll see you first thing tomorrow morning."

"Ja, I understand." Galvanized, Susie headed for the door. "I'm sorry." The words floated over her shoulder as she hurried out.

Nate met Thomas's startled gaze, and the boy came to him. "I— Is there something I can do?"

Nate shook his head. "I'll get someone in to replace her in a day or two. But not another teenage girl, that's certain-sure."

Thomas's face lost its apprehension, and he grinned. "Anna Mae's ferhoodled, acting that way. Susanna . . ." He paused, as if considering. "It was plain bad temper, saying that about Susanna. Susanna's a smart woman, and kind, as well."

Ja, that she was.

"We'd best get ready to open. If we get too busy in the front, I'll ask my mother to help out."

Thomas nodded and began picking up the boxes from which he'd been stocking shelves. The store seemed suddenly very peaceful.

Nate suspected he should have seen that Anna Mae was getting ideas and done something about it before now. That was the trouble with hiring young girls. They had too many dreams in their heads. Next time he'd look for a nice older widow.

Thomas had spoken the truth about Susanna, startled though Nate had been to hear him say it. Susanna was kind. That was a quality easily overlooked by young men starting to court, but it did more for a happy marriage, he suspected, than any flirtatious glances.

The truth was that Susanna hadn't been far from his thoughts in days. He couldn't deny he was thinking seriously about a future with her.

But they were neither of them teenagers, flirting at singings and trying out the idea of falling in love. At their age, anything they felt had to be serious enough to last a lifetime. Could he really make someone happy for the rest of their lives? He just didn't know.

No sooner had he removed the CLOSED sign from the door and unlocked it than the telephone rang in the back hall. A business had to have a phone, but he had to confess that he got tired of being at its beck and call.

"Nate?" Susanna's voice, sounding breathless. "I'm sorry to bother you. I know you're busy with the store—"

"It's not a bother," he said, cradling the receiver against his ear. "What is it?"

"When I reached the shop, I found a notice tacked on the front door." Paper rustled. "It's an orange form, something official looking. At the top, it says mold abatement procedures, and then there's a list of orders."

"Where are you calling from?" He'd read something about that in the newspaper this morning, but he hadn't paid much attention. He should have.

"I borrowed a cell phone from a man working next door. I wasn't sure what to do. I'm sorry."

"Don't be sorry. It's not your fault." But it was yet another problem to be dealt with. "Stay there. I'll come." He hung up on her protests.

"Thomas!" He leaned around the corner, catching the boy's eye. "I have to go out, I'm afraid. It's bad timing, but it can't be helped. Run over to the house and ask my mamm to come and mind the store for a bit."

Startled, Thomas nodded and slid out from behind the counter. Nate hurried to the parking lot. Billy Angelo, one of the teenaged Englisch boys who helped out with deliveries, was just getting into the truck. Nate grabbed the door handle and swung in beside him, receiving a startled glance.

"We'll have to put off the deliveries for a bit. Take me down to my mother's shop on the west end of Main Street. You know where it is?"

"Yes, sir." Billy put the truck in gear, looking cheered at the break in routine. "Problem?"

"Maybe," Nate said. And maybe he was being foolish, rushing down there to the rescue instead of telling Susanna he'd deal with the notice later.

But she'd sounded upset, and he wouldn't have been able to concentrate if he'd been worrying about her.

They reached the shop in a few minutes. He slid out the minute Billy stopped at the curb. Susanna stood on the steps, a piece of orange paper fluttering in her hand, bright against the somber navy of her dress.

"I shouldn't have called you away from the store." Her deep blue eyes seemed darker when she was worried.

"Ja, you should have." He took the paper from her hand. "I own the building, so anything to do with it is my responsibility." He scanned the sheet, trying to make sense of the legal-sounding language.

"Is it going to slow down work on the shop?" Anxiety threaded Susanna's words.

"Worse than that," he began, and stopped when he saw how stricken she was. "Ach, I'm getting ahead of myself. First I must look and see how bad the problem is. Then we'll see what comes next."

Susanna didn't look very reassured, but she put the key in the lock. He took a step back and gestured to Billy.

"Go around to the side and open the bulkhead doors to the cellar," he called.

Nodding, Billy started around the building.

"That will let the air in to help dry out the cellar. I probably should have thought of that before." He went in the shop ahead of Susanna.

"I didn't think of it, either," she said, "even when we were talking about the dampness." She looked so guilty he wanted to reassure her.

"There's no point in blaming ourselves. We can't think of everything." He picked up one of the battery lanterns they'd left at the shop, and started for the basement door.

Susanna came after him, and he waved her back. "There's no need for you to go down."

"It's my shop." The stubborn way her chin firmed said there was no point in arguing.

But he'd invested in it as well, and there might easily come a point at which he'd be ferhoodled to keep throwing money into it.

He started down the open wooden stairs, hearing them creak under his weight. A patch of sunlight crossed the floor below when Billy threw open the bulkhead doors. It revealed an ominous stain of black mold.

Nate swept the lantern's beam into the darker corners as he went down. He should have done something about this sooner. It was—

Thought broke off as the stairs cracked and lurched beneath his feet. He threw himself backward, had a quick image of Susanna reaching out to catch him, and the stairs collapsed beneath him. He went crashing down to the cement floor.

The impact stunned him, and dust rose in a cloud, making

him choke. He had to get up, but he was tangled in the pieces of broken steps. He couldn't tell if he was hurt . . .

Stop. Relax a minute. Think. He lay back on the damp floor, hearing a rush of footsteps above him in the shop as Susanna must have been running to the front door. The dust began to settle, and he saw Billy's white face looking down at him.

He was saying something, but try as he might, Nate couldn't seem to make out the words, and Billy's face spun around him. He closed his eyes.

"Is he dead?" The boy's voice cracked.

"Of course he's not dead." Susanna's voice now, and she was kneeling next to him, taking his wrist in her cool fingers. She must have run around to come through the bulkhead doors Billy had opened.

Susanna shouldn't be kneeling on that wet, dirty floor. He frowned, trying to move his hand.

"Just lie still." She pressed him back. "Let me see how badly you're hurt. Billy, try to get the boards off him, but don't touch him if you can help it."

"Yes, ma'am." The boy still sounded scared, but he acted in response to her voice.

Susanna's hands probed gently over Nate's hair, and he winced. "You've hit your head."

"I can get up—" he began, but when he raised himself on his elbows, the cellar swam around him. He sank back.

"No, you can't," Susanna said, her voice firm. She passed her hands over his arms and then helped Billy pull the boards from his legs.

Nate's mind was clearing, but he made no further attempt to get up. The crack on his head was probably nothing, but he suspected something was very wrong with his right ankle.

Susanna's hands reached his ankle and stopped, and he heard her indrawn breath. For an instant her fingers trembled against his skin.

"Do you have a cell phone, Billy?" Despite that betraying movement, she managed to sound calm.

"Yes, ma'am." Billy fumbled in his jacket pocket and brought out the cell phone that was like an extra hand to him.

"I want you to call 911. Say someone's injured and we need an ambulance at once."

"Billy can drive me." Nate managed to prop himself on his elbow.

Susanna put her hands on his shoulders, holding him, her face close to his. "Listen to me. We can't get you to the truck by ourselves, and if you try to do it, you'll damage yourself worse. Now lie still until they come."

Since it seemed evident that Susanna meant business, he let himself be lowered back to the floor. For such a quiet person, she knew how to give orders. And how to be calm in an emergency. She clasped his hand in hers, and he seemed to feel that serenity of hers flowing into him.

Billy's voice shook so much that the emergency dispatcher probably thought he was the injured one. He clicked off and looked at Susanna for orders.

She was frowning, and she focused on Nate's face as if gauging how alert he was. "Who is at the store now? Can you tell me?"

"Thomas. My mother. Maybe another driver if he finished his deliveries."

"Neither of the girls?"

"No." The incident with Anna Mae seemed long ago.

"That won't do," she murmured. She held out her hand for

the phone. "I'll take the phone. Billy, you go out on the walk and wait for the ambulance. Show them how to come in."

Billy nodded and fled.

Susanna punched in numbers. Thank the Lord Chloe had insisted Susanna memorize her new number in case of need. "Chloe? There's been an accident at the shop."

He could hear Chloe's high voice from several feet away.

"I'm fine," Susanna said. "Nate is hurt. We've called for an ambulance. I need you to go to the store and tell Dora, all right? Do it carefully. Assure her that he's not hurt badly, but he injured his ankle and it will have to be X-rayed. If she wants to meet us at the hospital, maybe you can drive her, ja?"

Nate could see Chloe's agreement in the way Susanna's face relaxed. That was kind of her, thinking of Mamm and not wanting to tell her on the phone. He might have his doubts about Chloe as a suitable sister for Susanna, but she would take care of his mother.

The wail of a siren sounded, coming closer rapidly. Nate lay still, his gaze fixed on Susanna's face.

"Everything will be all right," she said, patting his hand.

He nodded, but he knew it wouldn't. Surely after this, Susanna would understand. The shop would have to go.

Susanna opened the door to Dora's room and peeked inside. Dora had insisted she couldn't go to sleep in the middle of the afternoon, but she was already out, her kapp askew and her gray hair in disorder. Dora looked older when she was asleep, with all the energy and enthusiasm that usually animated her gone from her face.

As Susanna turned to go, her gaze caught on something that

froze her where she stood. She tiptoed to the sewing table that stood in the corner. *Her* quilt . . . the one her mother had made . . . She'd thought it was worth nothing but to be thrown away when she'd found it wet and dirty on the floor of her apartment.

She touched it lightly. Obviously Dora hadn't thought so. She must have washed it, and a fine sewing needle was stuck in the edge of a ragged square that Dora was clearly mending. A tear trickled down Susanna's cheek, and she wiped it away. Dear Dora, always thinking of others. Perhaps she meant this to be a surprise, so Susanna would have to do her best to pretend astonishment. Her father's Bible had been a total loss, but she would have her quilt, thanks to Dora's love.

Susanna tiptoed out, closing the door softly. She started down, comforted despite her fatigue. Good things and bad things, all wrapped up together . . . that was life, wasn't it?

The house was quiet around her, nearly as familiar as her own apartment now that she'd been here a week. Nate had refused all efforts to get him to go to bed when they got home from the hospital, but he was settled in the upholstered rocker in the living room, his foot on a padded stool. With any luck, he'd drop off to sleep eventually, given the pain medication the doctor had insisted he take.

Thank goodness for her sister on a day like this one had been. Chloe had been a rock, breaking the news to Dora, taking her to the hospital, bringing them home, dealing with all the phone calls that had to be made.

Donna had been waiting at the house when they got there, chicken soup already made on the stove, a loaf of her homemade bread ready to be sliced, and a casserole prepared for their supper. She had been full of questions about the accident, though, and Susanna had barely been able to answer them.

She still found herself shaking inside when she let her mind dwell on what had happened. She kept seeing Nate moving down the cellar stairs ahead of her, his tall, solid body blocking the glow of the lantern he carried. She'd sensed his irritation at this new problem, despite his efforts to hide it.

And then, so quickly, the tread he'd stepped on had shaken and cracked and collapsed, and Nate had fallen. Still on the landing she'd reached for him, frantic to catch him, but she couldn't, and her heart had nearly stopped with fear at the thought of what she'd see when the debris settled.

She was shaking again, and she moved into the kitchen and stood for a moment, hands pressed against the counter. Enough of this nonsense. Nate would be fine. He had a broken bone in his ankle, but nothing so serious that it would cause problems as long as he obeyed the doctor's orders. Getting him to behave might be the most difficult part of his recovery.

Dora had been so shaken at the hospital that the doctor had addressed himself to Susanna, apparently thinking she would be the person in charge. Maybe he'd assumed she was Nate's wife. He hadn't asked her name. The thought generated feelings she didn't want to examine.

In any event, the doctor had entrusted her with the medication, the instructions, and the precautions. Now the main issue was to get Nate to do as the doctor said.

Susanna ladled chicken soup thick with noodles, carrots, and chunks of chicken into a bowl, inhaling the rich aroma. She was hungry, as well as worried—that was what was wrong with her. As soon as Nate was taken care of, she'd have something to eat.

Picking up a tray with the soup and thickly buttered slices of bread, she tiptoed toward the living room. If he'd fallen asleep it might be best to let him sleep.

"You don't need to creep around." Nate's deep voice held an edge. "I'm not asleep. It's bad enough just to be sitting here doing nothing in the middle of a workday. I'm not going to take a nap like a boppli."

Susanna moved into the living room. Sunlight filtered between the plain white curtains on the windows and lay across the oval braided rug that covered the wide planks of the floor. She took the tray to the small table next to Nate's chair and arranged it within easy reach of his right hand.

"You can take it back. I'll come to the kitchen and eat like a grown-up." He groped for the crutches they'd given him at the hospital.

Susanna got to them first and put them out of reach. "No, I will not. And you'll sit here with your foot up as the doctor ordered."

"I'm not a child." He glared at her.

"Then stop acting like one," she said briskly. "I know you're used to being the boss, but this is one time when you'll have to obey the doctor. And if you're not quiet, you'll wake your mother, and I'll have to tell her you're not behaving."

Nate studied her face, as if judging how far he could push her. Then he leaned back in the rocker, a reluctant smile teasing at his lips above his short, fair beard.

"Didn't you mean to say I am used to being bossy?" he asked.

"Just a little too set on getting your own way," she said, handing him the soup bowl. "Eat something, and you'll feel better. You haven't had anything since breakfast."

"Neither have you," he pointed out. "Fix a tray for yourself and join me, and I'll be quiet and eat, ja?"

She considered arguing, but she was hungry, and at least if she ate with him, she'd be sure he was eating.

When she came back into the room a couple of minutes later with her own food, he was already spooning chicken soup into his mouth.

"Ready for seconds yet?" she asked.

He shook his head and pointed with his spoon at a chair. "Remember our deal."

She sat obediently. The first wonderfully aromatic spoonful of soup reminded her of how hungry she was. They ate in silence for several minutes.

Nate caught her gaze and grinned. "Feels sinful, doesn't it, eating in the living room? Mamm never let us."

"Neither did mine." Would her birth mother have done the same? Most likely. Mothers were mothers, she supposed, no matter where or who. "If I was sick, I got a tray in bed. Otherwise, eating was done at the table."

Nate dropped his spoon into the bowl and leaned back against the cushioned rocker, looking tired. The pills, maybe, she thought. Or the pain.

"It will be time for another pill in about an hour," she said.

"I'm all right." He turned his head toward her, face easing. "Speaking of being bossy, I heard you snapping out orders while I was lying on that cellar floor."

"Not snapping, I hope," she said. "Poor Billy looked nearly as stunned as you did."

"You are very calm in a crisis, Susanna Bitler. I didn't know that about you."

"I didn't feel very calm when I saw you fall." She couldn't

keep looking at him, not when she had that sick, helpless feeling at the image in her head. "I should have stopped you from falling."

She could feel him studying her, even without looking at him. "What do you imagine you could have done?" His deep voice was deceptively mild.

"If I weren't lame—"

"That's foolishness," he snapped. "You couldn't have kept me from falling, not if you'd had three arms and four legs. Besides, the whole business was my fault."

That brought her gaze to his face. "How could it be your fault?"

"I'm the one who should have checked those stairs before anyone went down them. The person who fell might have been you." His intensity was so strong that she felt it like heat on her skin.

"With everything else you've had to do, it's no wonder you didn't think about the steps. I certainly didn't." She took a breath, trying to calm herself. It would be so easy to let the pain and fear she'd felt at his accident make her betray her feelings. "Let's just blame it on the flood, and not either of us. Ja?"

"I suppose." He frowned at the cast on his foot. "I don't remember all they told us at the emergency room. Did the doctor say how long I have to wear this thing?"

"He said if you're careful to let the bone heal, they might be able to replace the cast with something lighter in a couple of weeks."

"Weeks," he repeated.

She could hear his frustration. "I'm sorry." What else could she say? "I'll be glad to work in the store. Maybe some of the others can put in extra hours. Anna Mae—"

"I fired Anna Mae this morning."

Susanna stared at him. "I don't understand. Why?"

Nate's head moved restlessly against the padded cushion. "She's been taking too much for granted. This morning, she said some things . . ." He seemed almost embarrassed. "Things she shouldn't have," he said, almost chopping off the words. "It's for the best."

Obviously he didn't want to discuss the matter. Well, it wasn't Susanna's business. Maybe Anna Mae had let him see too clearly that she had a crush on him. That thought hit too close to home for comfort.

"I'll work as many hours as I can. I have to do something to earn my keep." Susanna smiled, trying to turn it into a joke that she'd been living in his house for a week.

"You must stay as long as you need to. Mamm likes having you here."

And what about you, Nate? Do you like having me here?

But she couldn't ask that, not even in the flirting way that Chloe or even a girl like Anna Mae might.

"The landlord says it will probably be at least another week before I can get back into my apartment," she said instead. "He's had to wait for an insurance person to come before he can start the cleanup and repair."

Nate nodded. Amish didn't rely on insurance, of course, but other things slowed down the work, like that notice about the mold.

"I thought maybe I could do some work at the shop this week. I know some of the volunteers would help. If we could get rid of the mold ourselves—"

"No." Nate planted his hands on the arms of his chair. "All those rules and inspections—it's too complicated."

247

An argument hovered on her lips. Surely there was some work they could start. Nate seemed to think nothing would be done right unless he did it.

Still, it was his building, and that flash of ill humor was no doubt the result of his injury. He was in pain and frustrated as well, thinking of all his responsibilities.

She would just have to be patient, no matter how difficult it was. Hopefully soon they'd be able to get back to work on the shop. Eventually she would return to her own place, and everything would be as it had been.

She'd try to believe in her own words. But one thing, at least, would never go back to the way it had been before the flood. She could never go back to a time before Nate had kissed her.

CHAPTER SIXTEEN

The fields on either side of the country road seemed to blur into a green and gold haze. Chloe blinked, shaking her head. This long day had been trying, to say the least, but of course she'd been happy to help Susanna and Dora deal with the emergency.

Several times she'd heard the story of how Nate came to fall through the steps at the shop, and each time it made her shudder. It could so easily have been Susanna. Not, of course, that she wanted Nate or anyone else to be injured, but Susanna—she'd already been injured so badly.

Nate's broken ankle might well change the situation in regard to the shop. She'd had no opportunity to talk to Susanna about it, but it seemed to her this might push Nate further in the direction of getting rid of the building. If so, what would become of Susanna?

Susanna had asked her to get a message to Lydia, so she'd know what had happened. Chloe could have called Seth and asked him to tell Lydia, but her last couple of conversations with him had been so strained that she hadn't especially wanted to repeat the experience. If she went to see Lydia, she could deliver the news herself and find out how Jessie was doing after that . . . episode.

Chloe wasn't sure what else to call it. Jessie's outburst had been totally unexpected, and the look on Seth's face when he'd shut Chloe out . . . well, she kept seeing it every time she closed her eyes.

She loved Seth. She didn't have any doubts about her feelings, but she had plenty of doubts about his. And even if he felt the same, what good would it do?

Chloe's cell phone chimed, cutting off that futile line of thought. She stole a quick glance. Her grandmother. She'd better take it. Luckily she had almost reached the lane to Lydia and Adam's place. She pulled in, stopped the car, and grabbed the phone.

"Gran, how are you?" Her grandmother had been calling her more frequently in the past few days. A person might almost think Gran was interested in how her other granddaughters were faring.

"I nearly gave up on calling you. Why did it take you so long to answer?" Gran sounded almost plaintive. That was so opposed to her usual calm assumption of command that it startled Chloe.

"I'm in the car on my way to Lydia's. I had to pull over first."

"I see." There was a momentary pause. "She and the children are well?"

"Just fine." Chloe tried to keep any hint of triumph out of her voice. That was the first time Gran had taken the initiative in asking about them. "Susanna had a difficult experience today, though."

"She's not hurt?" The question came quickly.

"No, but her partner's son was injured. He and Susanna were checking out the mold situation in the basement of the shop, and the stairs collapsed under him."

"Susanna shouldn't have been doing such a thing." Gran clearly didn't care what had happened to an unknown-to-her Amish man. "Not with her disability."

"I suppose so, but the shop is her livelihood. Like a lot of people here, she's fighting to save it."

"It seems to me it might be advisable for Susanna simply to buy or rent another place and set up the shop on her own."

"Probably so." Chloe smiled as one of the buggy horses came to the fence next to her and put its head over inquiringly. "But Susanna doesn't have the money to do anything of the kind. I suggested she apply for a business loan, but in the aftermath of the flooding, the banks will probably be overwhelmed with applications."

Again there was a moment's silence. Then her grandmother cleared her throat as if she were about to address a group. "I've been giving this some consideration. I'll put up the money she needs for a new shop. You can let me know the specifics."

Chloe couldn't catch her breath. This was Gran, who'd spent the last thirty years denying the existence of her grandchildren.

"I'm not saying I want a relationship with either of them," her grandmother continued. "But I can't let Diane's daughter lose everything. Now, that's taken care of, and I don't wish to discuss it further. Are you still working with the flood relief?"

Chloe bit back the words of thanks that her grandmother didn't seem to want. "Yes, I am. Recovery is an enormous job. It's going to take a long time to get people back to a normal life."

"I'm gratified that you're doing what you can to help the less fortunate." The words were stilted, but her voice had warmed.

Chloe found she was smiling. For Gran, that was the equivalent of saying she was proud of Chloe.

"Thank you, Gran. I miss you."

"I miss you, as well. I hope you'll come home soon." Her voice seemed to tremble slightly on the final words.

Chloe's throat tightened. "As soon as I can."

"Goodbye." Gran ended the call abruptly, perhaps afraid she might show weakness.

Chloe sat motionless, gazing across the pasture to the orchard and beyond it to the Miller place. Seth's car was parked by the small barn. Seth might not recognize it, but he wasn't the only person torn by family needing him. Putting the car in gear, she drove on down the lane toward Lydia's.

The two boys came running pell-mell from the chicken coop when they saw her, and she hoped they weren't carrying any eggs.

"Daniel, David." She hugged them, loving the way they wrapped their arms around her. "How was school today?"

"We learned about writing letters today," Daniel said importantly. "Teacher said people really like to get letters."

"They certainly do. I know I'd love to get a letter from you."

Daniel grinned. "But we see you often, so I can tell you things."

"I want to tell something." David grabbed her hand, asserting his right to his aunt's attention.

"Sure thing." She swung their hands as they walked toward the kitchen door. "What?"

"I . . . um . . . I forget." His small face fell.

"That's okay. You can tell me when you remember, right?"

"Right." His grin was restored.

Lydia, probably hearing the commotion, had come out onto the back porch. "It's wonderful gut to see you. You'll stay for supper. There's plenty."

"I thought there might be." Chloe hugged her sister. She'd never yet arrived at an Amish home to discover that there wasn't enough to feed a crowd.

Lydia pressed her cheek against Chloe's and then drew back, studying her face. She turned to her sons.

"You two go and finish your chores now. You'll have time to visit with Aunt Chloe later."

Without the noisy protest some of her friends' children would have put up, the two boys nodded and darted off toward the chicken coop again.

"Komm." Lydia opened the door, her arm around Chloe's waist. "Something is wrong, ain't so?"

"Nothing too terrible." The kitchen was filled with the scent of cinnamon, and several coffee cakes were lined up on the countertop. "Smells good in here. It looks as if you're preparing for a party."

"It's just some cakes to send along to the shelter tomorrow." Lydia dismissed them with a wave of her hand. "Tell me."

"Susanna is fine. But she and Nate were going into the cellar at the shop to check on the mold, and the steps collapsed."

Lydia paled. "Susanna—"

"No, no, she wasn't hurt. But Nate fell and broke his ankle.

She went to the hospital with him, and she called and asked me to share the news with Dora and drive her."

"Poor Dora." Lydia's eyes mirrored empathy. "It's bad to hear your child is hurt, even when he's a grown man. And Nate . . . he's not the kind to make a gut patient, I think."

"No, that's for sure. He won't be able to do anything at the shop for weeks, maybe longer. I didn't get a chance to talk to Susanna about it, but I'm sure she's discouraged."

"She must be. But we can bring folks from here to work on it. Everyone wants to help."

Chloe had known that would be Lydia's response. "Maybe it's best to wait until we know more. Apparently there's some issue about a mold inspection before they can do much else."

Should she mention Gran's offer? Maybe not before she'd talked to Susanna about it.

Lydia nodded. "Always regulations, I guess. Well, in the meantime, we're planning a special auction to raise money for the families in Oyersburg, and vans will go every day taking anyone who is free to work."

It struck Chloe again how selfless people were being when faced with a crisis. "People are so kind." Her voice choked a little.

"That's why we're here, ja? To carry each other's burdens." Lydia glanced out the window, and amusement lit her face. "It didn't take Seth very long to notice your car. He's coming through the orchard now."

Chloe's heart gave a little thump. She had to see him—had to find out for herself what was going on with him.

"I'll walk out and meet him." Chloe made an effort to sound natural, which she suspected didn't fool her sister in the least.

"Take your time," Lydia said. "Supper won't be ready for another half hour or so."

Chloe made an effort to organize her jumbled thoughts as she walked toward the orchard. If she told Seth how she felt . . . but did she really want to do so? It might bring things between them to a head just when he was struggling with his sister's illness and his own future.

A fallen apple crunched underfoot, releasing its scent. Despite all the apples that had already been picked, the trees still seemed laden with fruit. Even though she knew nothing about orchards, it looked like a bountiful crop. Nature seemed to give with a lavish hand and take away equally.

Seth waited for her by the seat in the center of the orchard, not bothering to pretend he was coming for any reason except to see her. Even in his well-worn jeans and his flannel work shirt, Seth still carried the indefinable air of an urban professional. Was he really prepared to trade everything he'd earned to return to being Plain?

"I didn't expect to see you today," he said.

She met his gaze. "Didn't expect to or didn't want to?"

"Chloe, you know that's not true." He took an impetuous step toward her and stopped short, as if he'd run into something. "It's just that everything is so complicated right now."

"How is Jessie?" She couldn't pretend not to know what troubled him.

He rubbed the back of his neck. "Better, I guess. Mamm thinks she's regaining control more quickly now, but I don't know. There's no point in talking about it." He started to turn away.

She grabbed his arm. "Come on, Seth. Aren't we past the point of pretending?" She tugged him toward the seat. "Sit down and tell me what happened after Jessie had those hysterics at seeing us together."

He sat, reluctantly, and she took a seat next to him. She studied his profile, stern and determined in the afternoon sun filtering through the apple trees.

"Come on," she said again. "If I caused that—"

"You didn't. I don't know what did." He drove his fingers through his hair. "That's what's so frustrating. I thought she was getting used to the idea of . . . well, of you and me together. That she liked it, even. And then she exploded with no rhyme or reason."

"Does that happen often?" She'd known Seth's sister had emotional problems, but knowing and seeing were two different things.

"Not recently." Seth blew out a breath, as if trying to ease his tension. "That's what makes it so frustrating. The doctors say she's bipolar, but that doesn't really explain these fits of losing control."

Chloe groped her way, trying to find something she could hang on to. "I had a friend in college who was bipolar. When she was in the up phase nobody could stop her. She ripped through assignments, accomplishing more in a day than I did in a week. But then she'd be unable to sleep, and eventually she'd crash, sinking like a stone into depression."

"That's the pattern her doctor told us to watch for, and the medication does seem to be helping with it. But when she flies off the handle . . ." He lifted his hands in a gesture of helplessness. "Well, you saw. Nobody's been able to explain that to us. They keep saying it takes time."

Her heart ached for him. It must be maddening to be faced

with something he couldn't get a grip on. "I guess we start rely-ing on the idea that there's a pill or a treatment that will cure everything. It's a shock to find out it doesn't work that way."

Seth nodded, but she had the feeling he was listening to her with only half his attention.

"You see how it is. I can't leave my mother to deal with Jessie's problems alone. If I have to quit my job . . ." His voice ran out, as if he didn't really want to verbalize the possibility.

"Can't you go on the way you are? Working from here, going on business trips when you're needed?"

"The company wants more." His smile had a touch of bit-terness. "In this business, you're either out ahead of the curve or you're out of the race. I have to make a choice."

"If you talked to your employer—"

"Don't, Chloe." He cut her off short, shooting to his feet. "I'm sorry. I don't want to be rude. I know you're trying to help, but I have to figure this out for myself."

What about me, Seth? What about the feelings I have for you? What would you do if I came right out and said I love you?

She couldn't. Not now. It would be putting another burden on his back. Lydia's words about carrying one another's bur-dens came into her mind.

The trouble was that the other person had to be willing to let you share their burden. And Seth, it seemed, wasn't.

Nate pulled the crutches toward himself, careful not to make any noise. The slightest sound would bring either his mother or Susanna rushing to see what he wanted, and if they caught him, he'd never get over to the store today.

Good, he had the crutches without alarming anyone. He

wasn't sure which one was on duty at the moment, but between them, his mother and Susanna had kept him penned in this chair as if he were a babe in a cradle.

Foolishness. A broken ankle wasn't a big deal. The doctor wouldn't have given him crutches if he hadn't been intended to use them. There was no reason on earth why he couldn't get himself over to the store.

Just to make sure everything was running properly, mind. He wouldn't actually try to do anything, not until he could move around a bit more easily. But Mamm didn't see it that way. She hadn't even let him count the money last night, snatching the cash box away and saying he'd give himself a headache. He'd had worse lumps on his head playing eck ball than this one.

Getting the crutches properly positioned, he began to lever himself to his feet. But the chair rocked at his slightest movement, throwing him off balance, and he sat back down suddenly.

It seemed he'd underestimated how much he'd needed the help when Susanna had steadied the chair and given him a shoulder to lean on each time he'd gotten up. Well, Susanna wasn't here, and if she were, she'd figure out some way to stop him.

He couldn't help smiling. In the trials and upsets of the past week, Susanna had lost all her shyness where he was concerned. She'd revealed a strong, take-charge streak that startled him all the more because it was cloaked in such a soft, caring tone.

He managed to wedge the rocker against the table. Planting the tips of the crutches firmly, he tried again, and felt a wave of triumph when he actually stood upright by himself.

Turning carefully toward the door, he maneuvered the crutches. It had been one thing managing them in the hospital corridor. It was quite another, he found, to make his way around a room that suddenly seemed overly crowded with chairs and lamp tables and a braided rug that wanted to trip him up.

He took another step, then another, pausing after each to be sure he didn't hear anyone coming. Maybe they'd all gone over to the store.

The next couple of steps came with more assurance. He moved a bit more quickly. Almost to the door, and—

The crutch caught on the small table at the end of the sofa. It teetered, the books Mamm had stacked on it toppling to the floor. He tried to grab the table, lost his balance, struggled to get the crutch back under him . . .

"What are you doing?" Susanna's voice, and it was Susanna who rushed to him, grabbing him before he could fall. She braced her shoulder under his arm, supporting him better than any crutch could.

"What kind of foolishness is this?" She steered him back toward the rocking chair. "You should have called me if you needed something." She eased him into the chair and moved back a step, focusing on his face, her blue eyes dark with worry.

"I just thought I'd try it myself, that's all. A man's got to stretch once in a while."

Susanna's eyebrows lifted. "I don't believe that's it at all. You were trying to get to the store, weren't you?"

How was it she could see into his thoughts? "What if I was? I've just got a broken ankle. At least I can check on things. I'm not going to try and do any heavy work."

"And how did you plan to get down the steps? You haven't even tried steps yet, and you're not supposed to for another day."

"There's no reason why I can't do it today."

"And no reason why you should," she snapped back. "Your mother and sister are both minding the store right now, and they have plenty of help."

"Mamm shouldn't tire herself," he said, seizing on the first good reason he spotted.

"She's not. We're all looking out for her." The scolding look slid from Susanna's face, replaced by the smile that showed her dimple. "Besides, she's just as stubborn as you are. How could we keep her from helping?"

He didn't have an answer for that question, and it annoyed him. "Well, you should have," he said, knowing it was irrational.

Susanna shook her head slightly, apparently at his foolishness. "I'm going over to relieve her in half an hour. Then I'll send her back here, and since you're so good at getting her to do what you want, you can persuade her to take a rest."

He couldn't help it. He had to smile. "I guess you've had your hands full with the two of us."

She eyed him cautiously. "You could say that. Come now." She sat down in the chair next to him and drew it a little closer. "What is so important that you have to go over to the store this minute?"

"It's my store." He rubbed his palms on the arms of the rocker. "I've been focused on it for so long that I don't know how to let go, even for a day."

"The store filled your life up after your wife was gone." Susanna's voice was soft.

"Ja, I guess it did." Who would he be without it?

"Then you should understand how I feel about the shop. It's all I have."

Nate could read the longing in her face, and he suddenly found himself wishing that longing was for him, not for a shop that might be gone for good.

"It's different," he said. "I had to make a success to take care of my family."

"It's not different," she protested, leaning toward him, her hand on the arm of the rocker. "My mother is gone, and I have to take care of myself. And even if I have family now, I still need the shop." Passion filled her face, her voice. "Everyone needs something they can do, something to make them feel useful in the world."

"You are useful, shop or not." He put his hand over hers, holding it warmly. "You help so many people. You're a friend, and a sister. You have a life beyond the shop."

He leaned forward as he spoke, needing to show her, to convince her that she had value to so many others. Her eyes widened as they met his.

"Doesn't that apply to you as well, Nathaniel?"

Her question seemed to hang in the air between them. She was so close that all he could do was drink in the sweet scent of her. He wanted to pull her close against him, feeling a longing, a passion, a need that he'd thought he'd buried forever.

He lifted his hand, tracing the curve of her cheek with his fingertips. Her skin was so soft, so smooth, her eyes so deep a blue that a man could get lost in them, like diving into a deep blue pool.

He shouldn't. He had to. He cradled her face in his hand and then slid his fingers to her neck, drawing her closer until he could feel her breath on his face.

He kissed her . . . long, gentle, asking for a response and deepening the kiss when her lips softened under his. This was good. It was right. This was where they'd been heading for weeks, and they were finally here.

At last he drew back, leaning his forehead against hers, unwilling to have this moment end.

There was so much promise between them. It would be easy to let go . . . to release his caution, his common sense, and his fear. To let himself tumble into love with her.

But something deep inside made him hesitate on the precipice. What if he made a mistake again? What if he couldn't make her happy? It held him paralyzed, unable to speak.

Then the back door rattled, footsteps sounded, and Susanna sprang from the seat, her hands going to her hair, smoothing it before anyone should see.

The moment was past, and he was left longing to have it back again.

CHAPTER SEVENTEEN

Chloe spent much of the next day working the lunch cart in the area down toward the river, where people were finally able to start salvaging what they could. It proved to be more emotional than she'd bargained for. People needed a listening ear and a sympathetic heart as much as they needed sandwiches and coffee.

And when the trucks began to empty their loads of stoves and refrigerators, sofas and coffee tables, and all the other ruined furnishings of everyday life at the flood-ruined tennis courts where such a short time ago people had been playing, she found herself choking up as well. Those weren't just things—they were a symbol of normal life, now turned to scrap to be hauled away.

The bustle of hungry people finally diminished, probably because they were too tired or too disheartened to work any longer today. Tomorrow would be time enough to plunge back in again—for her, as well.

Chloe stowed everything carefully, closed up the cart, and slid behind the wheel. It was time to take the leftovers back to the consistory building, where the shelter had become the staging area for feeding people.

By the time she pulled into the parking lot, fatigue had set in. It took a moment to rally herself, and by then a volunteer had come out to help her unload.

"Hi, Mac." She opened the doors and began handing the leftovers to him. "How is it going today?"

Mac Evans, who proudly admitted to being eighty-one, gave her a grin that seemed to split his leathery face into a fine network of wrinkles. "Just fine, just fine. Give me a busy day anytime."

"You've had plenty of those lately." She picked up the cooler that held perishables and climbed down with it.

"Better to wear out than to rust out, I always say." He propped the door with his shoulder to let her enter the kitchen. "I'll get the cart shined up for tomorrow if you'll put stuff away."

"That sounds good to me." Chloe resisted the impulse to keep Mac talking. Friendly as he was, his job wasn't to take her mind off her troubles, so she headed for the walk-in cooler with her load.

Working the lunch cart had kept her safely away from Seth all day, and other people's problems had been a diversion from her own.

Too bad she was alone now, because that was when the memories were the strongest. She stacked packages of hot dogs on a wire shelf, aligning them as neatly as if they might explode if she didn't get them just right.

She could control the hot dog packages. She couldn't control her mind, which persisted in planting an image of Seth's face in front of her, his eyes pained, his jaw determined.

He wouldn't let her in. What was love, if not sharing your thoughts, your joys, your worries, and your grief with another person? She'd learned that from Lydia and Adam, she realized. They had given her far more than she had ever given them.

Seth wouldn't let her in. He wouldn't let her share a decision that affected the rest of his life.

Stop thinking about Seth, she ordered herself. She leaned her forehead against the inside of the door, as if the cold surface could freeze the thoughts away.

The clatter of the swinging door to the kitchen brought her back to her senses. Someone else was still here besides her and Mac. Nobody needed to see her being so . . . what was that word Lydia used? *Ferhoodled*, that was it. It was certainly a very expressive word for the scrambled nature of her thoughts right now.

Closing the cooler door, she stepped into the kitchen and found herself face-to-face with Jessie. For an instant Jessie's face expressed panic. It looked as if she'd turn and run.

Then she came a step closer and stopped, clasping her hands in front of her apron. "Chloe. I'm sehr glad it's you."

That was certainly a change in attitude from the last time they'd spoken. "It's good to see you, Jessie." She felt as if she had to edge her way through a minefield. "Have you had a busy day here?"

Jessie blinked, maybe at the friendly tone. She looked as if she'd been bracing herself for something, and Chloe wasn't sure what.

"A little." She shook her head, not meeting Chloe's eyes. "I must say how sorry I am. I should not have spoken to you that way." Her lips trembled, and she pressed them together, still not looking at Chloe.

How should she respond to the apology? Say it was nothing? But it had been something, and to dismiss it would be to belittle Jessie's feelings. She might not understand the forces that drove the girl, but Jessie was entitled to her feelings.

"I'm sorry, too," she said finally, trying not to analyze her words too much. "I want you to understand something, Jessie. Yes, I care about your brother." Her heart bled a little. "But that's not why I want to be your friend."

Jessie's eyes, startled, lifted to meet her gaze. "Why, then? Nobody else does." She lifted her hands in an expressive gesture, palms up. "I don't blame them. But why should you care?"

"Sometimes I think I know what it's like." She was treading cautiously, fearing she was going into forbidden territory. "I know how it feels when the people who love you try to . . . well, protect you too much. My grandmother used to hover over me as if she thought I couldn't be trusted not to make a mistake unless she was there."

Jessie seemed to consider her words. "What if you do make a mistake?"

"I've made plenty." *Including falling in love with your brother, it seems.* "But you know what? I've learned something every time, and I haven't made the same mistake again."

"It's different for you." Jessie didn't sound angry. She was simply stating a fact. "You're Englisch. You can do anything."

She had to smile at the naïve comment. "Maybe it seems that way to other people, but I love my grandmother, and I don't want to hurt her."

Chloe reached out tentatively to touch Jessie's hand. "You

have a heavier burden to carry than I ever did. But I think you can do it."

Jessie stared at her, and Chloe couldn't tell whether she accepted or believed the words or not. Then she turned away and hurried to the sink, her back turned firmly to Chloe as she began running water.

Well, she'd tried. Chloe pushed her way through the swinging doors. There weren't any easy answers for Jessie. Maybe there weren't any easy answers for her, either.

Chloe reached the front door just as it opened. It was Seth, coming to pick up Jessie, probably. He stopped at the sight of her. His tight face didn't give anything away.

"Chloe. I didn't think you'd be here."

In other words, he'd hoped to avoid her, just as she'd been attempting to avoid him all day.

"I dropped off the lunch cart. I'm on my way home." *Please, Seth. Talk to me. Tell me what's going on.*

But he nodded, holding the door for her.

A lady never shows her feelings in public. One of her grandmother's sadly outdated maxims, Chloe had always thought, but at the moment it came in handy. She gave Seth a meaningless smile, brushing past him to go out.

"Chloe, wait." He still held the edge of the door, his arm taut, his fingers white with his grip. "I . . . There's something I have to tell you."

"Yes?" She forced herself to look at him. *Tell me you love me, Seth. That's all I want to hear.*

"I can't go on like this, half in one world, half in another. It's not fair to anyone. I've submitted my resignation. I'm going home to stay."

She seemed to have lost the ability to breathe. That was it, then. He would live Plain, he would be baptized into the church, and he would try to be content. Maybe he could do it. She knew she couldn't.

She tried to force a smile, but her lips wouldn't cooperate. "I wish you well."

If she said anything else, she'd start to cry, and that wouldn't do either of them any good. She turned and fled.

Susanna was just about ready to lock the front door of the bulk foods store when Chloe came hurrying in.

"You're just in time." Susanna flipped the lock and pulled down the shade. "We're closing, but if there's anything you need for the lunch cart, of course you can have it."

"No, nothing." Chloe smiled, but she looked tired. There were dark shadows under her eyes that hadn't been there even during the worst of the evacuations.

Still, the ongoing stress was hard on many people. The adrenaline faded, and people just had to push through as best they could.

"You had a busy day?" Susanna led the way toward the counter.

"I'd like to talk." Chloe ignored the question. "Can you leave for a bit?"

There was a serious note in Chloe's voice and strain around her eyes. Susanna glanced quickly around the store. Thomas was tidying up the shelves while Susie swept the floor. They both knew exactly what had to be done at closing time.

"I must tally the receipts before I can leave, but I do that in the back room. Komm. It's quiet there."

Chloe nodded. "Fine, as long as it's private."

No sense in puzzling over what Chloe had on her mind. She'd know soon enough. Susanna took the cash box and led the way to the back room.

The small space didn't warrant the title of office, although that was its function. It had been carved out of a corner of the storeroom so it had no windows. File cabinets filled the end wall, and Nate's desk was a clutter of orders, receipts, and bills he hadn't been able to get to.

"I thought Nate usually did the receipts." Chloe paced the length of the room, which only took her a few steps.

Sitting down, Susanna cleared enough space to work and opened the ledger. Many Amish businesses had started using stripped-down versions of computers, but Nate clung to doing everything by hand.

"Dora and I are trying to keep him from doing too much. He insisted on coming in for a time today, and I think that taught him he wasn't ready yet."

Susanna couldn't help smiling at his reaction to being thwarted by his own weakness. Men could be like little boys when they were hurt.

She looked inquiringly at Chloe. Chloe seemed to have forgotten that she was eager for a private talk. She was standing in front of the bulletin board, staring at the lists of orders as if fascinated, her hands thrust in the pockets of her denim jacket.

The bulletin board shuddered at a thump from the other side of the wall. Chloe straightened it. "What on earth is going on over there?" She glanced around, as if orienting herself. "Is that next door?"

Susanna nodded. "It's so sad. Walker's Hardware is closing, another victim of the flood."

"They surely didn't have water up this high?"

"Not the store, but their house is down on Water Street." Water Street was aptly named in this case. The owners of those houses had paid dearly for their view of the river.

"A total loss?" Chloe had been here long enough to know what that meant.

"Ja. So sad. They've lived there all their lives. But Mr. Walker said their children have been wanting them to retire and go live near them, and he and his wife just don't have the heart to start over again."

"That's getting to be a familiar story." Chloe ran a hand through her already disheveled auburn hair. "How is Nate doing, other than being frustrated over work?"

"He'll be fine if we can make him take it easy." Susanna fought the urge to smile at just the mention of his name, even though her heart seemed to warm at the sound of it. He hadn't spoken yet, but he would, that was certain-sure. He wouldn't kiss her like that unless he wanted a future with her.

She pulled her thoughts away from rosy dreams and focused on Chloe. "You wanted to talk, ja? Sit. Tell me what the trouble is. If it's bad, we'll face it together."

Chloe took the only other chair in the room, a metal folding one. "It's not bad. I just haven't quite known how to tell you." She took a deep breath and seemed to compose herself. "I had a call from our grandmother yesterday."

Susanna nodded. That wasn't unusual, she'd think. Their Englisch grandmother seemed to keep a close watch on Chloe, even from a distance.

"She's well, I hope?" She still found it hard to even picture the woman, and even the words seemed a contradiction. How could she, Susanna Bitler, possibly have an Englisch grand-mother?

"She's well, I think. I've been keeping her posted on what's happening here with Lydia and her family and with you and the shop."

Susanna nodded to show she was following. Was the woman even interested? From what she'd learned, Margaret Went-worth hadn't wanted her or Lydia. Only Chloe.

"Now, listen to me before you say no." Chloe leaned forward, her hands on the edge of the desk. "Gran wants to give you the money to buy the shop and fix it up. You won't have to worry about what Nate wants. You can make the shop just the way it was before."

Susanna was too shocked to move for a moment. But then she shook her head. How could she accept money from some-one she didn't even know?

"Think about it," Chloe said, her voice persuasive. "This would be just as much a legacy from your birth mother as the farm and orchard were to Lydia. She didn't refuse to accept them, did she?"

Somehow it didn't feel like the same thing, but Susanna didn't know how to explain that to Chloe, who had probably always taken her grandparents' riches as a matter of course.

"I don't think I can."

"Give me one good reason why. Like it or not, Diane Went-worth was as much your mother as she was mine."

Put that way, it sounded logical, but . . .

"Anyway, I don't know that I'll need it. I might not need to buy out Dora's share of the shop. Things have changed between me and Nate." She was stammering a little, and her cheeks felt hot.

Chloe was staring at her as if she had sprouted wings. "You mean you and he actually . . . what you said the other day about having feelings for him . . ."

Susanna nodded, unable to hold back a smile. "I think so. I mean, he hasn't asked me yet, exactly. I know you don't like him. I'm sorry." Well, not sorry that she loved him, just sorry that Chloe had the wrong impression of Nate due to her.

"What difference does that make?" Chloe came around the desk and gave her a fierce hug. "It's what you feel that counts. Anyway, I only disliked him because of what he was doing to you. If he's finally woken up to what a wonderful person you are, that's great." Chloe took a step back and studied her face. "You're sure of your feelings?"

"I'm sure." She'd never been more convinced of anything in her life.

"Well, then. Just you wait until Lydia hears. She'll be so excited."

"Ja, but don't say anything, not to anyone, not yet. Promise?" Susanna wanted to hug the joy to herself a little longer, at least until Nate had actually said the words.

"Of course. I'm so glad you're happy."

But the momentary joy seemed to be fading from Chloe's face. Susanna clasped her hand.

"Something's wrong. I can tell. Is it Seth?"

Chloe's face seemed to stiffen, as if it were a mask she wore to hide behind. "He's given up his career. He's going back to the church."

For a moment Susanna could only stare at her. Poor Chloe. If only . . . "I'm so sorry for your hurt."

Chloe's façade didn't shudder, and Susanna could only guess

the cost of keeping it. "His family will be happy." Chloe spoke as if her lips were numb.

Susanna nodded. Wasn't that the dream of every Amish family with a son who had jumped the fence? That one day he'd realize what he'd lost and come back to take his rightful place? But she hadn't thought Seth's return would be at such a cost to her sister.

"Chloe, couldn't you—"

"No. I can't." Chloe's hands clenched into fists, and she turned away, probably so that Susanna couldn't see her face. "I could never become Amish. For one thing it would break Grandmother's heart. And for another . . ." She paused, and then went on, her tone painfully steady. "For another, unless two people really share their values, I don't think marriage will work. And we don't."

Susanna went around the desk, longing to put her arms around Chloe but afraid of being rejected. "I'm so sorry," she said again, feeling helpless.

Chloe straightened her shoulders. "I knew all along it could end this way. I can't wish I'd never met him, because then I wouldn't have found my sisters. But I should have been ready for it to turn out this way."

"No one can be ready for a broken heart." Susanna pressed her hand against her chest. Her sister's pain seemed to be echoing in her own heart.

Chloe was already at the door. "I can't talk about it anymore now. Maybe . . . maybe later."

She went out quickly and closed the door. Susanna took an instinctive step after her, but she knew it was useless. Chloe was one who would hold her pain to herself. And even if she weren't, what could Susanna say that would make her feel any better?

It seemed to her that both Seth and Chloe had been balancing between Amish and Englisch for as long as she'd known them. Now Seth had landed on the wrong side for Chloe.

Nate shifted his position slightly in the rocking chair, trying to ease the discomfort of the heavy cast propped on the footstool, and frowned at the official-looking letter that had arrived in the day's mail.

"I'm off now." His sister appeared in the doorway, her bonnet in her hand. "My family will want feeding, too."

"It was wonderful kind of them to spare you to cook for us. Not that you gave them a choice." He smiled, knowing her husband's mother had no doubt been happy to fix a meal for her son and grandchildren.

Donna grinned, her freckled face looking not so different than it had when she was chasing him around the apple tree in the backyard.

"Mamm Alice is making pot pie for her son, and he'll tell her it's better than mine even though we both know that it's not true."

Nate looked at her in mock surprise. "You mean you finally learned to cook?"

She swatted at him with the bonnet. "You just mind your manners. Tell Susanna everything is ready to come out of the oven. I finally got Mamm to go up and rest. She looked tired out, and it's no wonder."

"She does too much. She always has. And with all that's going on, I couldn't have picked a worse time to break my ankle." He glared at the cast. "And now this." He shook the letter he'd been studying.

"What is it?" Donna held out her hand, and he put the paper in it.

"More regulations, this time from the town. It seems like whatever you need to do to rebuild, there's some government rule about it. By the time I have all those things done to the shop property, I'll have more money in it than it's worth."

She handed the paper back to him. "By the sounds of this letter, you don't have much choice."

"There is another possibility." He hadn't talked to anyone about it yet, but Donna had a good head on her shoulders. "The town council is talking about using a grant they got to buy out some of the worst of the flooded properties in the west end. They'd put up an earthen levee and maybe turn the rest of the land into a walking path along the creek."

She frowned. "You mean Mamm's shop is one of the properties they want to buy?"

"It seems it's one they are considering. If I sold the building to them, I wouldn't have to deal with remodeling, because they'd just tear it down. No one else would be likely to buy it anyway, knowing how bad the flooding was."

"I guess that's true. But what about Mamm's shop? You and I might think Mamm would be better off without the work and worry, but she has to be convinced."

"It seems to me she's not really thinking about herself. If she didn't have Susanna to consider, I think she'd be happy to let the shop go."

Donna nodded. "Ja, I think so, too. But there *is* Susanna to consider."

He fixed his gaze firmly on the calendar on the opposite

wall. "I think it possible that Susanna might soon have other things to occupy her time."

Donna was quiet for a moment. Then she grabbed his shoulder and shook him, making the chair rock.

"Ouch. Watch what you're doing. I have a broken ankle, remember?"

"I'll give you a broken ankle," she retorted. "Are you telling me that you and Susanna—"

"Nothing's settled yet," he said hastily, unable to keep the smile from his face. "So don't you go blabbing about it to anybody."

"All I can say is that it's about time. You ought to start living again, and Susanna's a dear." She gave him a quick hug. "I've got to go, or they'll think I got lost. I won't tell a soul, but I'm happy for you." She planted a kiss on his cheek and whirled out of the room.

He sat, still smiling. If anyone could see him they'd think he'd taken leave of his senses. He hadn't. In fact, he'd come to his senses at last.

CHAPTER EIGHTEEN

*S*eth measured oats into a bucket and poured them into the feed pail in Blackie's stall. Blackie nuzzled his arm before dropping her head to begin munching.

Patting her neck, he noticed the graying hair around her nose. She'd been a two-year-old when he'd left home, and much of those last months he'd spent training her to the buggy. Now she was showing signs of age.

Star, the gelding, whickered and stamped a hoof, indicating his impatience.

"All right, I'm coming." Funny, that he'd spoken to the horse in English. He'd have to get used to using dialect most of the time.

Measuring out another pailful, he carried it to the stall and poured it in. Star tried to eat while it was still flowing into the feed pail.

"Greedy," he said, giving Star's neck a slap.

This might be his favorite part of his new life—these quiet moments in the barn at the end of the day.

Funny that Mamm hadn't reacted the way he'd expected when he'd told her his decision. She'd been happy, yes, but there'd been questioning, even worry in her eyes and in the way she asked if he was sure.

That was natural, wasn't it? It would take time for her to see that he was really serious, that he was doing the right thing. He'd spent too much time drifting between two worlds, never really Englisch, never really Amish. He was doing the right thing.

If only it weren't for Chloe.

That first day, when she'd thrown him out of her office, thinking him a con man, they'd struck sparks off each other. Once he'd become her guide to the Amish world of her family, he'd felt reassured because of that antagonism.

He should have known it was dangerous. He should have seen that antagonism was the flip side of attraction. But he hadn't, or maybe the truth was that he hadn't wanted to admit it. Now they were both paying the penalty for his carelessness. It seemed he couldn't make a move without hurting someone.

Chloe would get over him. A woman like her would have a string of guys after her in no time at all.

The barn door hinges gave a protesting squeal, and Jessie came in. She stood for a moment, her back against the door, watching him.

"So, did Mamm tell you my news?" He swung himself up to the loft as he spoke. Bending over, he loosened a hay bale, the scent of it old and familiar. He began tossing flakes of hay down into each stall.

"She told me." Jessie looked up at him, her face a pale oval in the light that filtered through the barn siding. "You were expecting a party, maybe?"

"What are you talking about?" Dusting the hay off his jeans, he scrambled back down the ladder to the barn floor, frowning at her.

"Telling Mamm you're back to stay. That you're going to get baptized and join the church. Be Plain again. You thought we'd celebrate."

He eyed her. What was going on with Jessie? "I thought you'd be glad to have me back," he said, his tone cautious. "Aren't you?"

She shrugged, as if to indicate that it wasn't important to her.

Her reaction nettled him, and he ignored Mamm's warning to be careful how he spoke to her.

"What's the matter with you and Mamm? Isn't this what you want? I thought that's what Mamm had been praying for all these years, for her erring boy to come back to the fold."

Jessie moved a little closer, and he could see the skepticism in her face. It bothered him. Usually his little sister looked at him with a bit more approval, as if her big brother could do no wrong.

"Mamm probably wonders if you really mean it," she said.

"I quit my job, didn't I?" What more did they want?

"You could get another." She sounded unimpressed. "Mamm knows you could."

"So I'll get rid of my Englisch clothes. My computer." He couldn't suppress a wince at the thought. Getting rid of his computer was like giving up a limb.

"You don't want to do that, ain't so?" She tilted her head, studying him as if he were a stranger.

He turned to check the latches on the stall doors, not eager to face that steady stare. "The computer is a symbol of who I was. Now I'm not going to be that person. Doesn't that show I mean it?"

Jessie took a quick step toward him and grabbed his arm, tugging him around to face her. "Just tell me. Are you coming back because you believe in being Plain? Or because you feel responsible for us?"

He tried to avoid looking at her. She tightened her grip as if she'd shake an answer out of him.

His control seemed to shatter. "What difference does it make? I'm back, that's all."

"It matters." Jessie's voice rose, but with anger, not hysteria. "If you want to give up your life because I'm sick, don't I get a say in that? Maybe I don't want you to. What about Chloe? Doesn't she get a say?"

He felt as if she'd slapped him. "I don't want to talk about Chloe. Anyway, this is my decision."

"Yours, yours," she mocked. "Is that all you can think about? You jumped the fence thinking only of what you wanted. Now you're coming back the same way."

"That's not true." He'd never expected to be having such an argument with Jessie, of all people. His little sister seemed to have done some growing up.

"Isn't it, Seth?" Her lips trembled suddenly, as if her anger had slipped away to be replaced by sorrow. "Mamm and I don't want you to sacrifice your life for us. You think that will make us happy, knowing you're miserable? And Chloe is a gut person. She cares, even when she doesn't have to."

Tears glistened in her eyes, and she wiped them away with

the back of her hand. Stunned, both at the words and at her obvious feelings, Seth put his arms around her.

"It's going to be all right," he said, the way he had when she was toddling around after him and skinned her knee. "It will."

She sniffled a little, hugging him tightly.

He wanted to take care of things for her. But how could he make it all right when he didn't know what all right was anymore?

He dropped a kiss on her forehead and managed to smile at her—his little sister struggling against huge odds toward maturity. Maybe she was doing better than he was.

"Go on in the house, okay? I'll be there. I just need a minute."

He managed to hold it together until she'd vanished behind the barn door. Then he sank down on a bale of straw and buried his face in his hands.

Was Jessie right? Was that really who he was—a man who put his own wants first? Had he been kidding himself about making this big sacrifice for his family?

He was scared. The fear bubbled up from somewhere deep inside him. He'd let his family down when he went away. He'd hurt them. He hadn't been there when Daad died, or when his older sister died. He'd let Mamm cope with Jessie's illness on her own.

What if he did that again? What if he made a life with Chloe and then let her down? His heart twisted, hurting so that he pressed his hand to his chest.

Chloe. He saw again the pain she'd tried so hard to hide. She hadn't succeeded. He'd seen it; he knew he'd caused it, and that terrified him.

He closed his eyes, and he couldn't see anything but Chloe's face . . . laughing at her nephews, earnest over her work, courageous when she fought the boat into the current to save others.

He saw her face when he'd told her he was staying, and suddenly he knew the truth behind the mask. Chloe . . . amazing, incomparable Chloe . . . loved him. Now, what was he going to do about it?

Susanna had been surprised when Dora mentioned she was going to her daughter's house after supper that evening, but glad Dora had felt like being out. She'd shooed her away when Dora had tried to help with the dishes and done the job herself.

It was strangely peaceful after all the busyness of the past weeks. The house was so quiet that Susanna could hear the rustle of pages as Nate read the newspaper in the living room. Content, that was what she was, with the familiar chore, the pleasant house, and the knowledge that Nate was only a few steps away.

The only cloud across her joy was for her sister. Poor Chloe. Her heart hurt for Chloe's grief. If only she could do something to ease her pain.

The thump of crutches announced Nate's arrival, and Susanna looked up. "You're managing much better on those, ain't so?"

"It's getting easier, I guess. Not fast enough for me, though."

That was predictable. "I think you wouldn't be happy unless you could be putting in a full day's work, even with the broken ankle."

"I shouldn't need my ankle to run the store," he said. Balancing himself uneasily on the crutches, he leaned against the counter next to her.

She felt all thumbs with him watching her dry the dishes. "Did you want something? Some more coffee, maybe?"

"No. Well, I do want something."

She reached for the towel to dry her hands. "Of course. What?"

"I want to know why you were looking so worried before I came in." He nodded toward the living room. "I was watching you, and you seemed to have the weight of the world on your shoulders."

"It's nothing," she said.

He clasped her hands before she could pick up another dish, holding them firmly. "Tell me. Did something happen at the store that upset you?"

"No, nothing . . . well, nothing about the store." She'd have to tell him. The touch of his hands seemed to be affecting her breathing. "Chloe stopped by to talk to me just when we were closing."

She felt the slightest possible withdrawal from him at her sister's name. Did he guess how Chloe felt about him?

"Is she having troubles?" He sounded concerned enough.

"It's Seth. I felt so sure the two of them would get together. I know they care about each other. But Seth has decided to go back to the church, and poor Chloe is brokenhearted at losing him."

Nate was silent long enough to make Susanna think how angry she'd be if he said something derogatory about her Englisch sister.

"I'm truly sorry," he said finally. "I thought, just from seeing them together, how well matched they were. And I'm sorry it's hurting you."

Susanna looked at him with gratitude. He'd said exactly the right thing. "I felt as if I should have found some way to make her feel better. Maybe I'm not a very gut big sister, but then, I haven't had much practice."

"No." He moved his thumbs along the backs of her hands, as gentle as if he was stroking a pet. "I'm sure you did what you could. Nobody can fix someone else's broken heart."

"I suppose. Maybe Lydia will do better. She's a comforting sort of person." Susanna had to shake her head at the strangeness of it all. "A month ago I barely knew them, but now I've accepted them as my sisters. I was so upset at first that I didn't think it could happen, and certainly not that quickly."

"It seems to me that things happen faster during a crisis." Nate hadn't let go of her hands, and he leaned closer to her. "We've all been caught up in the danger and the stress, and feelings come to the surface that might otherwise take months or years to grow."

Her heart thudded against her ribs. Was he talking about her sisters? Or about his feelings for her?

"The unimportant things get swept away," she said, trying to sound normal. "Only the important remains."

"That's exactly it." His voice seemed to have gone deeper. "Now I really want to talk to you about one of those important things."

Her ability to speak had gone entirely, and she could only nod.

"Ach, this isn't how I wanted to do it." He thumped his cast on the floor and then grimaced. "We should be out in the moonlight, taking a buggy ride, looking at the river, maybe. Not stuck in the kitchen with my foot in a cast."

Somehow his frustration wiped away her shyness. She looked up at him, lips trembling on a smile. "Does the place matter so much?"

"No." His expression cleared. "What matters is you and me. Susanna, you must know how I feel. I love you. I want you to marry me. Yes or no?"

A laugh bubbled up inside her because he sounded as if he were making a deal. But it was Nate, and that was how he thought. He loved her. He wanted her.

She tilted her face back to look up into his eyes. "I love you, Nate. So my answer is yes."

Nate's face broke into a smile, and then he pulled her close and his lips found hers.

There was nothing tentative or questioning about his kiss this time. He claimed her with his lips, gentle and demanding all at the same time, and she slid her arms around him, feeling the strong, flat muscles of his back under the smooth cotton of his shirt. He was hers, and she was his, and they belonged together.

An instant later she was glad she had hold of him, because the crutch slipped out of his control and went clattering to the floor. He nearly went after it, but she held him close until he could brace himself against the counter.

"All right?"

He grinned, laughter filling his eyes. "Ja, but this is no place for smooching. Leave the dishes. Let's go sit on the sofa where I can get my arms around you properly."

Her heart singing, Susanna retrieved the crutch and followed him into the living room. He settled on the sofa, set the crutches aside, clasped her hand, and pulled her down next to him.

"This is better," he said, and kissed her again.

Susanna gave herself to his kiss. This was the taste of belonging, of being loved and valued and wanted for herself, and she loved it.

Eventually her mind started working again. "Is this why your mamm went out tonight? Did you tell her you were going to propose?"

"You thought that was funny, didn't you?" His eyes crinkled. "Ja, she and my sister came up with the plan between them. They're both wonderful happy at the idea of having you in the family."

"I can't believe Dora didn't give any hint of it." Susanna's cheeks grew warm at the thought that Dora and Donna had known what Nate intended.

"Now, let's get down to business." He snuggled Susanna close to his side. "We need to make plans."

"Always a businessman," she teased, and felt his chuckle deep in his chest.

"Ja, I am. If you're agreeable, I want to talk to the bishop and make plans to get married as soon as reasonably possible. After all, we already have a home."

That had a lovely sound. "We will be happy, living here." This house was starting to feel like home to her in a way the small apartment never had.

"You won't mind that Mamm is living here?"

"Of course not. I love Dora." She wouldn't expect anything else. This was Dora's home, too.

"Maybe at the end of next month," Nate said, and it was

obvious that his thoughts had moved on. "Or early November. I'm sure the bishop will agree. We don't need a lot of fuss over a wedding. We're not youngsters."

"We're not exactly old," she pointed out. Of course Nate had been married before. He'd been the passionate young groom once, with Mary Ann. Naturally he'd think in more practical terms now.

Susanna tried not to mind. She was marrying the man she loved who loved her, something she'd never thought would happen. It would be foolish to quibble because he didn't speak of their wedding in romantic terms.

"Young enough but not too young," he said, giving her a squeeze. "That's the best part of life, ain't so? The business is already established, and we're only a step away from the store."

She nodded. "And not far from the shop, either."

Suddenly there was tension in the arm that encircled her shoulders. "I . . . I need to talk to you about the shop."

The unusual hesitation in his voice told her something was wrong. She drew away, turning so that she could see his face more clearly. "What about the shop? Is there a problem with the mold removal?"

"In a way." He wasn't looking directly at her, alarming her. "It's not just the mold. There are all kinds of regulations in force now that didn't exist when the building was put up. Every day it seems there's something else the government says has to be done."

She found herself wanting to put her hands over her ears, but she was a grown woman. She couldn't do that no matter how little she wanted to hear something. "What are you saying, Nate?"

He planted his palms on his thighs, a firm gesture that suggested he had something important to say. "The town is offering to buy up those buildings down along the creek. They want to put up a levee and turn the rest into a park. Given the expense and trouble of fixing up the building, I . . . well, I've accepted their offer."

Susanna could only stare at him. "I can't believe it. What about the shop? It's your mamm's and mine. You can't just sell it."

"I know you loved the shop, Susanna. But I explained to Mamm, and I think she understands. The building isn't worth saving."

So easy. Just as if it was any business deal. "How can you get rid of something that means so much to me?"

He reached for her hand, his forehead wrinkling, but she pulled it away. "I've explained it badly, but you have to understand. This is the best answer. And once we're married, you won't need the shop."

"Won't need it?" She felt as if she were looking at a stranger.

"I don't mean you shouldn't work if you want to," he said hastily. "You can help me in the store all you want. It will belong to both of us."

Susanna could only stare at him. Did he really not understand something so basic to her? She'd helped build the business. She'd put her heart into it, and he simply wanted to discard it.

"Komm, Susanna." He reached for her hand, but again she pulled it away. His face seemed to freeze. "Anyone would think the shop means more to you than I do."

She shook her head slowly. "If you don't understand something that means so much to me, how can you say you love me?"

"Susanna, that's foolishness. Selling the building is just business. It has nothing to do with my feelings for you."

"Business isn't everything." Her head was throbbing, her heart aching. She thought of what Chloe had said about people sharing values. Not only didn't Nate understand what the shop meant to her; he wasn't even willing to try.

"I'm sorry, Nate." The words came out of a throat gone dry. "This isn't going to work. I can't stay here. I'm going to my sister's."

"Susanna, stop. We have to talk about it. You can't just walk away."

She heard him fumbling for the crutches, but she didn't wait. She couldn't keep talking about it. He'd said he loved her, but he didn't understand the first thing about her. Nobody could build a marriage on such a basis.

CHAPTER NINETEEN

The knock on Chloe's door took her by surprise, and she glanced around the small living room. Her computer was on top of a couple of stacked books on the coffee table, she'd been organizing papers on the sofa, and manila file folders filled the only chair. She couldn't even claim to have been getting any work done, since she'd been sitting staring into space, thinking about Seth.

She opened the door a few inches, prepared to make short work of her visitor, and then swung it wide when she saw that it was Susanna.

"Come in." She clasped her sister's hand and pulled her into the apartment. "Excuse the mess. I didn't—"

The rest of the sentence was lost when she had a good look at Susanna's face. Lips pressed together to hold back sobs, eyes brimming with tears . . . this wasn't a casual visit.

"Susanna, what is it?"

The tears overflowed. Susanna put her hands to her face, her shoulders shaking. She must have suppressed her emotion by sheer force of will until she got here, and now the dam had burst.

"It's all right. You're here now." Chloe closed and locked the door. Putting her arm around Susanna's waist, she led her to the sofa.

"Here, sit down." She cleared the sofa by the simple expedient of sweeping all the papers onto the floor, where they drifted across the worn beige carpet.

Susanna sank onto the sofa and bent over, her face buried in her palms. Sobs ripped through her so that her whole body shook.

Chloe stood watching her helplessly for a moment. Then she sat down next to her and gathered Susanna into her arms. "It'll be all right. You're safe here. You can cry as much as you need." She rocked back and forth, rubbing Susanna's back with vague memories of Granddad doing so when she had nightmares as a child.

Whatever had happened, Susanna clearly needed comforting. Chloe had never seen anyone cry so hard. It frightened her to see calm, sensible Susanna lose control this way. Even when the flood was surging toward them, even when Nate had had his accident, she'd never fallen apart.

There was no point in trying to get any sense out of her until the storm was over. Chloe sat holding her, waiting it out.

Finally the sobs lessened. She could feel the moment at which Susanna became aware of what she was doing, could sense the embarrassment that seized her.

Susanna drew back, trying to hide a face blotchy and swollen from weeping. "I'm sorry. I . . ." She didn't seem able to go any further.

"You're going to be all right." Chloe rose, helping her up. "Come on. The bathroom is right through the bedroom. I want you to go splash some cold water on your face and bathe your eyes. I'll make a pot of tea, and then we'll talk."

She had to guide her sister's stumbling steps at first, but once they reached the bedroom, Susanna managed to attempt a smile. "I'm all right. Denke."

Chloe switched on the bathroom light and left her alone. If she were in Susanna's place, she'd want a few minutes to collect herself.

Chloe went quickly back to the minuscule kitchen that occupied one end of the living room. She put the kettle on the stove, filled a teapot with hot water, and got out a packet of the herbal tea Susanna had made herself. That had been one of the first steps in their friendship—the day Susanna and Dora had invited her into the back room at the shop for a cup of Susanna's special tea.

They'd come a long way since then. She was very afraid she knew what had so devastated Susanna that she'd come seeking shelter with her sister.

By the time Susanna came out of the bedroom, the tea was brewed. Chloe carried a tray with teapot and cups to the coffee table, and then had to set it down so she could move the computer.

"Sorry this is all such a mess. I was trying to sort out some things." That wasn't really too far from the truth. She'd been trying to sort out her feelings for Seth.

"I'm sorry. I shouldn't have burst in on you." Susanna's voice still had a tendency to waver.

"Who else would you come to but your sister?" Chloe poured tea into a mug and passed it to Susanna. "This will make you feel better. It's your special blend. You gave it to me one day at the shop, remember?"

Susanna nodded, eyes shimmering with tears again. But she seemed to have them under control as she sipped. "I'm sor—"

"No, don't say it again." Chloe settled down next to her. "You don't need to be sorry for anything. Just tell me. It's Nate, isn't it?"

Susanna nodded. "How did you know?"

"Because only a man can make you feel that miserable." As she well knew. "What happened? Did he back out of proposing?"

"No, it wasn't that. He did ask me, and I said yes." She clutched the mug with both hands, and even so it shook a little. "I was so happy. I never thought love would happen for me." The tea sloshed dangerously.

Chloe took the mug from her and set it down before it could spill. "That's just silly. I never met anyone more lovable than you."

Susanna shook her head, but there was the faintest hint of a smile, gone again as quickly as it came. "We were talking about the future. About getting married, living there in the house, what our life would be like. I mentioned the shop, and that's when he told me."

Chloe had begun to think it must be something about the shop. "Go on," she said, when it seemed Susanna had come to a full stop.

"He's sold the building to the town. They're going to tear it down, and some others along the street as well." Susanna's tear-drenched eyes were tragic. "He kept saying it was sensible, it was business, it was the best thing to do. He didn't even think to talk to me before he did it."

A knife seemed to twist in Chloe's heart. Like Seth, who hadn't talked to her before making the biggest decision of his life. But at least he hadn't tried to defend it as being sensible.

"Is the man blind?" Chloe could safely take out her own anger on Nate. "Doesn't he understand how much the shop means to you? Didn't he even think you should have a say in its future?"

"I guess not." Another tear slipped out, and Susanna wiped it away with a fingertip. "He says he loves me, but how can he love me when he doesn't understand something so important to me?"

"Oh, Susanna, I'm so sorry." What else was there to say? Her heart twisted with pain. At least Susanna had found out quickly, before she'd made a mistake that couldn't be rectified. "I guess we're the unlucky-in-love sisters. Thank goodness Lydia, at least, has her happy ending."

Susanna's laugh was partly a sob. "I just couldn't stay there a minute longer. I walked out without even a nightdress. What am I going to do?"

Chloe reached out to clasp her hands. "Short-term, you're going to stay here with me. I'll lend you a nightshirt and whatever else you need. And tomorrow I think we should give ourselves a day off from responsibility. We'll go and see Lydia."

"I . . . I was supposed to work at the store tomorrow," Susanna began.

"You don't want to go back there, do you?"

Susanna shook her head.

"Then, don't. We have to talk to Lydia. She'd be hurt if she thought we hadn't come to her when we're in trouble." And Chloe didn't know about Susanna, but she could certainly do with some of the maternal comforting Lydia did so well.

To her relief, Susanna nodded. "Ja, we have to see Lydia." Her face clouded. "My things . . ."

"I'll stop by the house tomorrow and pack up your belongings. You'll stay here with me until we figure out what comes next."

"It's imposing. You said yourself that the apartment is so small."

"Not too small to share with my sister. I'll be glad of the company." She hesitated, but maybe it would be good for Susanna to remember that she had options for the future. "And don't forget your legacy from the family." It had seemed to make an impression when she'd referred to it that way earlier. "You'll be able to rent or buy your own place and start your business. Half the stock is rightfully yours. You're the one who found the craftsmen, and you're the one who saved much of the stock from the flood. You wouldn't have to stay here. You could move over to Pleasant Valley and be close to Lydia."

Susanna put her hand to her forehead. "I guess I could. It's too much to think about tonight."

"Let me show you where everything is." Chloe rose, leading the way back into the bedroom. She pulled a nightshirt from a dresser drawer. "Luckily we're about the same size. I'll get out some clean towels."

It was going to be tight, sharing this tiny apartment with another person, but at least having Susanna to take care of was keeping her mind off her own troubles.

When she came back into the bedroom, Susanna was standing

at the table between the twin beds, holding the framed photograph that stood there.

"Is this your . . . our mother?"

Chloe nodded, coming to stand next to her. It wasn't the posed studio portrait that Gran had tucked away. This was a picture someone else had taken of Diane. She was sitting on a rock, wooded hills behind her. The wind was blowing her hair back from her face, and she was laughing.

Susanna studied the photo. "You have a look of her, I think."

"Maybe, but so do you and Lydia," Chloe replied. "Look at the dimple."

Susanna touched the glass gently. "What would she think of us, if she could see us now?"

The answer came readily, without the need for thought. "She'd be glad that we're together."

An hour later Nate still sat where Susanna had left him, trying to make sense of what had happened. How had something that seemed so right turned out so wrong?

Susanna was a smart woman. She understood business. So why didn't she understand his decision? He was only trying to do what was best for their future.

Memory flickered in the dim recesses where he seldom looked. He'd said something like that to Mary Ann once, back when they were first married and he was working around the clock trying to get the business established. *It's for our future,* he'd said. But they'd had no future.

He shoved that thought back in the corner. The situation with Susanna wasn't the same thing at all.

He heard the door open, and despite himself his heart leaped. Susanna had come back.

Then he recognized the footsteps. His mother had returned, not Susanna.

He heard Mamm cross the kitchen. She came to the living room door, a big smile on her face, all ready to congratulate them. Then she saw his face, and the happiness faded.

"What happened?" She came straight to him, putting her hand on his shoulder. "Something has gone wrong."

"Everything has gone wrong." He shook his head. "I don't want to talk about it."

"Don't be foolish. Of course you will talk about it." Mamm wouldn't take that for an answer, obviously. "Didn't you ask Susanna to marry you?"

"I asked her. She said yes."

"Well, then." Mamm dragged a chair over to sit in front of him, leaning forward to look in his face. "I won't leave until you tell me, Nathaniel. Out with it."

It was the tone she'd used when he was a small boy trying to hide something from her. He'd never succeeded.

"I don't know. Everything was fine. We were planning our future together. And then Susanna took offense at something I said. She was unreasonable. She just walked out."

"That doesn't sound like the Susanna I know." Mamm put her hands on his knees, studying his expression. "Now tell me what you did."

"I'm your son, Mammi. Shouldn't you be on my side?"

"Not if you've done something wrong. What were you talking about that Susanna took offense at?"

"I was trying to explain the decision I'd made about the

shop. You know, signing the papers to turn it over to the town." He'd explained the possibility to Mamm first off.

"Wait. Are you saying you already did it? Without discussing it with Susanna first? What were you thinking?"

"You agreed it was the sensible thing to do." He didn't like the defensive note in his voice.

"Ja, I said it was sensible, but I am not Susanna. The shop meant so much to her, even more than it did to me, I sometimes think. You shouldn't have decided without talking to her first."

His jaw hardened. "I'm the man of the family. It's my job to take care of everyone."

"That doesn't mean you should be telling everyone what to do." Mamm shook her head, clearly exasperated. "You can be the boss in the store, but even there you shouldn't be bossy. In a marriage, you have to be a partner."

The temper he was trying to control slipped. "Like Daad, I suppose. I'm trying to take care of the people I love, not let others do it the way he did."

"Nathaniel, if you were younger I'd take a switch to you for speaking that way about your father." Her face had paled.

"You know I'm right." Like it or not, it was the truth. "Daad never did a lick of work if he could get someone else to do it. He should have taken care of you."

Mamm pressed her lips together, the lines in her face growing deeper, and he was angry with himself for hurting her.

"Your father was the person he was. I knew his faults when I married him, but I loved him anyway. Ach, Nate, don't you know I want the best for you?"

"The best isn't someone who'd walk away."

"Are you talking about Susanna or Mary Ann?"

He could only gape at her. "You knew about Mary Ann?"

"Ja, I knew." Her lips twisted. "Maybe I did wrong not talking to you about it at the time, but I thought you were coping the best you could."

He shook his head. This was all too much to handle. "I don't want to talk about it any further, Mamm."

She got up slowly, her gaze fixed on him. "No, I guess talking isn't helping. But you'd best spend some time thinking about it. Because if they both left, maybe they both had a reason."

She turned away, leaving him feeling as if a load of bricks had just fallen on him.

Susanna was feeling a little nervous as Chloe drove up the lane to Lydia's house the next afternoon. She glanced at Chloe's face, but she had seemed distracted the entire drive.

"I wouldn't want Lydia to think I'm looking for pity." She startled herself by saying it. "I mean, coming in on her with my troubles."

"She'd be upset if we didn't." Chloe eased the car to a stop outside the back door. "Besides, I left a message on the machine in the phone shanty telling her what happened. She'll be expecting us."

Susanna supposed that was a good thing, although she felt a little disconcerted that Chloe had spoken to Lydia about her troubles. Still, maybe she assumed she would spare Susanna the telling again.

They got out and walked together to the door. Lydia stood, framed in the doorway, holding out her hands to them.

Susanna's uncertainty slid away as she was enveloped in Lydia's hug. This was her sister. Of course she had to share her burdens.

"I'm wonderful glad you came, both of you." Lydia led them into the house. "The boys won't be home from school for another two hours, so we have time for a visit."

The kitchen smelled of cinnamon and apples, and a rich, dark apple cake sat cooling on the counter. Susanna suspected you couldn't come into Lydia's house this time of year without smelling apples.

"The cake looks wonderful good," she said.

"We'll have some," Lydia said quickly. "But first, how are you?" Lydia held both her hands and studied her face.

"Better, I think." She wasn't, really, but at least she'd stopped crying at the drop of a hat. "Poor Chloe bore the brunt of it last night. She asked me to stay with her, and she even went over to Dora's to get my things today."

"It's just too bad Nate wasn't there," Chloe said. "I was looking forward to giving him a piece of my mind." Chloe looked capable of it, with her color high and her green eyes flashing. Susanna felt profoundly grateful that her path hadn't crossed Nate's.

"We would love to have you stay here, too," Lydia said. "Maybe you'd like to get away from Oyersburg for a bit."

"That's kind of you." Susanna's heart was full. It was good to be wanted. "Not right away." The future was a blank, and when she tried to see into it, she couldn't make out any possible paths.

"Sure?" Lydia said, squeezing her hands.

She nodded. "I need to make some decisions with Dora about the stock we took from the shop. We'll have to split it somehow, I guess." The idea seemed overwhelming. How could she split up something that had been her life's work?

"Give it a little time," Chloe said. "It will sort itself out. Dora wants to make things easy for you, I know. She told me how sorry she is for what happened."

Susanna nodded, choking up a bit. "She's a good friend."

Nodding, Lydia turned to Chloe. "What about you? How are you?"

Chloe's face seemed to stiffen. "I'm fine. I just hope this isn't awkward for you, being such close friends with the Miller family."

Lydia waved that away with a gesture. "I think Emma Miller is as befuddled as you are about Seth's decision. She's not sure Seth is doing the right thing. Or at least that he's doing it for the right reason."

Chloe shrugged, obviously determined not to talk about it. "He's a grown man. He's made his choice."

Susanna found that she and Lydia were exchanging looks. How long could Chloe try to hide her feelings? How much would it hurt her to do so?

"Emma thinks Seth is returning to the faith out of a misplaced sense of responsibility. What do you think, Chloe?"

"I don't know." Feeling moved in Chloe's face and was quickly masked. "We didn't talk about it."

"Maybe you should," Lydia said. "Maybe you should tell him how you feel about him."

Chloe seemed to be struggling to hold something back. And losing.

"If Seth has decided to become Amish again, I'm not going to ask him to change his mind. I do have a little pride."

"Ja," Lydia said softly. "You do. And that sounds like something your grandmother would say."

Chloe froze, her face immobile. Feelings seemed to rage in her eyes. Suddenly she turned and walked toward the door.

"Chloe? Where are you going?"

She hesitated in the doorway, glancing back at them. "Just where you want me to. To see if Seth is home."

Chapter Twenty

Seth straightened the framed family tree he'd just hung for his mother in the kitchen, glad to have something to occupy his hands. Too bad it didn't occupy his thoughts, as well.

His mind and heart had been in turmoil. How could he find a way out of the hole he'd dug?

It was one thing to fear Jessie was right, and another to be sure. Harder still to know what to do about it.

The need to see Chloe was eating at him. But what could he say to her? How could he convince her that he knew his own mind?

If he hurt her again . . . His mind winced away from that thought.

The back door flew open and Jessie burst into the kitchen, her cheeks pink, her eyes sparkling. "It's Chloe. Chloe is coming."

He froze.

She grabbed his hand and pulled at him. "Did you hear me? She's walking up through the orchard right now. Go to her."

He glanced at his mother. She nodded, smiling. "Go. Schell."

It was as if a spring had released inside him. He shot through the door, letting the screen slam.

Jessie was right. Chloe was walking toward him through the orchard, and the trees formed a green archway for her.

Seth's heart seemed to swell until it felt as if there'd be no room for it in his chest. He headed toward Chloe, his long strides eating up the ground. Suddenly he was running, his fears dropping away as he went like apples falling from the trees.

She saw him. Stopped. Waited.

He got to within a few feet of her and halted, breathing heavily, not sure how to get over the last hurdle. Chloe was staring at him, her eyes wide, her face vulnerable.

"You came," he said.

Chloe nodded. "I came." She took a deep breath, as if drawing courage. "I almost didn't, but Lydia helped me see the truth. I would regret it forever if I let pride keep me from saying this—I love you, Seth."

The last remnant of doubt evaporated. He reached out to her tentatively, knowing how hard it was for Chloe to set aside her pride and make herself vulnerable with no guarantee of return.

"Can you forgive me?" His voice went husky on the words. "I've been so stupid even my little sister could see it." The truth seemed so beautifully clear now. "I told myself it was wrong to try to exist between two worlds. I thought I had to go to one side of the fence or the other. But I don't. I can be a bridge between them . . . we can, together, if you'll have me." He held out his arms.

It was Chloe who took that last step between them. His arms closed around her with a huge wave of thankfulness, joy, passion. Their lips met, and he'd never tasted anything so sweet.

Finally. Finally he could kiss her, hold her, love her without feeling as if he was destined to hurt someone with every move he made. He deepened the kiss, holding her close and feeling as if they were two halves of a whole, together at last.

She sighed finally, her breath against his lips, and drew back enough that he could see her face. Sunlight filtered through the leaves overhead, gilding her skin with the rich glow of autumn. "No regrets?" she murmured.

Seth felt as if his heart would swell right out of his chest, and he wanted to laugh with sheer joy. "What is there to regret? The little fact that I don't have a job? Or that your grandmother will explode at the thought of us together?"

Chloe smiled with him. "We can't fail." She glanced up at the green arch overhead. "My parents were here once, in this very spot, loving each other and their children. Lydia and Adam pledged themselves to each other here. If they can figure it out, we can, too." She laid her palm against his cheek. "We'll find a way to be here for our families and still be true to ourselves. I promise."

She understood him, so clearly, that it was as if she knew his thoughts, and it both humbled and astonished him. How could he ever have thought that he could go on without her?

"Marry me," he said, holding her close. "Wherever we are together, that's home."

She tilted her head, smiling. "Yes," she said, and he kissed the smile on her lips. Yes.

Nate went back to the store in the afternoon. Maybe that would help keep his mind off what had happened the previous night. He'd been pummeled so by both his mother and Susanna that it was a wonder he wasn't covered with bruises. And all because he was trying to do what was right.

The store seemed fairly quiet. Since it didn't look as if there were any problems needing his attention, he headed for the office.

Thomas was seated at Nate's desk, his blond head bent over some papers. He looked up, smiling, when Nate came in.

"I thought maybe you'd be resting this afternoon."

"I'm fine." His irritation probably showed, but he'd be pleased if people would stop acting as if he was an invalid. "What are you doing?"

"Filling out the order forms," Thomas said, as if it was the most natural thing in the world.

"You shouldn't be doing that." Nate clumped his way awkwardly to the desk. "I do the orders."

Thomas rose, backing away from the desk. "I just . . . I've been doing the order forms since you've been laid up. I was just trying to help."

"I'll do it." Nate shifted his body to the chair. "If you want to help, you can go and sweep up in the front."

Thomas stood for a moment. Then he turned and went out without a word.

Nate turned to the order forms, frowning down at Thomas's neat printing and recalling the hurt in his eyes. The boy had been trying very hard. He was smart, honest, hardworking, and took the initiative, seeing things that had to be done without being told.

In other words, he was just the sort of person Nate wanted working in the store. What had possessed him to speak to the boy that way?

His mother's words about bossiness rang in his thoughts with sudden conviction. Nonsense. He was taking care of his family and running his business the best he could.

But he was restless, unable to settle down to work. Probably because of the cast, that was all.

Grabbing the crutches, he thumped to the door and looked around the store.

Everything was fine. The shelves were fully stocked again, now that the trucks could get through. Thomas was sweeping, while Susie helped a customer. It was a business a man could take pride in.

Pride, that most un-Amish of qualities. What would people think if they could hear his thoughts?

Surely it wasn't wrong to be happy about his accomplishments, was it? He'd like to be convinced of that thought, but he couldn't.

Walk humbly with your God. That was what the Amish lived every day. What he had promised to live.

It felt as if blocks were tumbling in his mind, falling away, revealing what he'd become in his desperate need not to be like his father. He looked aghast at the image.

Everything isn't about business, Susanna had said, pain in her gentle face. It was like a blow to the heart. He'd been so focused on his own goals that he'd trampled hers, and then he'd expected her to marry him.

The floor seemed to shift beneath his feet. He had to do something, now, and pray it wasn't too late. But first . . .

As quickly as the cast and crutches allowed, he went to where Thomas was working.

"Thomas, I have to go out. I know I can count on you to run the store while I'm gone."

Thomas stood a little straighter. "Ja, for sure."

Nate turned away, then remembered and turned back. "And if you have time, you may as well take over the order forms, too."

Thomas's grin nearly split his face. "I will. Denke."

Nate would clap the boy's shoulder, but he didn't have a spare hand with his crutches. At least that error had been easily fixed, and Thomas had a forgiving nature.

The bigger problem, the one that weighed so heavily on Nate's heart, might not be fixable at all, but he had to try.

"It's wonderful kind of you to come here to see me," Dora said.

Susanna looked around Gaus's Bulk Foods, her nerves jangling. "You're sure Nate won't be coming in while I'm here?"

"I promise." Dora dusted a speck from the cash box. "He's out, and he won't be back until much later."

"I'm sorry." Susanna felt her cheeks grow warm. "It sounds foolish, but I just don't want to run into him, at least not so soon."

Was it just the night before last that she and Nate had been so briefly engaged? So much had happened since then that it felt much longer. She and Chloe had stayed at Lydia's for a supper that had turned into a celebration of Chloe and Seth's engagement.

"I understand." Dora patted her hand where it rested on the counter. "I wouldn't have asked you to come here except that I can't get away right now."

Susanna nodded, still not sure why she was here. Dora's note, delivered by a small Amish boy, had only said that she must see Susanna this afternoon. Surely she didn't expect her to talk about what had happened between her and Nate.

"I just wanted to be sure that everything is all right between you and me, regardless of how foolish my son is." Anxiety colored Dora's words.

Susanna clasped her hand. "Of course we're all right. You must know how dear you are to me. After all we've done together, nothing can separate us."

Dora smiled, obviously relieved. "They were gut years we had with the shop, ja?"

She was talking about the shop in the past, and Susanna's heart ached a little more. "Aren't you sorry to see it go?"

"Ja, in a way." Dora spoke slowly, as if still sorting out her feelings. "I have regrets, but the flood has made me realize I need to take things a little easier."

"Then that's what you should do." Susanna certainly didn't want Dora thinking she had to do anything she didn't want to for her sake.

"I don't mind helping out in Nate's store," Dora said, glancing around at the well-ordered shelves. "And in your shop, too." She paused, and Susanna thought she seemed a little embarrassed. "I mean, assuming you open the shop somewhere else."

Susanna nodded, uncomfortable. She hadn't yet made up her mind what to do. The legacy, as Chloe called it, would allow her to do so, but she wasn't sure she wanted to stay in Oyersburg.

Of course, now that Chloe was so happy, Susanna didn't have to stay for her sake. She could open a little shop somewhere else, maybe even in Pleasant Valley, as Chloe had suggested, close to Lydia.

"I'm glad we're still friends," Dora said. "I wonder, now. Would you mind doing a little something for me since you're here? It wouldn't take you more than a couple of minutes."

"I'd be glad to." As long as she could be well away before Nate returned. "What is it?"

"You know my little black change purse, the one I always carry?"

Susanna nodded. Dora had had the same little snap bag since Susanna had known her.

"I left it next door this morning. Mrs. Walker wanted to show me the work they were doing over there, and I must have walked out and left it on the counter."

"I'll gladly fetch it, but won't the door be locked?"

"That's why I'm afraid someone will take it," Dora said. "The workers are in and out at all hours, and they keep leaving the door unlocked. Anyone could walk in."

Susanna nodded. "I'll try the door at least. If I can't get in, surely Mrs. Walker will see it and know it's yours."

"Denke." Dora seemed more relieved than was justified by a small change purse. "You'll go right now, ain't so?"

Smiling, Susanna went toward the door. Thomas jumped to open it for her, and she gave him a friendly nod as she walked out.

It was only a few steps to the storefront next door. The

plate-glass windows had been covered over with brown paper, so she couldn't see if anyone was there.

She tried the door. As Dora had feared, it was unlocked. She opened it and went inside. "Is anyone here?"

No answer, but plenty of light came through the paper on the windows. She glanced around, curious.

The store was much larger than it had looked when filled with all the paraphernalia of a hardware store. Now the shelves and cabinets stood empty, and the bare wooden floor echoed to her footsteps as she went to the counter in search of the change purse.

"I already have it." Nate stepped out from the back room, dropping the little bag on the counter. "Susanna—"

She turned away, shaking her head, feeling her cheeks go red with shock and embarrassment. How could Dora, her dear friend, trick her this way?

"Don't blame Mamm," he said, and moved as quickly as his cast would allow between her and the door. "I told her there was no other way you'd talk to me."

"There still isn't," she said, determined on that point, at least.

"Please, Susanna, just listen, then. Only for a few minutes. Then I promise I won't bother you again."

All of her anger had been spent. Now she just felt cold. Empty. Common civility demanded that she listen to him. Forgiveness would take a little longer. She gave a curt nod and clasped her hands together.

Now that he had his chance, Nate didn't seem to know where to begin. He gestured to the space around them. "What do you think of it?"

"Very nice," she said, her tone colorless. "Why does it matter?"

"I'm considering buying it, but I wouldn't do that without asking you first."

She stared at him blankly. "What are you talking about?"

"Your shop." His face was serious, his gaze intent. "This is for you, if you'll take it. I tried to get out of the deal with the town, but they wouldn't agree, so I thought maybe this was the next best thing. It's right on the busiest part of Main Street, and you can see it has plenty more space than the old shop."

She was shaking her head. "Stop, please. This doesn't make sense."

"Susanna, listen. I know it sounds as if I'm trying to buy forgiveness, but I'm not. Forgiveness can only be freely given, and I don't deserve yours."

"I forgive you." Her head was pounding so that she couldn't think. She just wanted him to stop. "Does that satisfy you?"

His eyes filled with something she realized was pain. "I was so determined to prove that I wasn't like my father that I let my business take me over. I turned into someone who couldn't think of anyone except in terms of business. That's far worse than anything my father ever did."

The genuine feeling in his face seemed to melt the ice around her heart.

"Don't say that about yourself. Think about what you did in the flood, giving away without ever counting the cost. You're a hardworking, generous man, Nate. You are." She could hardly believe she was defending him, but it was true.

"It doesn't look that way to me." His lips twisted. "I lost what I valued most because I was so intent on business."

Her heart thudded. He couldn't be talking about her, could he?

"I shouldn't have spoken to you the way I did." She rubbed

her temple, trying to understand. "I was just as bad, so preoccupied with my shop, so desperate to have it back the way it was that I couldn't see anything else."

Somehow he was holding both her hands in a warm grip. "It's not the same, Susanna. You gave your heart to your shop. I was at risk of giving my soul." His voice had roughened with pain. "Ach, Susanna, don't you see? You woke me up, made me start thinking about life again. Made me want to be a better man for you. I know I made a mess of it the first time, but can't you forgive me and give me another chance?"

Fear ricocheted through her. To risk her heart that he loved her, wanted her—

Somehow she managed to push the fear away. That was her hangover from the past, that conviction that nobody could want her. This was the future.

Nate loved her. How could she turn away from him again?

He was still waiting, patient, anxious. She reached out to press her palm against his cheek, searching for the words.

He found them for her. "I'll ask you for the second time, Susanna. Will you marry me?"

She smiled, feeling suddenly free of the past. "For the second and last time, yes, I will."

Nate drew her into his arms, and she went willingly, sliding her arms around him and feeling him warm and alive under her hands. He loved her. This was her future. Nate loved her, and they would make a new life together.

EPILOGUE

Susanna smiled as she looked around the crowded shop. She was having an open house to celebrate the new location of Plain Gifts, and folks had been streaming in all day long.

The Oyersburg Amish had turned out in force, as if today's event was a continuation of hers and Nate's wedding party the previous Thursday. And so many Amish from Pleasant Valley came that they'd had to hire a bus.

Their Englisch friends were there, as well, so many of the people with whom they'd worked during the trying time of the flood. Maybe everyone felt the need for a celebration of something. It would be a long while before the town was completely normal again, but it was good to celebrate the small accomplishments along the way.

Chloe appeared at her elbow, holding a serving tray of snacks and sweets. "I still say you should have delayed the opening so that the two of you could have gotten away for a honeymoon," she said. "You're newlyweds, and you're working harder than ever."

Susanna smiled fondly at her sister. "You're a fine one to talk. You and Seth are going to be married in just a month, and I haven't seen you go anywhere except to Philadelphia to bring your grandmother back for today."

She nodded toward the corner where Margaret Wentworth sat, very erect, seeming to supervise the proceedings. Daniel approached her with a plate of cookies, and she shed the grande dame manner to smile at him.

"What are you two plotting with your heads together?" Lydia came over to lean heavily against the counter.

"You should sit down," Susanna said, but before she could move to get a chair, Nate had brought one. He smiled at her over Lydia's head, one eye twitching in the slightest suggestion of a wink.

Her heart fluttered. Here she was an old married woman already, but melting the instant her husband looked at her.

"Well?" Lydia demanded, her arm curved protectively around her belly.

"No plots," Chloe said, leaning close to speak above the chatter in the room. "Susanna was chiding me for not getting away for some private time with Seth—"

"You started it," Susanna said. "You and your talk about honeymoons."

Chloe grinned. "I was about to explain that Seth has gotten so busy already that he doesn't want to take any time off yet. And I'm content to be here. Where else would I want to be?"

Seth had begun a new business right here in Oyersburg. The town would come back, he'd said, and there was no reason why he couldn't do for small local businesses what he'd done for big corporations in his last job. He seemed very content, happy to give up traveling all over the place for a quieter life and a slower pace.

Chloe was blooming, her happiness contagious. Between helping Seth get started, looking for a house for them once they were married, and helping Susanna get the shop completed, she still managed to find time to work on her research.

Chloe had echoed her thoughts, Susanna realized. Where else would she want to be?

Just two months ago she'd been in the old shop, contented enough but alone. Now . . . now she had family, friends, two dear sisters, a loving husband, and the shop. The quilt that her mother had made and her dear mother-in-law had saved now graced the double bed she shared with Nate. God had been so good to her.

"What do you suppose they'd think if they could see us now?" Lydia said, echoing the words Susanna had once spoken.

She didn't have to explain, not to them, that she was talking about their birth parents. Despite the fact that none of them could remember their faces, they seemed very close and very dear at times. They had done their best for their three little girls. No one could do more.

"They'd be happy," Chloe said, as she had before. "They'd be happy that we've found each other at last."

RECIPES

Three Bean Salad

This is my standard dish for times when the power is off, as in an emergency. No cooking required, and although it's better chilled, it can be served at room temperature.

FOR THE SALAD:
2 cups cut green beans, canned
2 cups cut yellow beans, canned
2 cups kidney beans, canned
½ cup minced onion
½ cup chopped green pepper
½ cup chopped celery

FOR THE DRESSING:
¾ cup sugar
½ cup cider vinegar
½ cup salad oil
1 teaspoon salt
1 teaspoon pepper

Drain the beans and place in a large glass bowl. Add the onion, green pepper, and celery. Mix the dressing ingredients together, stirring until the sugar is dissolved. Pour the dressing over the bean mixture. Cover and refrigerate. The recipe can be doubled or tripled as needed.

Church Beans

These beans seem to go by different names in different parts of the country. I've heard them called "funeral beans" and "church lady beans," and every cook seems to have her own variations in ingredients. I make this whenever I need to serve a hearty dish to a crowd.

½ pound bacon, diced
½ pound ground beef
1 large onion, diced
1 can (14-ounce) pork and beans
1 can (7- or 12-ounce) kidney beans, drained
1 can (8-ounce) butter beans or any white beans
½ cup brown sugar
¼ cup ketchup
2 tablespoons molasses
½ cup white sugar
½ teaspoon mustard

Preheat oven to 350°F.

In a large frying pan, cook the bacon until lightly browned. Add ground beef and onion, cooking while stirring until browned. Stir in the beans and add the rest of the ingredients, mixing thoroughly. Pour into a 2-quart-deep casserole dish. Bake uncovered at 350°F for 1 hour. The recipe can be doubled for a larger crowd, and it can also be cooked in a slow cooker on low for 4 to 5 hours instead of baked.

Aunt Erna's Banana Fudge Bars

This recipe is a good way to use up ripe bananas. It's delicious and the ingredients are ones I always have in my pantry.

⅓ cup melted shortening
3 tablespoons cocoa powder
1 cup sugar
¼ teaspoon salt
1 teaspoon baking powder
1 tablespoon milk
2 well-beaten eggs
1 teaspoon vanilla
½ cup flour
1 cup mashed bananas
1 cup chopped walnuts

Preheat oven to 350°F.

Combine the shortening, cocoa powder, and sugar by hand or at a low speed with a mixer. Add the rest of the ingredients except the bananas and walnuts and beat well. Stir in the bananas and walnuts. Pour batter into a greased 8-inch-square pan. Bake at 350°F for 45 minutes. Cool and cut into bars. This recipe can be doubled for a larger batch.

Dear Reader,

Susanna's Dream *continues the story of the three lost sisters and their efforts to create a bond after so many years apart. I hope you've enjoyed learning about the lives of Lydia, Susanna, and Chloe, and the family they've forged together.*

The flood in this story is based on Tropical Storm Lee, which caused devastating flooding in my family's small town and in others along the Susquehanna River basin. Although the names have been changed, the selfless actions taken by so many people to help others are genuine. We've seen again and again how generous and giving people are when they band together to face an emergency.

I would love to hear your thoughts about my book. If you'd care to write to me, I'd be happy to reply with a signed bookmark or bookplate and my brochure of Pennsylvania Dutch recipes. You can find me on the Web at martaperry.com and on Facebook at facebook.com/MartaPerryBooks, e-mail me at marta@martaperry.com, or write to me in care of Berkley Publicity Department, Penguin Group (USA) LLC, 375 Hudson Street, New York, NY 10014.

Blessings,
Marta Perry

An Excerpt from

THE FORGIVEN

First in
Marta Perry's fascinating new series

Keepers of the Promise

Coming in print and e-book
from Berkley Books
in October 2014

R hoda! Joshua! Come to supper." Rebecca Fisher stayed on the back porch until she saw her two kinder running toward the house. Rhoda came from the big barn, where she'd been "helping" Rebecca's father and brother with the evening chores. Rhoda adored her grossdaadi and Onkel Simon, and Rebecca was grateful every day that Rhoda had them to turn to now that her own daadi was gone.

Joshua had clearly been up in the old apple tree that was his favorite perch. Paul had talked about building a tree house there for Joshua's sixth birthday. That birthday would come soon, but Paul wasn't here to see it. Rebecca's throat tightened, and she forced the thought away.

"Mammi, Mammi." Joshua flung himself at her, grabbing her apron with grubby hands. "Guess who I saw?"

"I don't know, Josh. Who?" She hugged him with one arm and gathered Rhoda against her with the other. Rhoda let herself be hugged for a moment and then wiggled free.

"I helped put the horses in," she reported. "Onkel Simon said I'm a gut helper."

"Mammi, I'm talking." Joshua glared at his sister. "Guess who I saw?"

"Hush, now," Rebecca said, hating it when they quarreled, even though she remembered only too well how she and her brothers and sisters had plagued each other. "Rhoda, I'm wonderful glad you're helping. Joshua, who did you see?"

Probably an owl or a chipmunk—at five, Joshua considered every creature he encountered a real person.

"Daadi!" Joshua grinned, unaware of the hole that had just opened up in his mother's stomach.

"Joshua—" She struggled to find the words.

"That's stupid," Rhoda declared from the superiority of her seven years. Her small face tightened with anger. "Daadi's in heaven. He can't come back, so you can't see him, so don't be stupid."

"Rhoda, don't call your brother stupid." Rebecca managed the easier part of the correction first. She knelt in front of her son, praying for the right words. "Joshua, you must understand that Daadi loves you always, but he can't come back."

"But I saw him, Mammi. I saw him in the new stable and—"

"No, Joshua." She had to stop this notion now, no matter how it hurt. "I don't know what you saw, but it wasn't Daadi."

His small face clouded. "Are you sure?"

"I'm sure." Her heart hurt as she spoke the words.

"Please look, Mammi." He pressed small hands on her cheeks to ensure she paid attention. "Please look in the stable."

Obviously it was the only thing that would satisfy him. "All right. I'll go and look. You wash up for supper."

Josh nodded solemnly. Rebecca stood, giving her daughter a warning look.

"No more talking about this until I come back. You understand?"

Rhoda seemed about to argue, but she nodded as well. After pausing to see them headed for the sink without further squabbling, Rebecca slipped out the back door.

A quick glance told her there was no activity at the barn now. Probably her daad and brother had finished and headed home for their own supper. It wasn't far across the field to the farmhouse where she'd grown up.

That field would be planted with corn eventually. Daad had mentioned that only yesterday, and she'd thought how strange it seemed that Paul wasn't here to make the decision.

Turning in the opposite direction, she skirted the garden. The early onions were up, and in a few weeks the danger of frost would be over, and she could finish putting the rest of the vegetables in the ground.

Beyond the garden stood the posts from which the FARM STAY BED-AND-BREAKFAST sign should hang. She'd have to put it up soon. Her first guests were due the end of May, and she had to fight back panic at the thought of dealing with guests without Paul's support. The bed-and-breakfast had been their dream, and he'd enjoyed every minute of their first season.

Last summer she'd been too devastated by his death to think of opening, but now . . . well, now she owed it to Paul to make their dream come true as best she could.

The stable still seemed raw and new to her even though it had been up for more than a year. They'd gone ahead with the building even after Paul's diagnosis, as a sign that they had faith he would be well again.

But he hadn't been. He'd grown weaker and weaker, and eventually she had learned to hate the sight of the stable that had been intended for the purebred draft horses Paul wanted to breed. The stable had stood empty ever since.

Steeling herself, Rebecca swung open one side of the double doors and stepped inside. Dust motes danced in a shaft of sunlight. The interior seemed to echo of lost hopes.

Sucking in a breath, she forced herself to walk through the stable, her footsteps hollow on the wooden floorboards. No one was here. Joshua's longing for his daadi had led him to imagine what he longed for.

A board creaked behind her and Rebecca whirled, heart leaping into her throat.

A man stood in the doorway. Big, Amish, silhouetted against the light so that she couldn't make out his face. Then he took a step forward, and she could see him.

For a long moment they stood staring at each other. Her brain seemed to be moving sluggishly. He was tall, broad-shouldered, with golden-brown hair and eyes. He didn't have a beard, so she could see the cleft in his chin, and the sight stirred vague memories. She knew him, and yet she didn't. It wasn't—

"Matt? Matthew Byler?"

A flicker of a smile crossed his face. "Got it right. And you're little Becky, ain't so?"

"Rebecca Fisher," she corrected quickly. So Matt Byler was back home at last. Nothing had been seen of him since his family had migrated out west when he was a teenager.

"You married Paul Fisher, then." He came closer, making

her aware of the height and breadth of him. "You two were holding hands when you were eight or nine, the way I remember it."

"And you were . . ." She let that trail off. Matt had been a couple of years older than they were, and he'd been the kind of boy Amish parents held up as a bad example—always in trouble, always pushing the boundaries of what it meant to be Amish.

Now Matt's smile lit his eyes. "You remember me. The troublemaker."

"I . . . I wasn't thinking that," she said. But of course she had been. It was the first thing anyone thought in connection with Matt Byler. "Are you here for a visit?"

Matt didn't have a beard, so obviously he hadn't married. That was more than unusual for an Amish man of thirty. Surely his unmarried state wasn't for lack of chances. A prudent set of parents might look warily at Matt as a prospective son-in-law, but the girls had always been charmed by his teasing smile.

"My uncle needs some help with his carpentry business, and he asked me to give him a hand."

Everyone knew that Silas Byler had been struggling to keep his business going since his oldest son had so unexpectedly left the community. How strange life was that Isaiah, who'd never caused his parents a moment's worry, should be the one to leave, while bad boy Matthew came back to take his place.

"I'm sorry about Isaiah. It was a heavy blow to your aunt and uncle, ain't so?"

Matt nodded with a wry twist to his mouth. "Funny, isn't it? Everyone was so sure I was the one headed over the fence."

"You did a pretty good job of making folks think so, the way I remember it," she said.

"Ouch." Matt's teasing grin appeared. "You've developed a sharp tongue, I see."

"I've just grown up," she said. "I have two kinder of my own now. Little Joshua must have seen you here at the stable. He thought it was his daadi."

His face sobered instantly. "I'm sorry, Rebecca. Truly sorry. My uncle told me about Paul. You have my sympathy."

"Denke." She shouldn't be angry with Matt over Joshua's vivid imagination, but if she were being honest with herself . . . "Was there something you wanted here, Matt?" she asked abruptly.

He looked a little taken aback by the blunt question. "I'm looking for a building I can use for my furniture business. Onkel Silas told me about the stable and how Paul was going to . . ." He didn't finish the thought. "Anyway, he said you weren't using the stable and might be willing to lease it to me."

Everything in Rebecca recoiled at the thought of putting another person's business in Paul's stable. "No." Her tone was sharper than she'd intended. "I'm sorry. It's not available."

Matt's eyebrows lifted. "It's standing empty. I can pay you five hundred a month for the space."

"It's not available," she said again, annoyed at him for putting her in this position, and unable to keep from thinking about what she could do with five hundred dollars a month.

Matt studied her face, his eyes intent and questioning. "You don't like the idea of turning Paul's stable over to someone else. I can understand that. But you have two little ones to raise. Can you afford to have it sitting empty when it could be earning money for Paul's kinder?"

The fact that Matt was probably right didn't make her feel any more kindly toward him. "I don't think that's your concern."

"Maybe not. But it is yours, Rebecca." He held her gaze for a moment longer, and she felt as if he was looking right into all her grief and uncertainty. Then he took a step back. "I wouldn't do any harm to the place. Think about it."

He turned and walked away. He was silhouetted in the doorway for a moment, and then he was gone, leaving Rebecca unsettled and upset.

Photo by Lorie Johnson Photography

A lifetime spent in rural Pennsylvania and her own Pennsylvania Dutch roots led **Marta Perry** to write about the Plain People who add to the rich heritage of her home state. She is the author of more than fifty inspirational romance novels and lives with her husband in a century-old farmhouse.

Visit the author online at martaperry.com and facebook.com /MartaPerryBooks.